FROM
SNOW
TO
ASH

Anthony Sharwood is a Walkley Award–winning journalist specialising in sports, the outdoors, weather and climate. He started his career writing longform magazine and newspaper features and has spent the last ten years as a writer and editor on leading Australian news websites. He has also presented television shows, radio programs and a podcast.

A skier, hiker and lifelong lover of Australia's High Country, Ant's brain was pretty much fried after a decade of digital journalism. The Australian Alps Walking Track was a chance to escape, to cleanse, to reset. *From Snow to Ash* is his second book and documents that trek. Ant lives with his wife and two teenagers in a Sydney suburb nobody has ever heard of.

FROM
SNOW
TO
ASH

Solitude, soul-searching and survival
on Australia's toughest hiking trail

ANTHONY SHARWOOD

hachette
AUSTRALIA

Published in Australia and New Zealand in 2020
by Hachette Australia
(an imprint of Hachette Australia Pty Limited)
Level 17, 207 Kent Street, Sydney NSW 2000
www.hachette.com.au

10 9 8 7 6 5 4 3 2

A catalogue record for this book is available from the National Library of Australia

ISBN: 978 0 7336 4528 0 (paperback)

Map courtesy of Australian Alps National Parks Co-operative Management Program
Cover design by Luke Causby/Blue Cork
Front cover photo: Getty Images/Justin Bailie
Back cover and internal photos: Anthony Sharwood
Typeset in Bembo Std by Kirby Jones
Printed and bound in Australia by McPherson's Printing Group

The paper this book is printed on is certified against the Forest Stewardship Council® Standards. McPherson's Printing Group holds FSC® chain of custody certification SA-COC-005379. FSC® promotes environmentally responsible, socially beneficial and economically viable management of the world's forests.

*To the firefighters, park rangers, ecologists, trail-clearing volunteers,
High Country hut conservators, and everyone who works in or out
of uniform, paid or unpaid, to preserve the mountains.*

Though nothing can bring back the hour
Of splendour in the grass, of glory in the flower;
We will grieve not, rather find
Strength in what remains behind;

William Wordsworth, 'Ode: Intimations of Immortality from Recollections of Early Childhood'

CONTENTS

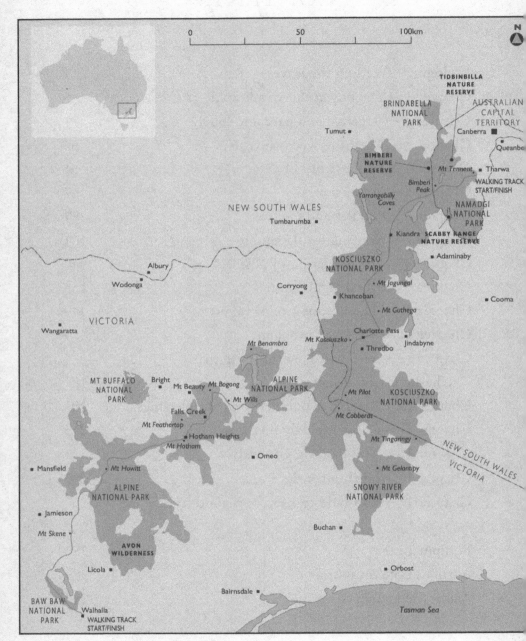

0   50   100km

N

TIDBINBILLA
NATURE
RESERVE

BRINDABELLA
NATIONAL
PARK

AUSTRALIAN
CAPITAL
TERRITORY

Tumut

Canberra

Queanbe

BIMBERI
NATURE
RESERVE

Mt Tennent

Tharwa

Bimberi
Peak

WALKING TRACK
START/FINISH

NEW SOUTH WALES

Yarrangobilly
Caves

NAMADGI
NATIONAL
PARK

Tumbarumba

Kiandra

SCABBY RANGE
NATURE RESERVE

KOSCIUSZKO
NATIONAL PARK

Adaminaby

Albury

Corryong

Mt Jagungal

Cooma

Wodonga

Khancoban

Mt Guthega

VICTORIA

Mt Benambra

Mt Kosciusko

Charlotte Pass

Jindabyne

Wangaratta

Thredbo

MT BUFFALO
NATIONAL
PARK

Bright

Mt Beauty

Mt Bogong

ALPINE
NATIONAL PARK

Mt Wills

Mt Pilot

KOSCIUSZKO
NATIONAL
PARK

Falls Creek

Mt Feathertop

Hotham Heights

Mt Cobberas

Mt Hotham

Omeo

Mt Tingaringy

NEW SOUTH WALES

VICTORIA

Mansfield

Mt Howitt

Mt Gelantipy

Jamieson

ALPINE
NATIONAL PARK

SNOWY RIVER
NATIONAL
PARK

Mt Skene

AVON
WILDERNESS

Buchan

Licola

Orbost

Bairnsdale

BAW BAW
NATIONAL
PARK

Walhalla

Tasman Sea

WALKING TRACK
START/FINISH

The Australian Alps Walking Track

READING THE LEAVES

The moment I started worrying was when charred black leaves began twirling down from an uncertain sky, dotting the snow grass tussocks like chocolate shards on cupcakes. Where had the leaves come from? What did they mean? Were they a gentle reminder of distant danger or a sign of imminent peril?

The Grey Mare Trail in the north of Kosciuszko National Park traversed the sort of country I'd been dreaming about for weeks. The terrain was undulating but not steep, the trail well marked, the creeks still flowing after a month without decent rain. You could put a lot of miles behind you in country like this and I was doing just that. But those black leaves, crinkly and powdery to the touch. They worried me. There was ash too, gently floating to earth like grey summer snowflakes.

It was 31 December. My plan was to travel another 20 kilometres to Happys Hut by evening and have a Happys New Year, because there are worse ways to build an itinerary than on puns. I checked my phone one last time while I still had a flickering bar or two of reception. The nearest fire on the New South Wales Rural Fire Service Fires Near Me app was still 50 or 60 kilometres away, down near Tumbarumba on the western side of the mountains. To borrow from the old terrorism ad, I was alert but not alarmed.

About seven kilometres north of Mt Jagungal, by a narrow unnamed creek flowing through open heathland, I paused for the first brief break of the day, glugging greedy mouthfuls of water between strips of jerky. I wasn't carrying much jerky. Always seemed to go for it when I felt uneasy. This little flesh-fest was a psychological boost as much as a protein hit. Hikers go to the wilderness to be humbled by nature, inspired by it. The jerky was a sign I felt threatened by it. Up the hill from the rest spot, the Grey Mare Trail met an offshoot called the Doubtful Gap Trail. I paused again to look at the sky. You'd better believe I was feeling doubtful as those singed leaves and ash floated to earth.

Throughout the trek, I wasn't discouraged by the solitude, by the wandering mind, by the doubts that crept in daily, unstoppably, like bugs to a sealed tent. Even as fire spread around three states on the maps on emergency apps like pools of grey blood, its smoke often cloaking the peaks and valleys through which I walked, I never seriously second-guessed my plans because the Alps, mercifully, had not been directly threatened by the worst December blazes.

But that ash. Those blackened leaves. They were unnerving.

They weren't snow gum leaves, that much I knew. Snow gum leaves have a distinctive grain, their veins curving along the length of the leaf in near parallel arcs. Even in their singed state, these leaves clearly had the pattern common to most eucalypts, where the veins fan out towards the edge of the leaf from one long central strand. That meant they were from a distant lowland forest to the west and had risen on hot updrafts, travelling my way on strong upper atmospheric winds.

I touched a leaf. Cold. Another. Also no warmth. These leaves couldn't possibly start a spot fire, could they? And if they weren't from around here, surely there was no immediate danger. Right?

I had no answers. All I knew was that the day felt wrong. Gloomy and wrong. You might think it's easy to dramatise that feeling in hindsight, but I shared my mood on social media before setting out from O'Keefes Hut that morning.

Smoke from a fire near Tumbarumba has blown in. No danger up here for now, but the mountains have a very bleak feel today, which grabs hold of your mood. Onwards, and good luck to all firies and people in harm's way today.

Turns out I was about to become one of those people in harm's way. Much sooner than I could have imagined, those delicate black leaves helicoptering their way to earth would be swooshed aside by the blades of an actual helicopter descending to pick me up.

What I saw from that rescue chopper was terrifying.

CHAPTER 1

THE BOY AT THE WINDOW

I am walking away from myself and towards myself.

Away from a workplace I can't face anymore for reasons which are nobody's business, but if you've ever repeatedly felt your good intentions evaporate as the working day groans into action, you'll know exactly how I feel.

Away from a fidgety, alt-tabbing mind which has forgotten how to switch off.

Away from distracted parenting and partnering, from

irregular sleep cycles, from a life lived around the clock yet in many ways not well lived.

Away from the looming threat of unemployment, a word which is cool and liberating when you're in your twenties, with no one depending on your labour and the income it brings, but terrifying, humiliating and potentially catastrophic when you're a middle-aged man in the suburbs of a major city with a mortgage, a wife, two teenaged kids and a whippet, and when you live in an age where knowledge and experience are commodities devalued by the day.

I'm walking away from certainty, from comfort, from familiarity, from ease.

And I'm walking on Australia's toughest and most beautiful mainland hiking trail – the 660-kilometre Australian Alps Walking Track – towards a skinny, wiry-haired boy staring out a window.

When I was seven, my parents separated. My brother and I moved with our mother from Sydney to Canberra, a city where we had no connections, no history, no prejudices and no expectations. Our three-bedroom brick house on the western fringe of the city overlooked street upon street, suburb upon suburb, of similarly unambitious houses. Beyond them, the fledgling capital abandoned its flimsy pretence of being a real city, giving way to a range of low grassy hills, then dark mountains which dominated the horizon. I had never seen mountains before, or none that I'd noticed.

One winter morning, not long after we'd moved, there was snow on the mountains, reaching about halfway down.

Like most Australian kids I had never seen snow, or even thought about it in my own country. But there it was. Snow. In plain sight through my window. The mountains had my attention.

As we settled into our uprooted lives, I learned the unwritten schoolyard codes. I wore shorts on even the frostiest days because wearing long pants was a crime punishable by social banishment if you were lucky, fists if you weren't. I let the older kids win at handball because I wanted to feel the ball slapping my hands, not my face. I climbed the gravelly rock face in the cutting beside the freeway because falling would be bad but being ostracised for dodging the neighbourhood initiation rite would be worse. In spring, I joined the boys in the street throwing rocks at swooping magpies, a ritual I regret to this day. And in all seasons, I learned to stay in the blind spot of the school principal, a former military man who doled out the cane as routinely as the milkman delivered milk.

Home was a haven. I had my family and I had my mountains. After school, I would often retreat to my bedroom and spend hours staring at those dark shapes on the horizon. One day, I held a piece of paper to the windowpane and traced their outline. I practised drawing the pattern by memory till I got it right. I can still draw that crenellated outline today.

Like most Canberrans, we called those mountains the Brindabellas. In fact, they were the Tidbinbillas, which are lower and drier and one valley closer to Canberra than the much snowier and mostly hidden Brindabellas, but which are still a mighty range, high enough to catch snow and hold it for several days after each winter storm. Not that I knew their real name back then. Nor did I understand that they were the last of the Australian Alps, the end of a mostly unbroken chain stretching nearly all the way to Melbourne. And I had no idea that one day I would try to walk those mountains, all of them.

Throughout those early Canberra years, Mum worked seven days a week in the business she'd started to keep the family afloat. My dad visited occasionally from Sydney in his old red Datsun 120Y. One weekend, I asked him to take me and my brother to the mountains. He inquired about the route. I told him to get onto Streeton Drive, a major local thoroughfare named after the Australian artist Sir Arthur Streeton. 'Don't tell me to get onto the street and drive!' he barked back.

We hiked a peak called Camels Hump in the Tidbinbilla Range. The view from the 1400-metre summit was even better than I'd imagined. In the distance to the east was our home suburb. Somewhere among those roofs, I thought I spotted our house, or at least the place where it likely stood. To the west was a deep valley and behind it the higher, more impressive Brindabellas. To the north was the rest of the Tidbinbillas, the range I'd stared at every day for five years, the familiar ridgeline unrecognisable from this angle, picket-fenced with spindly white-barked snow gums. That initial up-close encounter was enthralling. It was like holding hands for the first time with a childhood crush, delighting in the gentle clench of her fingers.

Dad had learned to ski when he lived in Canada. Back in Australia he bought a membership in a ski club with lodges at Perisher and Thredbo. Once each winter, he'd take us to the snow. I fell in love with skiing, a way of gliding across a landscape that felt close to flight, and I developed an obsession with snow itself – its feel, its texture, its depth or lack thereof, its very presence in a land that was so hot for most of the year.

In summer and autumn, we'd stay in one of the lodges and hike around the Kosciuszko area. In these years, I came to understand the mountains and how to walk them. I learned to avoid the candle heath, a wetland shrub with creamy flower spires which is also known as dragon bush on account of its pineapple-top foliage which could shred your legs if, like all the kids in my neighbourhood, you wore shorts to everything but weddings.

I developed a reverence for the sphagnum bogs, the delicate, spongy, fluorescent yellow pillows of moss which are the secret to the everlasting streams of the Alps, storing precious water and releasing it drop by drop in its own good time. To tread heavily upon sphagnum is vandalism. To destroy it, as the wild horses do, is worse.

By assessing the shade of green, I learned how to gauge from a distance whether bushes were knee high and walkable or two metres tall and impenetrably scrubby. My favourite bush was alpine mint, a neat shrub with a deep menthol aroma and dark green leaves tightly bunched like flower buds. It's easy to walk through and resilient enough to flourish from valleys to peaks, thumbing its nose at the other alpine plants with their strict altitudinal zones.

I found mountain music in the squeaky-gate cry of the gang-gang cockatoo, the 'faaaaaarrrk' of the ubiquitous little ravens, the lonely squeal of yellow-tailed black cockatoos who somehow stay aloft despite their impossibly languid, apathetic wingbeat. I was ever on the lookout to catch a fat spotted alpine grasshopper in my hands, always trying but failing to scoop up translucent mountain galaxias fish from a gravelly high alpine stream.

And, of course, I fell in love with snow gums. If there's one thing that makes the Australian Alps unmistakably and irreplaceably the Australian Alps, it's snow gums. From the gnarled, tortured stumpy midgets on all but the highest peaks, to the slender, ribbony, long-limbed beauties lower down, these unique eucalypts are the emblem of our Alps. Their best feature is their bark. It can be bright orange, red, or yellow, beige or dark chocolate brown or olive green or white. It all depends on the altitude and weather conditions.

Here was a part of Australia that looked and smelled like no other, in both summer and winter. And I knew that I'd spend a lifetime walking and skiing as much of it as I could.

But life happens and dreams often don't. And though I visited the mountains most years to ski and hike, I more or less stuck to the same familiar areas, never venturing out for more than a night or two. Then, a few years ago, I read about a trail called the Australian Alps Walking Track, which traverses the entirety of the High Country between Gippsland and the southern outskirts of Canberra. The idea formed quickly: I would walk the track one day. I would piece together the puzzle that lay behind the dark mountain range of my childhood, mountain by mountain, stream by stream, valley by valley, range by range.

People fly around the world these days and Instagram themselves with all sorts of spectacular landscapes in the background. They're on the rock tongue at Trolltunga or in a thermal pool in Iceland or on some beach in Thailand staring at an offshore island that looks like the cocktail umbrella in their drink. I wanted to plunge deeper. I wanted to immerse myself in the landscape of my dreams rather than just touch it. To know it, not just observe it. To cross it in its entirety, not just visit the photogenic sections. The project felt particularly urgent because the mountains themselves, like me, were entering a precarious phase of life. The Australian Alps are like our inland Great Barrier Reef. Morbid as it seems, I wanted to see them before they became something else.

Even as a boy, I understood that the mountains were fragile. Long before talk of a changing climate, I understood that this tiny part of Australia – which comprises a mere sixth of 1 per cent of the landmass of the world's hottest, flattest and driest continent – was a hiccup of nature, a remnant, a miracle. There are so many threats to the mountains, from the modern human development of ski areas to the cattle which denuded the grasslands and muddied the clear waterways from the early 1800s until they were finally banned in the mid-twentieth century, to the feral deer and horses which do the same damage today, to a warming climate. And then there's the biggest enemy of all, which is of course related to the changing climate: fire.

The Australian bush burns. This is normal and necessary in most places, as the bush relies on periodic blazes for regeneration, for life itself. But the eucalypts of both the subalpine and alpine areas of the High Country are different. They must burn less frequently because they take longer to regenerate. Before this century, the High Country typically burned every 50 to 100 years. Tragically, the recurrent alpine megafires of the 2000s are turning snow gum woodland to grassy meadows, and tall, elegant alpine ash forests to scrub.

Dr Tom Fairman of the University of Melbourne undertook part of his PhD research into snow gum forests. He found that high fire frequency increases snow gum mortality, and that grasses overtake landscapes formerly carpeted in heathy bushes. He and his supervisors coined a term for the denuded alpine woodlands: 'subalpine savannas'.

Fairman's research on alpine ash trees on the lower slopes of the Alps paints just as bleak a picture. The alpine ash and its close cousin the mountain ash are the world's tallest flowering plants, soaring as high as 90 or 100 metres and living up to 500 years. But it takes an alpine ash tree 20 years to produce seed – and it can't resprout like other eucalypts. If an ash forest burns twice or more in that time period, forget it. With no seed in the canopy or soil, you're very likely looking at a future acacia shrubland. This is now happening across the mountains, and it's hurting not just the forests themselves and the animals which depend on them, but the people who study them, live in and around them, visit them, hike through them, ski through them, love them.

'There's a sense of loss seeing the forests in transition,' Fairman told me. 'I try not to dwell on it.'

'We risk losing the Australian Alps in the state they're in. It looks like all the natural controls have been switched off,' another leading alpine ecologist, Phil Zylstra, explained.

'The old snow gum forests I remember are becoming rare,' High Country volunteer firefighter Cam Walker despaired. 'I've seen the Alps burn, and burn hot, three times in 15 years. It's terrifying that one person can witness so much change in 15 years, which is a blink in the life of these mountains.'

The spring of 2019 was unusual in the Australian Alps. A weather pattern over Antarctica called the polar vortex broke down, forcing stormy weather systems in the Southern Ocean further north than usual for that time of year.

'The breakdown of the polar vortex in the spring of 2019 was remarkable. The phenomenon that caused it – a process called sudden stratospheric warming – has only been observed a few times in the southern hemisphere,' meteorologist Ben Domensino from Weatherzone explained. The upshot was repeated cold snaps in the Alps. Ahead of the cold snaps, hot winds blew. In the unstable zone between hot and cold air masses, dry lightning storms brewed. Heat, fire, snow. This was the story of the 2019 spring in the Victorian High Country, well after the ski lifts closed and long before the first alpine flowers bloomed. Heat, fire, snow. Sometimes the unseasonal snow flurries extinguished the fires. Mostly, they didn't.

The first fires started in October. In November, a severe outbreak of dry lightning struck Victoria's alpine region. Fires soon raged around the state's highest peak, Mt Bogong. On 1 December, yet another storm dumped snow 50 centimetres deep at the ski resort of Mt Hotham, one of the heaviest out-of-season snowfalls anyone could remember. Firefighters would be desperately defending Hotham village barely a month later.

While the weather danced its crazy dance, I stayed focused on my preparations to walk the Australian Alps Walking Track. This would be my summer on the track, fires or no fires, blizzards or no blizzards. Or would it? Even without the threat of extreme weather, was I really capable of this walk?

There's a strong argument that the Australian Alps Walking Track should be as well known as Spain's El Camino, America's Appalachian Trail, New Zealand's Milford Track or Tasmania's Overland Track, to name just a few of the world's most famous hikes. But most people have no idea the AAWT exists, and that includes most Australians. It may surprise you to learn that no peak on the Appalachian Trail is as high, or as likely to see snow in summer, as the top dozen peaks along the AAWT. The AAWT runs beneath one of the world's busiest domestic air routes between Australia's two largest cities, yet it traverses five designated wilderness areas, where even the most basic timber signs are forbidden as they constitute a human incursion. Along the predominantly north–south axis of the AAWT lie the bones of numerous ghost towns from the nineteenth-century gold rush, one of which – Kiandra in New South Wales – was the site of the world's first ski club, the Kiandra Snowshoe Club, formed in 1861. The AAWT passes by dozens of restored cattleman's huts, vestiges of the grazing era, which are wonderful emergency shelters. And it passes through the traditional country of at least 18 distinct Aboriginal clan groups.

The AAWT is a track that deserves to be attempted by tens of thousands of hikers each year in the warmer months. (Only a handful of people can handle it in winter, as it requires cross-country skiing expertise and elite survival skills.) Yet the full five-to-seven-week hike is attempted by as few as 100 groups or individuals annually. On my trip, I met just three other parties, two of them soloists like me.

Why so few hikers? And why so little recognition? Partly it's because the AAWT is tough. Seriously tough. Its total vertical ascent and descent is more than 28,000 metres, which is like climbing and descending Mt Everest from sea level three times. The track is also extremely remote in places. For much of its length, you can't just hop on or off the AAWT. Though it passes close to several ski resorts, the official route passes through no towns or settlements, and often goes days without crossing even the quietest back road. That means you must supply yourself with food drops in predator-proof containers hidden in the bush. The famous American and European through-hikes are dotted with towns, serviced huts or resupply facilities at least every few days. On those hikes, the principal requirements are good planning, resilience and shoes as comfortable as gloves. On the AAWT, you need those things and much, much more.

But the main thing that makes the AAWT so taxing on both mind and body is not the terrain or its inaccessibility. It's the misleading word in its title. That word is 'track'. The AAWT is not that. Not as one unbroken entity anyway. It's more like an accepted route. An idea. A join-the-dots of existing fire trails and hiking trails in varying states of repair and disrepair and, sometimes, no trail at all but just a spur or ridge or creek or valley to follow. To undertake the AAWT, you need a compass and at least a dozen local maps. GPS is also extremely useful, but you need to understand that even with your navigational aids you will lose the trail at times, and be forced to rely on bushcraft and common sense. You must prepare for swift river crossings with no bridges, weather that can and will do what it wants in any season, and drinking water that is not always easily found. And you should know that every single day on the trail, you will face moments of decision-making that will impact your distance travelled, your comfort level and perhaps even your survival chances. In short, an attempt on the AAWT should be classed as something between a long hike and an expedition.

Accomplished outdoorsman and leading trekking guide publisher John Chapman, along with his wife, Monica, and friend John Siseman, wrote the official guide to the AAWT, simply called *The Australian Alps Walking Track*. It's an impressively thorough book containing detailed track notes, maps, suggested walking itineraries, history and more. Attempting the walk without it would be unthinkable.

'The AAWT was never created or envisaged as a maintained, easy-to-follow walking track,' Chapman told me. 'The real issue has always been that the walk has the word "track" in its title and many walkers therefore expect it to be an easy-to-follow, well-marked track, like they find in many other places. We have always made it clear in the guide that this is not the case. Monica regards it as more of a concept of bushwalking though our alpine country. It really is more a traditional bushwalk that requires certain skills rather than a long-distance trail like the great American and European routes.'

The British author and mountaineer Robert Macfarlane, who has written extensively and elegantly on wild places and why we visit them, wrote in his book *The Old Ways: A Journey on Foot*:

> Paths are the habits of a landscape. They are acts of consensual making . . . without common care and common practice they disappear: overgrown by vegetation . . . Like sea channels that require regular dredging to stay open, paths NEED walking.

He's right. Paths do need walking. They also need maintenance. And despite the best intentions and ongoing hard work of many, the AAWT has barely enough of either. A National Parks employee I met on my hike said his office would love to devote time and resources to maintaining their particular section of the AAWT, but they have other priorities, like controlling feral animals which degrade the sensitive alpine environment, and feral humans who are even worse, treating national parks as their personal rubbish dump, fire pit, hunting ground and off-road rally course. Then there's fire prevention and fighting, which is pretty much a full-time distraction outside of the four-month snow season.

As things stand now, the AAWT still has some sort of identifiable trail on the ground for about 80 to 90 per cent of its length, due largely to the dedicated work of volunteers who organise weekend sorties with brush cutters and machetes. Will it ever become a clearly marked trail for its entire route? Possibly not. It certainly won't happen anytime soon.

The idea of a track across the Australian Alps was first floated in the late 1970s, as an extension of what was then the Victorian Alpine Track. But who would be responsible for a track that passed through two states and a territory? The breakthrough came in 1986, when Victoria, New South Wales and the Australian Capital Territory signed a memorandum of understanding with the federal government to co-operate in managing the alpine national parks. The Alps had never previously been managed as one biogeographical entity. The Australian Alps National Parks Co-operative Management Program changed that.

The Program soon settled on a route for the Australian Alps Walking Track. It would run from the small town of

Walhalla in Gippsland to the Namadgi National Park Visitor Centre near the village of Tharwa on Canberra's southern outskirts. Distinctive yellow trail markers were made. Signage was erected at key points. On the ground, not too much else changed.

Every few years, the Program updates its AAWT strategic and operational plan. The current plan explicitly states that the AAWT is not intended to be an Overland or Milford style of track where facilities are provided along the way. It says the bulk of the walk will continue to be a 'remote natural' experience for people 'with extensive overnight bushwalking experience and the skills to navigate and be self-sufficient'.

But there's a difference between a remote, natural track and a track that's often just not there. And here's the rub: despite the existence of an overarching body, state managers remain responsible for their respective sections. Politically, there are no votes in maintaining hiking tracks, so the upkeep of the AAWT remains in the classic bureaucratic crack of being everybody's and nobody's business.

John Chapman's book warns hikers about the toughness of the AAWT. It calls it a 'serious and strenuous undertaking', cautions against walking alone, and stresses that it should definitely not be attempted by people with no previous experience of a long through-hike.

People like me.

I took that on board and decided to give it a crack anyway. And as I tweeted from the trail head in Walhalla the day after that early December High Country blizzard: what's the worst that can happen on a 660-kilometre track half-covered by snow and blocked by fires in two places?

That's the point where you'd expect a line like, 'I was about to find out'.

And yeah, I was.

CHAPTER 2

NEGATIVE AND HARD AND LONELY

The shed is a crude structure, sharing its brick rear wall with an outhouse. The side walls are cheap timber cladding, defenceless against the incursions of a creeping vine. The front wall disintegrated in a recent rainstorm when the timber double-door blew off its hinges and took half the frame with it. Heavy rain drums on the tin roof, spattering the interior from a corner with a bad seal. The concrete floor is wet and there are so many mosquitoes, it's like someone just blew on a big black dandelion.

Of all the High Country huts I stayed in or visited, none were half as rough as the garden shed in my small backyard in an unfashionable Sydney suburb you've never heard of. But this shed will do as a workspace. Comfortably. That's one thing a long period in the wilderness does for you – you put up with flawed things. Scarcity becomes sufficiency. When the fourth wall is broken, things become more real. Theatregoers, that one's for you.

I'm out here in the shed now. My desk is a Formica workbench and the chair is not quite high enough, even with two cushions. The computer screen is cracked and the laptop battery won't charge properly. The wind howls and the dog next door barks. In front of me is the whiteboard on which I planned my AAWT trek. In the fading black chicken scratch I call my handwriting, the headings read: GEAR LIST/STILL NEED/ITINERARY. Some things, I got right. Snap-lock bags were a good inclusion on the gear list. I included them to hold food but ended up mostly using them to scoop water out of streams too shallow to dip bottles into. Absolute godsend. As for my itinerary, ha! Mt Skene to Mt Hotham in six days? Good one. The whole itinerary was laughably ambitious. Mountains on a map and mountains you climb are escalators versus staircases.

I'm piecing the hike together, trying to make sense of all that isolation and remoteness at a time when, suddenly, half the world is isolated and working remotely due to Coronavirus. I'm reading an online interview with Cheryl Strayed, author of the terrific book *Wild*, which became an excellent movie with Reese Witherspoon (aren't they all?), and which should not be confused with the movie *Into the Wild* about the young dreamer played by Emile Hirsch, who dies in an abandoned bus in Alaska after mistakenly eating poisonous plants while moody acoustic Eddie Vedder music plays.

'The beautiful thing about going alone is that every triumph is yours, every consequence of every mistake is yours, everything that you have to figure out is on you,' Strayed told a journalist about her hike on America's Pacific Crest Trail that inspired her book. 'That's a really powerful experience. And sometimes it is beautiful and positive and exciting, and sometimes it's negative and hard and lonely. I wanted that. I welcomed that.'

Me too. I also wanted and welcomed the hardships and triumphs of my own decisions on the trail, even if at times it was negative and hard and lonely. Before the AAWT, I'd only done short solo hikes of one or two nights' duration, but I was experienced enough to know that it's on you. All of it. Each literal and metaphorical fork in the road is yours to navigate. How far to aim each day? Your choice. Where to eat, drink, to camp, pitch your tent? All up to you. A short cut through scrub or extra miles on a marked trail? Only you can decide. I craved that autonomy. I needed it.

In regular life, we are at the mercy of other people's decisions. In our workplaces, people barely qualified to tie their shoelaces rise through the ranks because they use the latest jargon and are good with calendars. The more meetings you schedule, the more you must be doing. The more you act the part, the more people believe it. Out in the natural world, there's no faking it.

Pretending you're an expert does not work. Your well-laid-out CV does not impress nature. Your grandiose job title will not help you stay dry and upright when crossing a swollen river with a 20-kilogram pack. You cannot power dress a snowstorm into submission or fix a tent that rips in 100 kilometres per hour winds with corporate jargon, no matter how physically or metaphorically agile you are. You cannot climb a mountain by being adept at climbing the corporate ladder. There are no key stakeholders to think about in the outdoors. On a long solo hike, the only key stakeholder is you.

So I'm here in a shed with three walls but I'm back on the trail. It's day one. Six months of planning and training are behind me and my dad has driven me to Victoria. It's been a good trip. Three days on the road with the man who first took me to the mountains. Bonded like we hadn't bonded in years. The snow chain hire guy in Cooma thought we were crazy. Nobody hires chains in summer. And this wasn't just any summer. This was a summer when the Monaro plains around Cooma were dry to the point of scarification. Grass had turned to stubble and stubble had turned to dirt in what would prove to be Australia's hottest, driest year on record. And here we were, hiring snow chains. But I'd been watching the long-range forecast closely for ten days. A major cold front had been brewing and was now imminent. We were taking back roads to drop food in high, remote locations. Let chain guy laugh. We might need those chains. And we did.

Walhalla may be the start (or finish) of Australia's greatest hike, but it's the sort of town where people stroll. Set in a narrow valley accessed by roads that'd make a rally driver car sick, it's barely three hours from Melbourne but feels hidden from the world and divorced from all history except its own. Walhalla had a population of 5000 in the gold rush of the mid-to-late 1800s. These days it's closer to 20, but it feels like more because the restored period streetscape has made the town a popular tourist spot.

Walhalla's two signature buildings are the Star Hotel, a gem of rebuilt Victoriana with its freshly painted creamy timber façade and cast-iron filigree balcony railing, and the rotunda in the small park opposite.

The AAWT starts at the rotunda with minimal fanfare. It feels like there should be a band permanently playing, wishing northbound hikers well and congratulating successful southbound through-hikers. Instead, there's just a small yellow triangular AAWT symbol on a low post beside the rotunda, and a sign that says:

Old steel bridge 7 km
Mt Erica 23 km
Mt Bogong 267 km
Mt Kosciuszko 445 km
Namadgi National Park (ACT) 680 km

John Chapman's book says it's 660 kilometres, not 680 kilometres, to the track's end at the Namadgi Visitor Centre. Either way, it's a long stroll.

I clumsily farewell my dad. Men are so bad at hugging. He's taking highways instead of back roads now, which is good, but it's going to be a long drive home for him.

And that's that. I'm outta here. It's 3 p.m. There are 13 kilometres to my campsite. It won't get dark till much later this evening but it's time to hoof it. From the rotunda, the track ascends steeply for 100 steps or so. I don't look back until it levels out along a flat path. Long ago, this path supported a tramway whose carriages transported logs to the hungry furnaces of the mines, a shockingly wasteful alchemy of trees into gold.

So, how do I actually feel being alone on the AAWT after planning it for so long? In the world of sports journalism, where I've worked for many years, reporters often ask athletes how they feel after they've won a big thing they've trained for years to win. It's a fantastically inane question because, seriously, how do you think they feel? They feel happy. They feel elated. They feel 'stoked' if they're a surfer or snowboarder. They'll also tell you that they 'can't believe it', or that 'it hasn't sunk in yet'. I once interviewed a sports psychologist for a story on how long it actually takes for a really big thing to sink in for athletes. She told me it averages at about three weeks. So, hey, maybe somewhere approaching the New South Wales border I'll work out how I feel about tackling this thing. But right now, if I had to pinpoint an emotion, I'd say stoked.

Only kidding. I actually feel a little sombre. Melancholy, even. This I was not expecting. Maybe it's the grey day. Maybe it's the thought of weeks of solitude and everything that could go wrong. Maybe it's the daunting look of the high Baw Baw Plateau ahead, with its tablecloth of deep summer snow. I'll be up there tomorrow.

The mood eases as I walk. This former tramway is an excellent, unchallenging way to start the trek. For nearly two hours, the track hugs the contours of this steep lowland valley, occasionally winding into gullies of tree ferns and temperate rainforest with small, clear creeks, then back into dry, scrubby forest. As if to reassure me that good things lie ahead, the track presents a lyrebird, the talented forest mimic, famed for imitating everything from the calls of other birds to the buzz of chainsaws, with which it is all too familiar. The track delivers trigger plants by the hundreds, cheerful, single-stem plants which pollinate by slapping bees with a tiny ladle-shaped whacker when they alight on one of the delicate pink flowers. And the track offers up a black snake, but not a big one, because it wants to warn of dangers ahead but not totally scare the $90 beige Columbia Omni-Shade hiking pants off me.

The track has a sidekick in this early section. It's the Thomson River, Melbourne's primary water source, which is dark and brooding and in no hurry to get anywhere fast. Spanning it up ahead is the old steel bridge mentioned on the sign in Walhalla. Constructed in England in 1900, it's actually called the Poverty Point Bridge, a nod to the abandoned township of Poverty Point which once stood here and was named, you'd have to say quite cruelly, for the living standard of its residents.

There were all sorts of tragedies on this part of the river back in the day. Six immigrant Italian timber-cutters drowned in one boating accident. Another time, an enormous eucalypt fell and slid down the hill, wiping out an entire household. When you see the old photo of the bridge with ladies in white dresses and gentlemen in suits and a hillside almost entirely denuded of its giant eucalypts, you can imagine how that happened. A degraded forest is always more dangerous than a pristine forest.

All going well, in a few days I'll cross back over the Thomson on a log bridge where it's a swifter, clearer, more inviting stream. Exploring rivers at various stages of their life is one of the best things about hiking. Rivers run young and old at the same time. They are nature's time machines.

After the bridge, the AAWT climbs an unexpectedly tough section called Fingerboard Spur, an apt name because it's tapping you on the shoulder, a reminder that this track goes up and down like a yo-yo in an elevator all the way to Canberra, so hey, get used to it. At the top of the hill, the track crosses one of just six sealed roads on the entire journey then descends to a grassy campsite beside the Tyers River East. It's drizzling at the campsite but not enough to make life unpleasant. The river gurgles healthily and the forest smells like compost. There's a school group at the campsite. They give me Aldi imitation Tim Tams then leave me alone. I heat a foil pouch of curry in boiling water. It's spectacular. All food tastes better outdoors, especially actual food. I am no fan of the freeze-dried meal sachets sold in hiking stores. They are junk. All of them. The worst are the ones that sound the best, like coq au vin, which contains neither identifiable coq nor anything but the vaguest, slightly acrid, hint of vin. Many seasoned hikers dehydrate their own food. That was a level of culinary commitment beyond my energy and time. My solution was ready-to-eat curries sourced from the south Asian grocers of Sydney. I wanted to eat as much vegetarian food as possible, because there's that Netflix documentary about the ultramarathon runner who ran the entire 3500-kilometre Appalachian Trail in about three minutes on a plant-based diet. Who doesn't want to be that guy? But, for the sake of variety, I bought a mix of meat and veg. Some I sampled in advance, others were left as a mystery for the trail. Of those I tried, my favourite was the chicken karahi by the Pakistani company D'lish, which describes itself thus on the packet:

D'lish Chicken White Karahi is prepared with delectable mixed spices so that you may enjoy a great time together. This incredible meal will enable you to spend an incredible time anywhere you want.

Could the description be more relentlessly upbeat? Or, as it happens, accurate? I really am having an incredible time with my fragrant chicken karahi and the babbling Tyers River East and my knock-off Tim Tams and the thought of 13 solid kilometres behind me and a mere 647 to go.

And in the morning, the chirpy feeling vanishes quicker than the stars.

'For northbound walkers, this is the start of the longest single climb on the AAWT,' Chapman warns of the 1125-metre ascent from my riverside campsite to Mt Erica on the Baw Baw Plateau. A gate with an AAWT sign on it, crushed like a dead praying mantis by a fallen tree, is an omen of what lies ahead. The first half-hour is delightful, through mountain ash and native cherry with globular stoneless bright red native fruits that can be eaten. Not game to try.

Then the trail gets steep and slippery, with fallen trees turning it into an obstacle course. There are four ways to deal with tree trunks blocking a track. There is the straddle, where you step over it. This is harder than it sounds with a 20-kilogram pack on your back. There is the sit swivel, where you place your backside on the tree and swing your legs round. There's the belly swivel, similar to the previous manoeuvre but inverted and ungainly. And there's the crawl, slow, unpleasant, muddy and belittling, even with no one around. The crawl is also an invitation for leeches to hitch a ride. Hop on board, guys. I'm already losing time log-dodging, what's a few more minutes brushing you off? There goes my plan to have morning tea on the summit of Mt Erica. It'll be lunch or afternoon tea now.

Eventually the trail comes out on Mt Erica Road, an unsealed road on which only one car passes in the hour it takes me to get to the terminus at about 1100 metres above sea level. I stop at a picnic table in the forest to eat a wrap with a pouch of tuna and sundried tomatoes. Down lower, the air was moist, almost warm. It's cool here. An extra layer, maybe? Let's see if the track can warm me up.

The path is narrow again, boarded in places to stop it turning to mud. As it ascends, the trees change. Gone are the tall forest giants, replaced by thin-limbed snow gums. There's a real bite to the wind up here. How high am I? About 1300 metres, according to my GPS app which also tells elevation. This is the start of the snow line. At first, it's easy walking through the snow. It's satisfyingly crunchy underfoot. As it gets deeper towards the top of Mt Erica, it becomes a slog.

Like all peaks in the Baw Baw area, Mt Erica is a scarcely identifiable summit, an easily missed pimple which barely protrudes from the plateau. In this respect, it is typical of the Australian Alps, which are mostly not craggy or dramatic like the world's great mountain ranges, nor half as high. Indeed, the continent's highest peak, 2228-metre Mt Kosciuszko, is itself a minor protrusion, so unremarkable to the eye that debate rages over whether it was actually the mountain that Polish explorer Pawel Edmund Strzelecki climbed in 1840 and named after a compatriot whose name is an even higher-scoring Scrabble word than his own. Some say Strzelecki climbed Mt Townsend, 19 metres lower but a more dramatic peak.

One who definitely got it wrong was Austrian-born artist Eugene von Guérard, whose painting *North-east view from the northern top of Mount Kosciusko* hangs in the National Gallery of Australia. The 1863 artwork clearly shows the view from Townsend. No one who's climbed both Kosciuszko and Townsend could possibly say otherwise. More on that when we get there. If we get there. Suffice it to say for now that our Alps roll more than they rock. With a notable exception or two, they are rounded rather than jagged. And nowhere is this truer than the gently undulating tableland of the Baw Baw Plateau. But it's still a tough climb. Long way up. And, as mentioned, it really is chilly up here today.

Before the hike, I watched a lot of YouTube videos about through-hiking. There are videos about gear you absolutely must bring, gear you absolutely mustn't bring even though the previous video said you definitely should bring it, videos on what to wear, what to eat, how to poop in the woods – everything. One video urged hikers to dress lightly on climbs, so you don't sweat too much. Made sense. With that in mind, I've been wearing just a light shirt all day with a thin rain jacket tied around my waist. I put the jacket on. Not much of a difference but it'll do for now. Got to keep moving. My planned campsite near Mt Whitelaw is still about 12 kilometres off. Tired now, though. The climb has taken its toll. So have the last couple of kilometres of snow-covered track. And now the snow's really deep. Okay, and the trail just disappeared. Nope, not there anymore. What can you say? Day two on the AAWT, no one about and I've lost the trail in deep snow in the first week of the Australian summer. Hello, negative and hard and lonely.

The good news is there is a difference between losing the trail and being lost. I know where I am, at the site of a former shelter called Talbot Hut, of which only the chimney remains. Chapman's book says the AAWT branches off to the west just up the hill from here. Must have missed the junction. Wonder how far back it was? Seriously cold now as I thumb through the book. Can barely flick between pages with numb hands. Starting to shiver. Two hikers approach. They are women who say they're camping the night at the hut site. One sets up their tent while the other guides me to the spot where the AAWT turns off. No wonder I missed the fork – there's no official trail marker. Or, if there is, it's buried. I try to express my thanks but more or less just grunt. No doubt she thinks I'm too proud or stubborn to show gratitude. In truth, I'm shivering pretty badly and trying to hide it. There's also a bit of a disconnect between my brain and mouth. This, my wife might argue, is no cause for alarm. Regular programming. But this is not normal.

Hypothermia is like a crumb on your lip – it's difficult to spot the signs yourself. But I'm mountain-wise enough to recognise its early onset. It was stupid of me not to wear more layers in this wind, climb or no climb. I quickly layer up with a thermal undergarment and fleece jacket. I eat a muesli bar and pick up my pace. It's tough in the deep snow but I've got to get my blood flowing. This is a moment for necessity, not comfort. The track dips a little in elevation, just enough that the snow thins out. It dips a little more and the path turns to mud. The path is quite the scene here, a dark serpentine strip between snow-covered bushes, slender snow gums forming an arboreal tunnel.

Peter Maffei, president of the volunteer group The Friends of Baw Baw National Park, says there are parts of the plateau that are old and otherworldly, like something you might see in a movie. He says there's one spot that locals affectionately call Hobbitland. Think I might have found it. If I haven't, it'll do.

Early evening. I won't get close to Mt Whitelaw, so I decide to camp at the first suitable location. I just need somewhere sheltered from the wind. Snow-free would be a bonus. I find both in a protected glade surrounded by myrtle beech and mountain tea-tree. It's a really beautiful little clearing. It's the sort of place where the hobbits would meet for tea each afternoon with the sylphs, elves and fluffy bunnies. I pitch the tent on smooth tussock-free grass beside two small granite boulders. They make perfect furniture, one for cooking on, one for sitting on. Dinner is hot miso soup with noodles, dessert is a choc-coconut bar and an apple, and bedtime is well before dark, swaddled in my sleeping bag, ahead of a night forecast to dip well below freezing.

'Everything that you have to figure out is on you,' Strayed said. 'That's a really powerful experience.'

It is. And it is.

CHAPTER 3

WHAT THE WEEDS REVEALED

It's warmer today. The snow is rapidly vanishing, and the bitter winds have gone to annoy New Zealand for a few days. Summer is muscling its way back onto the Baw Baw Plateau. I am well slept and I really feel like walking on this glorious Thursday. So I walk. The first hour is carefree rambling on a well-marked trail winding through snow gum woodland and intermittent frost hollows – shallow depressions where cold air pools on winter nights, preventing the growth of trees.

Walking really is the most underrated activity. It's the simplest physical activity of all, and the one which arguably first made us human. Think of all the single-person transportation devices. The bicycle, the motorbike, the Segway, the skateboard, the scooter, the ski. They all propel you in ways that are efficient or thrilling, but they distort the passing landscape or distract you from it. Walking is uncomplicated. Unimpeded by mechanisms that constrict your body and steal your attention, walking is an activity that is free in every sense of the word.

Walking is a workout for the senses. When you walk, you view the world as an ongoing story, not just a scene. As a hiker, you smell the landscape: the menthol of alpine mint bush, the earthiness of mud, the timberyard aroma of a freshly cracked snow gum branch. You hear the world as a walker. The squelch of boots on snow patches, the drawn-out whistle and crack of the whipbird. Filling your bottles with the minerally water of an alpine creek, a walker tastes the world. And you touch the landscape as a walker, as brambly bushes brush your forearms, and when you settle beside a creek to eat Vita-Weats with Laughing Cow cheese, carefully sliding your backside onto a snow grass tussock so it cushions you instead of prickling.

Walking is a mind cleanser. It's like meditation standing up. When you walk, you travel at the speed of thought. You fall into a rhythm, the meandering mind in step with the winding track. We spend our lives funnelling our thoughts, setting them to a task. We talk of chasing our dreams but have forgotten how to daydream. Walking calms us. In a digital age, when our thoughts pinball around, walking encourages the mind to drift rather than dart. To flit and flutter like a mint green butterfly in bushes in alpine heathland. 'Methinks that the moment my legs begin to move, my thoughts begin to flow,' the American philosopher, nature lover and hiker Henry David Thoreau wrote. Thoreau knew a thing or two.

So, then. With the nervous skittishness of day one and the cold of day two behind me, what sublime reflections waft through my mind on this truly exquisite morning of day three? I'm thinking about work. Depressing, but it was always going to happen.

I'm actually thinking about the bigger picture, about my career. I started as a long-form writer for magazines then became a digital specialist because magazines were dying and the internet was booming. Lately, I've been writing quick news and sports hits for websites as well as snappy copy for television. In many ways, my career path has mirrored the ever-increasing pace of the modern media, and of modern life itself. When I started, I would sometimes take a week to write a story. Now, it can be a minute. Some days, I still produce quality work. Other days, the information I convey is of no practical use to anyone. I am a waster of your time, and of my own. A master of the dark art of clickbait.

I used to be excited by the immediacy of digital journalism. Get the tone right and you'd be a star on social media for, oh, at least two hours. Now, it just exhausts me. Maybe it's burnout due to the added responsibilities of partnership and parenthood, which my predominantly younger colleagues don't have. All I know is I used to want to be a rock star. Now I just want to be a rock. Or hide under a rock. Or something.

The trail passes over Mt St Phillack, another nondescript peak which would be challenged for prominence by your average lump. It then threads through a thickly forested section where the path is strewn with bark freshly torn from the trees by the strong winds of the past few days. Long strands repeatedly catch my boots and drag along behind me. A couple of times I pause to shake them off but that becomes a full-time job, so I stop bothering and let them trail along until they free themselves.

When I was very young, my dad took my brother and me to the rugby league grand final. For the record, the Parramatta Eels beat the Newtown Jets 20–11, securing their first premiership. But I don't actually remember the game. Indeed, I recall only two things from that day. There was Jetpack Guy, who took off with an enormous whoosh and flew clear across the ground. To this day, Dad goes full Darryl Kerrigan when talking about him. And there was Bagpipe Guy. Before the game, a pipe band marched a long, slow lap of the Sydney Cricket Ground. At one point, a streamer hooked itself around his shoe. It was a long streamer and it looked extremely comical as Bagpipe Guy trudged along in step with 'Scotland the Brave' or whatever they were playing, without missing a note. It must have distracted the hell out of him, and he must have had a strong urge to kick the streamer off, but he did nothing. He marched his whole lap like the streamer was never there. Would it have ruined his playing if he'd shaken his foot? Could he not have passed off such a manoeuvre as some sort of Highland fling? Was he even aware of the streamer? Perhaps he was blissfully oblivious. Maybe he just didn't care. This is the 38-year-old conundrum that occupies my hiker's mind as I approach the turn-off to Baw Baw village, which I may or may not need to visit today. My charging cord is giving me grief and may need replacing. I've got a solar charger affixed to the top of my pack with a cord dangling down into my shirt pocket in a nifty little set-up, but the phone's not charging properly. I thoroughly tested my phone battery and the solar panel before I left, so the problem has to be the cord.

Baw Baw is open for summer mountain biking. Like most Australian ski resorts, it is trying to reinvent itself as a year-round destination. This is crucial for ski resorts worldwide in an age of dwindling snow, and particularly urgent in Baw Baw's case as it's the lowest of the mainland Australian ski resorts. Its summit is just 1566 metres above sea level, although 'summit' is a generous description for a high point that would struggle to find steady work as a mound. Baw Baw has been treading an increasingly fine line with snow coverage. It tends to close and reopen several times each season and reportedly came close to ceasing operations entirely in 2013 due to financial issues. For now, it struggles along. Other Australian downhill ski resorts have not been so lucky.

In 2006, a watershed moment occurred in the Australian Alps that was every bit as significant as the first mass coral bleaching on the Great Barrier Reef in the late 1990s, but was never reported in those terms. Indeed, it was scarcely reported at all outside of small regional newspapers and snow industry websites. The winter of 2006 was warm and dry across the Australian Alps. For the first time ever, the winter snowpack fell short of 90 centimetres, topping out at just 85.1 centimetres at Spencers Creek, the highest of three New South Wales sites at which hydro-electric operator Snowy Hydro has taken controlled snow depth readings since 1954 so it can predict the spring inflow to its dams.

The season was bad in Victoria too, especially up at Mount Buffalo National Park, an isolated, boulder-strewn massif cut off from the rest of the High Country. It's the only significant chunk of Australian Alps bypassed by the AAWT, but it's still beautiful and historic. Buffalo was the site of Australia's first ski lift, a humble rope tow installed in 1937. By 2006, Buffalo skiers had been anguishing over dwindling snow for years. There are old black-and-white photos of people skating on the man-made reservoir Lake Catani, but by the turn of the millennium the ice was more likely to be as thin as milk skin on hot chocolate. Then came the double whammy. First, the tiny Cresta Valley ski area barely opened its lifts all winter, with meagre snowfalls. Then, in December, fire ripped through the national park, destroying virtually everything. While Buffalo continues to flourish as a destination for cross-country skiing and family snowplay, its ski lifts have never reopened. The nearby Mount Buffalo Chalet survived the 2006 fire, but the grand European-style alpine hotel, built in 1910 and much loved by generations of Melburnians, also closed for business soon afterwards and remains shuttered. Thus did Australia lose its first downhill ski resort to the warming climate. The only question was which one would be next.

That would be answered in January 2020, when a ferocious fire levelled Selwyn Snow Resort in New South Wales. The small, beginner-orientated resort was where I taught my kids to ski. It was affordable and friendly, the vibe chilled but not cool. You could be a great big dorky dad at Selwyn and blend right in. Now it's ashes. Selwyn's owners have announced plans to rebuild, but not until after the 2020 winter. So, provisionally at least, two of the nine mainland Australian downhill ski resorts are victims of a warming climate. We are watching them disappear before our eyes.

For now, Baw Baw remains fully operational. It specialises in the beginner's market, which means it needs less snow than the bigger resorts. Another selling point is its proximity to Melbourne: it's the only downhill ski resort within easy day-trip distance of one of Australia's two largest cities. And, as mentioned, there's the summer trade, which might just be a godsend for me.

This phone cord situation is a worry. It's new, so why is it not working? I'm testing the cord while eating a peanut butter wrap at a small trackside grassy flat. Okay, it's charging now. Jiggle, jiggle. Yep, definitely still charging. Hmm, perhaps no side trip to Baw Baw village is required.

If you look at the Baw Baw Plateau on Google Earth, you'll notice it looks smoother, less furrowed than the surrounding forested country. The nearby terrain is crinkled tinfoil after it wrapped a sandwich. Baw Baw is tinfoil straight off the roll. But its smooth featurelessness does not equate to blandness. 'It's a subtle landscape,' Peter Maffei says. That it is. Subtle and sublime. Rosellas chirrup and dart through the snow gum canopy. The trees are tight, intimate, but not spooky or conspiratorial. The shafts of light that filter between them are golden and pure. Flowers flower. Bees buzz. Frogs enthusiastically ribbit in the gurgling creek. Are they *frosti*, I wonder? Sadly, that's unlikely. The Baw Baw frog, aka *Philoria frosti*, is critically endangered. Its numbers dropped alarmingly recently, victim to some sort of fungus. There are now thought to be only a few hundred of the brown-and-yellow amphibians left in the wild. Fortunately, Zoos Victoria has a program to keep them croaking so they don't croak for good.

Peter Maffei has walked the plateau for decades and never seen a *frosti*, which disappoints him a little. But there's another thing he's never seen on Baw Baw, which he's extremely glad about: fire. Incredibly, the plateau has not burned since the Black Friday fires of 1939, which started on Friday 13 January and ignited the entire Victorian High Country. Almost all of the High Country has burned since then, much of it multiple times, some of it several times already this century. Yet Baw Baw remains an island of unburnt good health. And while the plateau's eponymous ski hill sits firmly in the firing line of a warming climate, its forests have not been in the literal line of fire for 80 years.

The 2009 Black Saturday fires came close. Ten years on, the cross-country ski trails of nearby Lake Mountain are still starkly scarred with grey alpine ash. But, somehow, Baw Baw escaped. The alpine ash forests surrounding the plateau are mostly unburned, and so is the snow gum woodland on top of it. Seems likes Hobbitland really has magical powers after all. Spoilsports that they are, the experts say another factor is at play.

'When alpine ash gets mature, it gets to a very low flammability stage,' alpine ecology and fire dynamics expert Dr Phil Zylstra explains. Zylstra's work shows that the less frequently alpine ash forests burn, the less likely they will burn badly in the future. That's because the understory layer naturally thins out over time, making the inevitable small and medium-sized fires much less likely to become megafires which crown, roaring through the treetops and killing everything.

This is an important and challenging concept. The prevailing narrative, echoed by Australians of all political stripes during and after the Summer of Fires, is that we must burn the bush more often under controlled conditions to stop uncontrolled bushfires. But it's not that simple, especially in the subalpine forests. As Zylstra wrote in the literary journal *Meanjin*:

Recently, I looked at every fire mapped across these mountains for nearly 60 years, and I found one thing in common from the foothills to the peaks: fire has always followed fire. For a couple of years, it brought quiet, then the undergrowth made the forests up to eight times more likely to re-burn for the next couple of decades until it self-thinned.

Zylstra is Honorary Research Fellow at the Centre for Sustainable Ecosystem Solutions at the University of Wollongong and Adjunct Associate Professor at Curtin University. The only thing longer than his job titles is his hair. He's a mathematician by training. In 2018, he published the results of a study in which he'd modelled a staggering 36 million data points from 58 years of mapped fire history over 1.5 million hectares.

The key takeaway?

Remarkably, he found that the areas that hadn't burned for the longest time were the *least* likely to burn again. Again, this is a massive challenge to the prevailing narrative of burn, baby, burn to prevent major fires.

'If the forest gets more flammable as it gets older, you would expect it to burn more into those older areas,' Zylstra tells me. So where was it burning more into?

'My research showed that for every single forest, there was this mid-range that the fires always favour. You had this short period of grace after a fire where you had bare ground. Then you had a few decades of really flammable forest. And then when it was older than that, the fires tended to burn around those patches or just creep into the edges.'

A keen hiker, Zylstra is the son of Dutch immigrants. They initially settled in Adaminaby, a town on the north-eastern fringe of Kosciuszko National Park which would be severely threatened by fires in January 2020, but he grew up in Blacktown in western Sydney, which he describes as 'the wrong place to like science and write poetry and that sort of stuff'. Repressing both his intellectual and lyrical urges, he moved to the mountains as a young man to work with sheep and cattle, having developed a love for the alpine region during boyhood family camping trips.

Then, one day, he had a bit of a realisation.

'We were sitting having smoko in a shearing shed one day and I just said to the others, "You know, I reckon I'm going to go to uni one day and do a science degree." An awkward silence followed. '"Scientist, eh? We might be sittin' with the next Einstein!"' his colleagues joked.

But Zylstra was serious. He went and got his degree and soon faced a dilemma.

'There was a job going with National Parks, and funny thing was, I'd grown up in this community where National Parks were the enemy and they were the reason for feral animals and weeds and bushfires and all those sorts of things,' he says. 'You just absorb that thinking and if anyone says differently, you think they're mad. That's where I was at. I didn't want to work for Parks at the time, but it was the only job going.'

About a year into his Parks job, he had another lightbulb moment.

'I'd done a lot of work with native grasslands while I was studying, and I used to look at grazing management with native grasslands. So one day I was waiting for somebody in a paddock just bordering the national park. While I was standing there, I was making a habitual identification of all the grassland plants around me, and I suddenly realised they were nearly all weeds. I'd never seen this in the park. This was private land bordering Kosciuszko National Park and it was a huge moment of revelation for me. This was a typical paddock – it was actually a pretty good paddock – and yet it was far, far more weedy than the park. I'd never taken that in. It really got me thinking that I had some unconscious bias in there.'

Overgrazing, Zylstra explains, is a bit like over-burning. It encourages the wrong type of vegetation. It hurts the land in all sorts of ways when it just needs to be left alone. Zylstra is a deep thinker on the environment. He's a micro-scale analyst with his millions of data points but he's a macro-scale thinker too, being widely read in everything from Indigenous firestick farming methods to the history of British forestry practices which were imported to Australia with disastrous effect.

'I think this all comes back to the role that we see for ourselves in the natural world,' he says. 'I grew up in a very religious environment and we were constantly taught that we are in charge of the natural world, we are the peak of it, God's put us there and we've got to subdue the natural world.

'And because of this mentality, we've got the view that the natural world is playing up against us, and we've got to stomp down and take control. We have to be stronger and more forceful. It's an authoritarian view, where we see ourselves as these beings that rule the world around us, and we've got to make it submit to us.'

Citing direct conversations he's had with Aboriginal elders, Zylstra explains that the popular understanding of Aboriginal firestick farming techniques is grossly simplified. He says they never ran around the bush burning it willy-nilly, and that they burned small, targeted areas, mostly on established travel routes. He argues that modern Australians need to burn small areas rather than vast tracts of bush in the name of fire prevention.

'In 60 years of prescribed burning, we still don't have a single study to show that burning big remote areas saves houses from fire. What we do have is studies showing that burning close to those houses can be helpful, and that's where any burning needs to happen.'

It's a simple, cost-effective thesis which is yet to strike a populist chord.

It also makes me think about my own situation. Let's use a little fire lingo to help draw out the parallels with the Zylstra hypothesis. I was burnt out at work. Like the forests, this made me much more likely to flare up. And I did flare up. And when that happened, it was extremely hard to put out such a big fire.

Back on the AAWT, the trail is good. It's a little overgrown as it descends the northern edge of the Baw Baw Plateau, but nothing unmanageable. I'm lucky. A day or two earlier, the track would have been impossible to find under snow. Now at least I can spot it if I pull aside the occasional bush. Intuition helps. You look at the contours of the landscape ahead and think, 'Where would I put the trail?' And that's where it usually is.

At least a couple of times a year, The Friends of Baw Baw National Park runs working parties clearing the trail up here with as many as 20 volunteers. Sometimes, equipment and extra labour are provided by one of two state government bodies – Parks Victoria and the Department of Environment, Water, Land and Planning – and sometimes not. But the Friends do it anyway. One volunteer generally clears about 100 metres of overgrown track a day, Peter Maffei says. So a full working party on the four-day Easter long weekend might clear eight kilometres in total. It's a slow, tough labour of love. No wonder they can't keep areas like this remote section totally free of bushes.

No matter. Progress may be slow but my evening target is near. I'm headed for Stronachs Camp, a small grassy clearing where they built a sawmill after the 1939 fires to process whatever timber was salvageable. I'd wanted to get further. I was ambitiously aiming for a grassy campsite on the banks of the Thomson River but was forced to recalibrate by a good ten kilometres because of slow-going, and because the AAWT sneers a big evil grin at anyone who sets the daily distance bar too high. No matter. I arrive at Stronachs right on dusk, hungry, thirsty, but in good spirits. Everything is okay. Hang on – no, it's not.

My phone cord has broken. The bit that plugs into the phone has snapped clean in half. I see now why charging was erratic. The attachment must have been in the process of destructing. Pretty sure I've got to own this. Dangling the charger from the solar panel into my pocket was a silly idea. The physics were all wrong. It tugged while I walked and placed too much load on the flimsiest part of the cord. Anyway, the 'why' is not important. It's about the 'what', as in, what exactly have I lost here? Can I get by without my phone?

No calls is a biggie but not a game changer. No photos, ditto. I can also survive without GPS as I have a compass and maps and Chapman's book with its detailed track notes. I also have an emergency beacon if things get really bad. So all things considered, I can live without my phone until I take a quick track detour into Hotham ski resort, which is still at least ten days away. But do I want to? I could get to Baw Baw village and back in a day if I set off early tomorrow. One day's walking in exchange for a phone that works. Maybe that's the smart move.

First things first. I pitch the tent and go looking for water, which Chapman's bible says can be found in a creek ten minutes down the lonely logging road adjacent to the campsite. The Bible: that's what I'm calling it henceforth. I walk out to the road and whoa ... hello. That I was not expecting.

CHAPTER 4

THE INSANITY
OF CHOICES

It's the first human I've seen all day. I wave. She waves. She draws near. *Hi. Hi.* Her name is Simone and she is the first AAWT through-hiker I've met. She has walked an obscene distance to make it to this forest clearing this fine summer's evening and plans to walk much further tonight, under the light of her headtorch. I suggest a cup of tea and a hot curry before she takes off. Who'd say no to that?

The curry is a good one. A veggie thing in a spicy, golden sauce. It's the first hot meal Simone has had in days and she devours it. Simone is a cold-soaker. One of the videos I watched before this trip was about through-hikers who use cold water to rehydrate their dinner in sealed containers. It saves on the weight of a cooking apparatus and fuel, but it must be miserable eating clammy wet muck after a long day on the trail. But for hardcore through-hikers, the rule is simple: travel light. If you can live without it, don't take it. Naturally, then, I'm not remotely hopeful when I ask if she happens to have a spare phone charging cord.

'You mean you're not carrying a spare one?' she laughs. You'd think I'd forgotten to bring pants. Just like that, Simone gives me her spare cord. Yes, this really happens. Five minutes after my first serious gear failure, the first person I've seen all day replaces it. She also tips a litre of water into one of my bottles so I don't have to find that creek. What strange magic is this? Trail magic, that's what. And it's as real as the trees and the rocks.

Simone tells me about trail angels. She says one time she was really thirsty when a trail angel cleverly disguised as a horseman gave her a whole bag of oranges. She ate them all on the spot. Then there was the time in Tasmania when the route back to her car was blocked by a police operation to apprehend a criminal. A pair of trail angels, in character as a local hiking couple, escorted her to their car, which was parked in an accessible place, drove her to their home in Hobart and let her stay for two nights. They even washed and pressed her clothes, gave her fresh undies, then drove her four hours back to her car when the criminal had been captured.

'New undies was a first but very much appreciated,' she says. I bet.

And now the hiking boot is on the other foot. Simone has become an angel herself, distributing phone accessories to clueless first-time through-hikers. She decides to stay the night. We don't have a fire going – through-hikers usually don't – but over hot tea cooked on my Jetboil stove, she reveals a little about herself. She hikes fast. Really fast. She is as dogged as the tortoise and as rapid as the hare. That blizzard a few days ago? She and another solo hiker called Ferg gutsed their way right through it over several marathon days on the most exposed section of the entire AAWT, where to stop would have been to freeze. As for tomorrow, she plans to wake at dawn and hike the entire 46.3 kilometres to Walhalla in a day. All of it. It took me two-and-a-half days. Admittedly, I was going uphill with a full pack and she'll be going down, but still. Simone is several types of supernatural beings rolled into one.

Before going to bed, Simone gives a briefing on the trail ahead. She says the two or three kilometres from Stronachs are a mess of fallen trees and obscured track, and that the whole track is tough in different ways for the next ten days or so until you reach Mt Hotham, after which it's pretty easy. She says it's a good idea to try the AAWT north to south on your first attempt, rather than south to north like me, because the first two weeks at the Canberra end are much easier and you can ease your way into the tougher sections. Simone would know: she's walked the AAWT three times.

Three times?

'Three times,' she answers, like she's walked her dog around the block three times.

Simone has an even bigger trek in mind for late 2020. She plans to walk from the tip of Cape York to the tip of southern Tasmania, which means she'll cross the continent on its longest north–south axis. Presumably she'll hop a ferry from the mainland to Tasmania, though I wouldn't put it past her to swim the 250 kilometres across the heaving waters of Bass Strait in a single afternoon, cold-soaking a lovely container of seaweed to eat on arrival in Devonport or Ulverstone while she drip-dries on the beach.

Simone says the organisation for the trip is doing her head in. She'll need hundreds of maps and will have to organise six months' worth of food and replacement gear to be sent by post. She's already reading up on croc safety. Never scoop water from the same part of the river twice: that's the first tip. Sneaky bastard crocs watch everything.

'Most people underestimate what they can do. I downplay stuff and then push through the insanity of my choices,' she says before disappearing into her tent. She's up and gone at dawn and I don't see her again.

* * *

In the morning, it's time to push through the insanity of my own choices. Simone was right; the track north of Stronachs is a nightmare. I want Baw Baw back. Sure, in places it had treefall, or there were bushes obscuring the track, and at times there was mud and snow and leeches. Minus the snow, all that and more await me here, in this nameless patch of bush on the northern flank of the plateau. It's an obstacle party and every stumbling block, snag, hindrance, impediment and encumbrance is invited.

Treefall is a natural occurrence in any bushland, but this forest was selectively logged a few decades back. It also burned. Those two factors meant that the few trees still standing were left without the protection of their arboreal accomplices and had little chance against winter gales. So they fell across the track, one by one, year on year, in a tangle of trunk and branches and upended roots. It's like fighting through a bird's nest in Brobdingnag. I'll let that line breathe for a moment while I haul myself over a log that was once a tree as high as a 20-storey building.

Okay, so if you've never read *Gulliver's Travels*, Lilliput is the land of the little people and Brobdingnag is where the giants live. The eighteenth-century classic masquerades as a satirical rollicking travelogue but if there's a greater work of misanthropy in the history of literature, then I haven't read it. Towards the end of the book, Gulliver visits a land where horse-like creatures are more intelligent and refined than people. When he gets home, he spends hours each day in the stables talking to the horses, having more or less written off humanity.

Are all solo journeys expressions of misanthropy? Possibly, though I think you can have the urge to flee the world without hating it. At some point, we all dream of fleeing our families, our jobs, our friends, our homes, our situations – all or any of it. Can we reconcile ourselves to our place in the world when we return? That depends on where the trail leads, doesn't it?

Right now, the trail is leading pretty much nowhere. Literally. If I could just get some of those Brobdingnagians to come along and play a nice game of pick-up-sticks, I could do a little hiking here instead of wrestling my way through this land-based logjam.

This I know: if I continue on a northward bearing, I'll eventually meet an old logging road called the Upper Thomson Road. From there, the AAWT follows vehicular tracks for 25 kilometres to tonight's campsite at the site of a former gold mining town called Red Jacket, or the slightly closer Blue Jacket. Either will do. I'm admirably ambivalent when it comes to abandoned settlements named after colourful garments. I need to get at least as far as Blue Jacket to keep to my schedule. My first food drop is at a 1570-metre peak called Mt Skene, and I've given myself six days to get there. I'm carrying a day of emergency rations so I can be a little flexible. Still want to make it on time, though, so I can reach the second drop at Mt Hotham on time, and then the three drops after that, and then get back to work on time and so on. Mind you, work schmerk. What's the point of work you no longer believe in? Feeding the family and paying the mortgage: those are two reasons. But you can do that other ways than working in a digital newsroom, living and dying a dozen weekly deaths as the analytics chart surges and dips with reader numbers. In a way, I feel sorry for the younger journalists. They've never known the quiet dignity of writing a story without knowing how many people liked it or were concurrently reading it, or how far down the digital page they read. Believe me, you don't want to know how far people read into your stories before they clicked a cat video. I'll just say this: put all the important stuff early. That was always a rule of journalism, triply so now.

Maybe I'll drive buses or mow lawns or something when I get home. Maybe I'll chainsaw dead trees to pieces on the northern fringe of the Baw Baw Plateau. It wouldn't pay well but it'd provide a much-needed public service, which is more than I can say about most jobs I've had in the last ten years.

I'd better get a wriggle on here. Literally wriggling. And squirming, clambering and crawling. Whatever it takes. The trees don't just slow progress, they conspire with the undergrowth which has grown back fiercely – à la Phil Zylstra's analysis of post-fire forest regrowth – to obscure the track. Here and there, helpful hikers have tied ribbons or lengths of cord to standing trees to mark the way. Occasionally, the track even puts in a brief cameo. 'Aha!' my brain exclaims. 'You've found the track now. All will be good.' Then the track disappears again. Then I spot it again and the goldfish brain goes, 'This time you won't lose it!' Then another tree blocks your path and the trail goes AWOL again. Then you see a sign nailed to a tree warning of the dangers of treefall and your perfectly sensible brain goes, 'If someone has gone to all the trouble of walking out here to nail this sign up, why not also nail a few official triangular yellow AAWT markers to the largest, most sturdy trees while they're at it?' The answer, no doubt, is that the Department of Treefall Notices is not the same as the Department of Yellow AAWT Signs. How good is bureaucracy? Did I mention I left Stronachs without brewing coffee this morning? My goldfish brain and my sensible brain both feel like they have been stung by jellyfish.

The slope steepens as I bash and crash onwards, occasionally on what might be the trail, mostly not. And just like that, there's the old logging road. I've arrived at civilisation, or at least something that once served it. Phew. By the road, a knee-high timber post with a triangular yellow AAWT marker points back into the bush. Good luck anyone going that way. 'Can't this trail just be easy for a day?' I ask the yellow marker. Yes, I'm talking to a triangle. In *Into the Wild*, it takes Chris McCandless weeks in Alaska to start having in-depth conversations with himself and/or inanimate objects. Four days into this trip and I'm Tom Hanks talking to his volleyball Wilson. At least the triangle doesn't answer back. When the shapes start talking, you really know you've lost it.

In truth, this is a good moment. If there's one constant companion on this track, it's not loneliness or flies or trees or mountains or clouds or sun or the weight of my pack on my shoulders. It's stress. Seems like there's always something to worry about. All that stuff I wrote about your thoughts freeing themselves and flitting about like butterflies when

THE INSANITY OF CHOICES

you hike? The feeling appears then vanishes like a lyrebird in the scrub. I've been weighed down by worry every day. On day one, it was the enormity of the whole trip. On day two, there was the huge climb and cold to contend with. On day three, there was the phone cord drama. Today, there was that horizontal forest. Then there are the constant lesser worries. How far to the next reliable creek? Do I have enough phone charge? Should I stop, take off my gaiters and unlace my boots to remove that tiny pebble? What's the weather doing? What's the cricket score? Why do I care what the cricket score is? Is my chest strap too tight? Is that sneeze the onset of a head cold or am I just allergic to something? Will there be a log bridge down at the Thomson River or will I have to wade? If I have to wade, how deep will the water be? The hiking mind can be as busy as a social media feed.

But, right now, all that matters is I'm through that forest. Life is good. A good life is always a better life with coffee. I take off my pack and boil up a brew with the last of my water, save for a swig or two, perched on my haunches in a roadside culvert.

A few years ago, after giving Rupert Murdoch ten of the best years of my professional life, I took long service leave and went to the French Alps with my wife and kids. We based ourselves in a large town just over the border from Italy. Friends from England visited one weekend, flying in to Torino. When they left, I drove them to Torino airport in a rental car. It was the first time I'd driven in Europe and it was extremely nerve-racking because Italy manufactures many of the world's fastest cars and every single driver thinks they're in one, including the truck drivers. On the way back, I pulled in at a petrol station for whatever excuse for coffee they could offer. Inside, a man in a crisp white shirt and black bowtie was working a classic espresso machine behind a marble bar. I sat down on a padded swivel stool and ordered an espresso. It arrived with the most satisfying clink of saucer on stone. That was a memorable coffee.

This one is better. I have real coffee grounds and mountain water and a filter attachment to my Jetboil stove and milk powder. And I have the satisfaction of getting through that nameless forest. You can have your skim decaf mochafrappiato or whatever you're sipping now on your 9.30 a.m. 'I've checked my emails and gossiped with my colleagues and seriously considered doing some work but not quite yet' coffee run; your coffee is nowhere near as good as my back-end-of-Baw-Baw brew.

I take out the map. All around me is Nowhere Country. Miles and miles of very little, with only a single town far from the trail, Woods Point, population 37 plus or minus the lyrebirds. This was all Somewhere Country back in the gold rush days of the 1860s. Not now. When people dream of walking the High Country, nobody fantasises about the country north of Baw Baw and south of Mt Skene. In truth, this is not even really High Country, not that there's a strict delineation. The winter snowline in the Australian Alps is around 1200 to 1400 metres above sea level, give or take, depending on how far north or south you are and whether you're on the western flank or the slightly warmer, drier eastern slopes. However you define it, this ain't it.

Ahead of me now is lower country, with thickly timbered valleys dipping below 500 metres and ridges rising to 1100 or 1200 metres. There are no prominent peaks and the only geographical landmarks of note are three rivers – the Thomson, Jordan and Black. From what I can tell, the country ahead is neither pretty nor ugly. It's just country, nameless and utterly un-Instagrammable. But there's something exciting about it. As much as I yearn to be walking among the snow gums and alpine grasshoppers, this Nowhere Country is enticing. The singer from the folk band America rode a horse without a name across the desert, but I bet that desert had a name. All those empty expanses of ice in Antarctica have names. How often in life do we go somewhere without a name?

I finish the most satisfying cup of coffee in history, heave my pack onto my back, strap up at the hip and chest and stride off, expecting to meet only one other person in the next three days.

After a couple of kilometres on the Upper Thomson Road, a track called the Trig Point Track descends to the Thomson River. It's so steep and gravelly and skiddy, I have to use my hiking poles as brakes, but even that fails to stop me splatting on my backside twice. This puts me in an exceptionally sweary mood for the next hour or two. A fly kamikaze-dives down my throat, I swear like a rugby league player who's just won the grand final. My phone's out of charge, I curse like a garbageman whose thumb just wedged in the truck's grinding apparatus. A snake crosses my path, I urge it to go listen to some funk music. This trail really is stressful. But it also has a knack of knowing when you've had enough. Sometimes the trail itself is the angel.

The Thomson River is wonderful. It's swift and narrow and clear and much friendlier than its bottomless, brooding older self at Poverty Point near Walhalla. I strip to my undies and have my first proper wash in four days while charging the phone in the sun on Simone's cord, which of course works perfectly. Lunch is wraps with sundried tomatoes and tuna from a foil pouch. The river has an excellent new log bridge, complete with a chain that functions as a handrail. Thank you, somebody.

Afternoon. The trail heads upwards towards an unseen peak called Mt Easton. Relentlessly. The sun is hot and the struggle is real. Did you learn how to read a contour map at school? Do they still teach that stuff? They clearly never taught it to anyone who made the rough vehicle tracks around here, because they blaze straight uphill rather than curling around the mountain. There's a hilariously blunt assessment of this area in an article on the Bushwalking NSW website. Hiker Roger Caffin wrote, 'It wouldn't be so bad except that some of those Victorian fire trails were made by a raving lunatic on a bulldozer who only knew one direction: the steepest.' Amen, brother.

Before lunch, I needed my poles to stop myself hurtling forwards; now, I need them to stop slipping back after each step. By the way, take poles if you get into hiking. The staff at my favourite hiking store, Trek & Travel, said young people in Europe buy trekking poles to preserve their knees so they can hike for life, whereas in Australia it's still mostly older people who buy them. They said be like the Europeans and buy poles before your knees go. And buy them because you'll need them for a hundred different reasons. They were right.

The track briefly levels out in an ugly patch of burnt, scarred bushland in a saddle halfway up the mountain. And there he is, in a blue synthetic sweat-wicking shirt and grey bush hat, with perfect white teeth and a beard still struggling to outgrow its bumfluff phase. It's Ferg.

Ferg Dale is a 19-year-old university student who's doing the whole AAWT in the first half of his long summer break. Simone said I'd run into him. Ferg offers some of his mum's wonderful homemade jerky. That cow can contentedly ruminate in bovine heaven, knowing its dried flesh tasted absolutely delicious.

Ferg grew up in Yackandandah in the foothills of the Alps in north-east Victoria, a town whose heritage main street is as pleasing to the eye as the name Yackandandah is musical to the ear. Like many teenagers in his district, he spent time at a local outdoor education centre called Mittagundi. He fell in love with the place, and with the outdoors, and worked there when he was 17 and 18. A year ago, he walked a 100-kilometre section of the AAWT and thought, 'I could keep going.' And here he is, with one hell of a story to tell.

Ferg set off in early November and hiked through three multi-day snowfalls. The worst was the third, when

30 centimetres of snow fell in one night at his campsite near a large exposed peak called Mt McDonald. By that stage, he was fortunate to have formed an impromptu hiking party with Simone.

'We were really lucky,' he says. 'We were both just really lucky we had another person with us when the conditions were really bad, otherwise we would have been in trouble. It got to the point where it had been snowing for four days and everything we had was soaking wet, so we kind of just had to be warmed by our body heat as we walked. That was all we had to keep us going – our body heat. We were also able to motivate each other, check in on each other, help each other up some steep bits.

'Up on that ridge on McDonald, I was like, if one of us trips over and hurts ourselves, it's going to be really bad, but also really dangerous for the other person because if we'd stopped for even or one or two minutes, hypothermia would have set in pretty well immediately. I was thinking, "God, this could basically go really badly." Mt McDonald was a living hell. Then going up Mt Sunday, mountain ash was all across the track. But we got all the way to Rumpff Saddle, just below Mt Skene, in one day. We just walked and walked and walked and it was by far the hardest day of the whole trip. We hadn't seen sun for four days and I was just so wrecked. At times, I was keeping Simone going. At other times, she helped me. By the end of the day, I was lagging so much that I couldn't even walk along the flat road into Rumpff Saddle. Then around 7 p.m. or something, I saw the car. My uncle was delivering a food drop to Rumpff Saddle and he had a fire going and some pasta and craft beer. I've never been so relieved in my life.'

Wow. Just wow. Remember, this is the AAWT we're talking about here. No help, no roads and no natural shelter or huts in that section either. I'd been dangerously cold in a protected forest up on Baw Baw when the summer blizzard had more or less petered out and stopped summer blizzarding. I can't imagine what those two endured. But they made their choice to hike on, and they pushed through the insanity of it. I bet Ferg's craft beer at the end of his ordeal tasted even better than my coffee.

CHAPTER 5

IMMERSION

I love survival stories. Can't read enough of them. When an adventurer with a gripping survival tale is on the media circuit, I'll often branch out from my news or sport duties and grab an interview with them. A few years ago, I interviewed two famous adventurers within a few weeks of each other. Each got their own article and I also wrote a third piece comparing their two experiences in the nearest thing to a 'think piece' I'll ever be accused of writing.

The first adventurer was Joe Simpson. He's the British mountaineer whose ordeal beneath a previously unclimbed face of a 6344-metre peak called Siula Grande in the Peruvian Andes was documented in the book and documentary *Touching the Void*. Simpson reached the summit with his mate Simon Yates but broke his leg on the way down. The two climbers were tethered together with ropes. As Yates tried to help Simpson down the mountain, he accidentally lowered him off a cliff. A storm set in. The climbers could not see or hear each other. Yates couldn't pull Simpson up. Death by exposure was imminent for both. In desperation, Yates cut the rope, sending Simpson on a plunge into the unknown. Mathematically, this gave him a better chance of survival than dangling until hypothermia claimed him, but you can imagine the ethical debate it created in climbing circles. It rages to this day.

Simpson survived his fall, landing in a crevasse on a glacier. He was battered and cold, but conscious and lucid. With his broken leg, Simpson could not climb the near-vertical walls of his crevasse. Then he had a revelation: God would not help him. Only he could help himself. As an experienced mountaineer, Simpson understood the internal layout of glaciers. His crevasse could be a dead end, but there was also a chance it was part of a maze of sub-glacial passages. He knew that if he descended to the bottom, he might die slowly and alone in cold and darkness, his body never to be found. But he might find a friendlier arm of the crevasse with less steep walls, which could lead him back to the surface. The gamble of his life paid off. Simpson descended then crawled up a different passage. Days later, delirious and near death from exhaustion, he emerged at the base camp, just hours before Yates, who had believed him dead, was about to leave. For what it's worth, I'm with Yates. He was starting to slip off the mountain himself, and what choice did he have? Simpson also staunchly defends his climbing partner, arguing he would have done the same in his position.

The second adventurer was Aron Ralston, the American who famously became trapped by a boulder on a solo trip through a Utah canyon and was forced to hack his arm off to free himself. His book was called *Between a Rock and a Hard Place* and if you've heard a better title, I'd like to hear it. The book then became a movie called *127 Hours*, and if you've ever heard a brilliant book title turned into a blander movie title, I'd like to hear about that too.

Ralston had studied mechanical engineering, so during his entrapment he used his free arm to rig up various mechanisms with rope and other equipment to try to move the boulder. Nothing would work. Crazed by thirst, hunger and the prospect of a slow death, he decided to cut his arm off with his multi-tool. But he couldn't do it. Not because he wasn't tough enough to try, but because – maybe put your lunch aside for a moment – while his multi-tool was sharp enough to carve flesh, it was not strong enough to cleave bone.

Then God intervened. Yes, Aron Ralston had the completely opposite experience to Joe Simpson, who abandoned higher powers and took salvation upon himself. And what God told Ralston was to stop trying so hard to solve the problem. Use the Force, Luke. Well, use gravity; let your body fall forwards, and allow the torque to snap your bones, Aron. Which he did. And hey presto, now his arm was much easier to saw through. How's that sandwich going?

So there you have it. Two adventurers, two disaster scenarios, two revelations, same happy outcome. Simone and Ferg went to a place almost as dark and leaned on each other. There's no formula for how you get through this sort of thing, and that's one of the appeals of the trail. Stuff gets thrown at you. Okay, what have you got?

Let me be clear: I am not out here courting disaster. I hope never to be faced with a survival situation. But part of the motivation behind this trek is to feel, just once, a little of what adventurers feel, from the planning of the trip, when an idea begins to morph into something daunting and all-consuming, all the way through to the aftermath, when readjusting to so-called 'real life' can feel like the comedown from a drug.

At some point in life, most of us stop adventuring. We settle into familiar patterns and behaviours. Our perspectives become our perspectives, our people our people, our beliefs our beliefs, our habits our habits. Many of us seek activities that help us feel edgy, challenged, pushed to our limits. The extreme fitness movement seems to tap into that urge. Run seven desert marathons in seven days, as my periodontist did last year. Now, what did you learn about yourself? Well, you learned that you either can or can't run seven desert marathons in seven days. What you didn't learn is what happens when you go to a wild place and there's no one to cook your dinner or give you medical treatment at the end of an exhausting day. What you didn't feel was wild and free and open to random encounters. Hardship is packaged up and sold these days, but you can't package real adventure, with its randomness and problem-solving.

I'm not having a go at anyone here. Extreme athletes, professional and amateur, inspire me. Trail runners with support crews are running the AAWT in under two weeks now. I haven't bumped into one, but if I do, they'll have my respect and a curry if they want one. Curry and running. What could possibly go wrong? I guess I'm just trying to say that modern life has lost that element of randomness. In a hyper-individualistic age, we fight wars and ideological battles to protect a thing called freedom, but what do we do with all that freedom of choice, of belief, of movement, of expression? We herd ourselves. We seek the familiar. This is especially true in the online realm, where we live so much of our lives. We dare not date someone without digitally stalking them first. We Google Street View every hotel before we stay in it, virtually visiting it before we've left home. In my shed here in Sydney, there's an upmarket magazine that comes with the weekend paper. On the back cover is a full-page ad for a guided trek on Spain's El Camino – 18 guests, two guides and a whole lot of luxury. New Zealand's Milford Track and Tasmania's Overland Track offer similar guided trips. We want wildness, but a controlled wildness. A luxury version of wildness, free from risk. We are drawn to a thing called wilderness, but reject its key element, which is wildness.

Back out on the AAWT, I've reached the top of this wildly steep track bulldozed by a raving lunatic and am now heading east on a timbered ridgeline on a fire trail called the Casper Creek Track. Do you know how good it feels to walk on level terrain after a major climb or descent? It's like reconciling with a lover after an argument, with all that entails. Over my right shoulder, I can see the Baw Baw Plateau. From the Walhalla end, the plateau was never visible in its entirety. From here, it appears as one unbroken massif. It is enormously satisfying. I crossed that. All of it. I've never looked at a geographical sub-region before and said that.

Onwards to the second of the three major river valleys here in Nowhere Country. The descent to the Jordan River is disgustingly steep. Raving Lunatic With Bulldozer did some of his looniest raving and dozing right here. The dry, gritty track is so slippery that it's easier to walk through the forest beside it. The snakes are unimpressed. One, then another, scuttles through the undergrowth as its late afternoon bask is rudely interrupted. An old schoolfriend of mine had a fat blue-tongue lizard that used to bask regularly on the warm concrete by his front door. One day, it was out on the back porch instead. 'That lizard doesn't put all its basks in the one exit,' my friend's dad quipped. Apologies for the Dad joke without warning. I'm actually not too worried about snakes on this trip because I feel protected by my gaiters. Snakes bite in a downwards motion, not sideways into your leg like a dog. So if an angry serpent strikes, I'm trusting it will sink its deadly venom into coated nylon, not flesh. That's what I tell myself as I tromp down through the forest. If nothing else, the gaiters make outstanding placebos.

The Thomson valley was open and sunny and welcoming. The Jordan valley is closed in and claustrophobic. You can hear but not see the river. When I pull into the Blue Jacket campsite, it's a fight through thorny blackberry to get water. Blackberry is a Weed of National Significance. There are 32 WoNS in Australia. Here, the blackberry has WoN the battle. Okay, that's two Dad jokes in one chapter. Your recycling bin is the one with the yellow lid. Blackberry is actually a problem in all sorts of ways. It shelters and feeds four-legged pests like foxes. It also helps turn small bushfires into big ones. Apart from all that, it's a bastard of a thing to walk through. For the second time in a day, I'm grateful for my gaiters. Alongside trekking poles, they're top of the list of equipment I was seriously considering not taking but incredibly glad I did.

Tricky river access aside, Blue Jacket is a lovely grassy campsite amid tall trees, with no obvious remnants of the former town. A historical marker sign at the campsite says:

Like many early gold mining towns of the era, after the short rush, many commercial undertakings were in financial difficulty. Most of the residents moved away. Some lost themselves in drink after never recovering their debts. Others turned to criminal activities. The town never held the status of its neighbours and faded like a true ghost town of the Gippsland goldfields.

The sign also says that Blue Jacket and its near neighbour Red Jacket took their names from either a sunken ship or garments worn by the early settlers. You can just imagine the broke, drunk gold miners smashing empty rum bottles over each other's heads in furious argument.

'Town was named after a ship!'

'No, it was a shirt!'

'Ship!'

'Shirt!'

Ker-*sploink*!

* * *

The morning air spends two minutes trying to be cool then relents. The blizzard is as distant a memory as the days when this valley had a post office and pub. The track follows the river to Red Jacket, crosses the Jordan then immediately heads uphill. The scrub is thick, my body drenched within minutes. Soon, bushes claim the track. Another bout of sweariness is upon me. Damn this effing track. Really, just screw it to hell. Luckily, there's an option. There's a 4WD track nearby called the Victor Spur Track which heads to my lunchtime destination of Mt Victor at 1185 metres. It's about three kilometres longer than the track that is theoretically but not actually at my feet, but whatever. I bash northwards through the scrub and find the road. It's wide, smooth and shady. For the first time on this trip, I fire up Spotify. Doesn't do the trick. The music sounds tinny and try-hard. A long hike doesn't need a soundtrack. The bush is the soundtrack. The sound of your feet. The strain and creak of your pack straps. And then, the most musical sound of all. Water. At a bend in the road, a creek tumbles into a roadside ditch. I was banking on a creek to refill my water bottles about halfway up this hill. What I didn't expect was a cascade. This must be a spring as there's not much of a gully above it. Its provenance is unimportant. What matters is – *ahh!* – I'm having a lovely impromptu shower and a drink. I've been pretty diligent on this trip so far about popping a purification pill into each litre of water but I'm tilting back my head like a Pez dispenser and sucking that beautiful clear water down. I fill my bottles and continue. I'm carrying a two-litre bottle and a 1.5 litre bottle. By the top of the hill, the two-litre bottle is empty. Not good. Got to get to Black River by this evening, or close enough to it to refill early tomorrow after a dry camp.

I'm up on a rough dirt road that goes from who-knows-where to who-even-cares. Burnt forest, not much shade. Nowhere Country is Nothing Country up here, bleak and uninspiring. A ute roars past. First human in 24 hours. No wave. I empty two Hydralyte sachets into my 1.5 litre bottle, turning it into an orangey electrolyte drink. It's refreshing but I have to conserve it. Three glugs every hour. That's all I can afford. Temperature's high. At least the wind is up, and cooling on account of my sweat. Ever seen a kangaroo lick its paws on a hot day? Same principle.

The AAWT veers off the gravel road with its corrugated surface to a potholed track called the Mt Selma Road. Water very low now. Got to keep walking. If I'm anywhere near Black River this evening I'll make Mt Skene before dark tomorrow. I trudge on. Had enough of this day. The track loops around a 1260-metre peak called Sunflower Hill which has the first snow gums since Baw Baw. I stop for a pee. Weird colour. Oh, that's not good. Is it the Hydralyte powder causing this? No, my pee is dark red, not orangey. It's almost the colour of cola. There's a bar of phone reception up here. Let's ask Dr Google.

The first hit is from the Mayo Clinic, an American not-for-profit medical centre with loads of helpful info. It says I have gross haematuria, a fancy way to say blood in the urine. It's gross, all right. The possible cause of said affliction could be one of many. Could be a urinary tract infection, or a kidney infection or kidney stone. No, please not that one. Not out here. I could also have an enlarged prostate, kidney disease or cancer. Good-oh. Then, right down the bottom under the subheading of *Strenuous Exercise*, it says:

It's rare for strenuous exercise to lead to gross haematuria, and the cause is unknown. It may be linked to trauma to the bladder, dehydration or the breakdown of red blood cells that occurs with sustained aerobic exercise.

Runners are most often affected, although anyone can develop visible urinary bleeding after an intense workout. If you see blood in your urine after exercise, don't assume it's from exercising. See your doctor.

Since seeing my doctor right now is not an option, I'll chalk it down to that. It has been a strenuous day. The morning climb was relentless, and this afternoon has been hot, exposed, windy and waterless. I don't want to harp on about this. I realise you've probably worked a ten-hour day with domestic responsibilities either side, and you're probably just cracking your first very well-earned pinot for the evening. I know you've done it tough too. I'll simply say this: a good friend and cherished colleague has just sent me a message.

'Are you feeling clearer? Is the trip all you dreamed of? What are your plans when back?' she asked.

I tell her that once in their career, every sports journalist should feel what an athlete feels. I tell her that you can write player profiles and match reports about epic five-setters and dramatic overtime thrillers all day long, but until you've made decisions under physical and mental duress – which is what high-level sport is all about – you're reviewing restaurants you've never eaten at.

I try to pee again. Drips. Still bloody.

Onwards.

As harsh afternoon yields to gentle evening, there's a puddle shaped like Australia on the path. I photograph it with a reflection of nearby trees, so it looks like the whole of Australia is a land of forest. Nice thought. In reality, forest covers 17 per cent of the continent's landmass, according to the Department of Agriculture, Water and the Environment. Ecologists say it was roughly double that when Europeans arrived in the late eighteenth century.

How much of that 17 per cent is alight at the moment? All I know is that for now, there are still no major fires near the Alps. I also know that I'm not drinking that puddle water. John Chapman once drank from a pool with a dead goat in it on a hike in South Australia, but the author of The Bible carries proper filtration. I have only purification pills. I splash a little water on my face, careful to ingest none of it. I also half-fill my two-litre bottle so I have some water to cook with tonight, and perhaps to drink after I've boiled it.

The light is beautifully soft now and the wind has dropped. Nowhere Country just got lovely again. The views go forever and the people look like ants and it's Mother Nature at her finest. Only kidding. Those are my three most-hated travel clichés. Just checking whether your pinot has kicked in and you're still awake. In the middle distance looms a grey-haired peak, or so it looks with its mane of trees that burned in the 2003 fires and have long since died and turned into silver ghosts. Map. Compass bearing. Yep, it's Mt Skene. Somewhere up there is my food drop with a bottle of Sarsaparilla and two packets of Twisties and a week's supply of who-cares-what-else because all I can think about is the Sarsaparilla and Twisties.

Time out. A quick break. I'm 86, maybe 87 kilometres into the hike. My food drop at Mt Skene is at the 110-kilometre mark. A few more kilometres tonight, then down-and-up the valley of Black River tomorrow. After a final half-hour of walking, I set up a high camp on a ridge overlooking the valley of Black River. Long way down but that's tomorrow's problem.

Right now, it's about enjoying the evening. You can forget to do that out here. The wind has died and the tent is set up on soft green grass and a Pakistani Haleem curry – a rich slurry of stringy chicken, lentils and broken wheat – is warming up and my pee is now more Fanta than Coke, and seriously, what's the worst that can happen tomorrow?

Ask a silly question.

The Bible says there's an overgrown track along the river. No sign of it among the blackberry bushes. About a kilometre down the invisible track is a notoriously overgrown trail up a steep spur on the other side of the river. So basically I'm seeking a concealed path leading to a track that's almost certainly not there. It's my understanding that federal politics works more or less in this way.

The Bible suggests wading the river if you can't find the riverside track. Okay then. The river is fantastically refreshing but tricky. It's full of fallen timber. I am a contestant on one of those TV shows with a pool full of inflatable obstacles, except the obstacles are hard and pointy and scratchy and … bugger! My backpack has snagged on a branch. Jiggle, jiggle. Nope. Yank, tug. Won't budge. I'm thigh deep in a swift current on slippery river stones and I've got to slip my arms through my pack's straps without dislodging anything valuable. As I perform this manoeuvre, one of my prized carbon-fibre trekking poles plops into the water and starts to float away. What? Who knew they floated? Stop floating! I've got my backpack off now. I heave it onto the bank and dive into the river. It's me versus pole now. But pole is swifter.

Pole is Michael Phelps and I'm Eric 'The Eel' Moussambani from Equatorial Guinea, the guy who was the world's slowest swimmer at the Sydney Olympics, except that's not actually the best analogy because this river is probably full of really swift eels. Anyway, my pole is gone, halfway to Adelaide in the Murray River system by now.

Sigh.

I wade back against the current. What comes next is unclear. I'm not in the mood for that trackless spur anymore. Climbing 700 vertical metres up the overgrown scrubby spine of a peak called Mt Shillinglaw does not sound like a pleasant afternoon. Not now. Not without my pole. I look at my map. There's a track called the N15 that starts on the opposite bank just downstream. If I bash through the blackberries and giant tree ferns, I can cross the river and take it. There's just one catch: extra distance. Both the AAWT route and the N15 hit the road that goes to Mt Skene, but the N15 intersects with it a lot further south, adding ten, maybe 12 kilometres of walking. That means I'll fall short of my food drop before dark. What to do?

The answer comes from something Ferg mentioned yesterday during our brief encounter. He told me he had nearly fallen down a disused mineshaft halfway down Mt Shillinglaw. Seriously, there was a great big gaping hole underneath a bush and who knows how deep it was? You'd be lucky if they found your fossil. No, thanks. I'll take the N15. It sounds nice and sensible, like a computer chip or a Hyundai.

The track is easy to locate. It also offers a gift in the form of a sturdy stick which happens to be exactly the length of my remaining pole. Stick, you've got a new job now. You're coming to Canberra. Stick doesn't argue so I jam a light cloth into the cleft at the fat end where it's split and tape it up, first with black duct tape, then with sweat-absorbing sports strapping tape. Beautiful. What a lovely pair. Stick, meet pole. Pole, meet stick. You're partners now so learn to get along.

Bottles in the river. Glug, glug, glug. Okay. Off we go.

Since it's only about the sixteenth-hardest climb of the week, I'll spare you the details of the ascent up the N15 track from Black River to the Jamieson–Licola Road. Suffice it to say that despite having taken a good, long drink at Black River, my pee changes colour again. But I reach the road and am suddenly hungry. That's a thing that happens in the outdoors. Hunger comes as swiftly as a rain squall. I stop to cook an early dinner. I've got bits and pieces of food to last another day or so, but my last remaining main meal is freeze-dried roast chicken and vegetables. It's awful. Blech. That chicken might well have been the meanest bird in the henhouse. It might have been the sort of chicken that pecked other hens for sport and pooped in their pellet trays out of spite and cruelly mocked their extravagant red combs. It still didn't deserve to be turned into this gunk. But I feel better after shovelling it down because calories are calories. Onwards. It's about 20 kilometres to Mt Skene, which means it's out of reach tonight, but I'll walk as far as I can then camp by the road and try to make up the distance tomorrow. At a high point with two bars of phone reception, I ring my mother. She's fretting over the fires currently burning in other parts of Victoria and New South Wales. I tell her I'm fine, but did your mother ever listen to you when you called her from the Jamieson–Licola Road and assured her there were no fires near you?

Cows walk onto the road. They take fright and gallop ahead. The road curves in and out of treed gullies. One of them has a trickle running through it. It's not much but both bottles are now full.

When my dad and I drove this road six days before to deposit the food drop, we saw no other cars in three hours. But that was a snowy Tuesday. It's a fine Sunday afternoon now, so I'm semi-hopeful of a passing car to run me up to Mt Skene. Would that be cheating? I reckon not. Not with the extra kilometres I'm covering. Don't care anyway.

But there are no cars. Not on this goat track between Smallsville and Piddletown, and I say that with all due respect to Jamieson, population 301 at the 2016 census, and Licola, population 21, which just this week made the news as the first Victorian town to go fully solar powered and off the electricity grid. Several times, I think I hear a car engine. Nope, it's the wind. Hang on, that's definitely a car. Nope, cow snort. In The Bible, John Chapman is overly apologetic to hikers for those sections where the AAWT follows roads. He clearly regards any road walking – even on backwoods thoroughfares like this – as an inferior activity to bush hiking. That's a little harsh. There's actually something lovely about walking along a quiet road in the twilight. For once, navigation and the state of the route ahead are not an issue. It's also a reminder that you're not rushing like everyone else in this world. Which, when you think about it, is pretty much the point of hiking.

I've travelled maybe seven or eight kilometres with another dozen to go when 14 cows snort in unison. No, they don't. It's actually a car this time. The ute doesn't stop immediately because the driver thinks my flag-down is a friendly wave. But he's stopped now. In a delightfully old-fashioned gesture, the driver introduces himself with his surname. I think about doing the same but realise how silly it would sound so offer my first name. He reciprocates. He is Trevor, a farmer from the Jamieson side of the range, who drove three hours to a shooting competition in Gippsland this morning and is extremely pleased with his efforts. If I heard him right, he shot a can off a fence from a thousand yards, not once but twice. What he didn't do today was clean his car. Not today, and possibly not ever.

Have you ever seen that TV show about hoarders? You could make a whole episode about Trevor's car. On the floor and the dashboard are tin cans and tools and blankets and clothes and thingamajigs and whatchamacallits by the dozen. In every crack and corner are blobs of brown cotton-candy cobweb. It's such a pigsty, it's almost a work of art. Only a teenager's bedroom comes close. But messy cars go as fast as clean ones, and within 15 minutes we're up Mt Skene. My food drop is beside a roadside sign. Should be just in the bushes here.

Two brothers, Mark and Andy Oates, did the AAWT from south to north in the winter of 2018. They're proper outdoorsmen – one an outdoor education guide, the other a paramedic – and extended highlights of their trip are on their website and YouTube. It's truly inspirational stuff. They struck a massive winter blizzard here at Mt Skene. The snow was two metres deep and they spent three incredibly frustrating hours digging for their food drop. I find mine in about three minutes. It's not quite where I thought it would be, but so it goes when you bury something in snow and the snow melts.

'You've got a lot,' Trevor says as I tip the food onto the snow grass.

True. Because food is life, and that's doubly true when you're hiking.

'You got a tarp to sleep under?'

Trevor kills me. My tunnel-shaped tent with retractable poles is made of breathable seam-sealed nylon ripstop fabric and neatly folds into a bundle smaller and not much heavier than my sleeping bag. Trevor can't have set foot inside a hiking store since the last time he cleaned his car. Lovely guy, though. I donate my bagged rubbish and the plastic 25-litre water drum that housed my food, and wave as he drives off. I stuff the fresh food supplies, batteries, paracetamol tablets, hand sanitiser and other essentials into my pack, then hike up to a small grassy clearing near the summit of Mt Skene.

What a spot. That high ridge above Black River last night was good but this is better. I have travelled 110 kilometres. My pee is close enough to yellow again, the sky is purply pink and these Twisties and Sarsaparilla are what God serves as hors d'oeuvres at the annual trail angel conference in trail heaven. Looking at the ranges stretching to the horizon, I feel both serenity and excitement. There's the satisfaction of achievement and the thrill of what's to come. I've never been here but can identify some of the peaks. To the north-west, there's The Bluff, Mt Stirling and the tip of Mt Buller. North along the ridgeline, the dominant summit is Mt McDonald, where Simone and Ferg endured such hardship. When you read as many books about the Australian Alps as I have, a map forms in your mind. Then you come out here and you experience it in three dimensions. No, four dimensions. The fourth dimension is feeling the landscape. Walking it. Immersing yourself in it.

* * *

Back in my shed in Sydney, rain beats down on the tin roof and against the timber walls. Really got to trim that vine. It's prying the timber slats wide apart, creating gaps for wind and rain. I call Ferg. I want to ask him the old sports journalism 101 special: how did he feel when he was out on the AAWT? Not just in that snowy survival battle, but the rest of the time. How did being a solo adventurer make him feel?

'I thought I knew the mountains in Australia, but I didn't really know them at all until I was this intimately associated with them on the AAWT,' he tells me.

I hear ya, mate.

'A big project like the AAWT ... it gives you so much drive to plan something that allows me to experience all these moments that basically make me happy to be alive.

'One time I was in my tent and there was heavy thunder and lightning outside and it was just getting closer and closer and the thunder was earth-shatteringly loud, and I could taste metal and there was nothing I could do. Nothing. So I lay there in the tent feeling the rhythm of my heartbeat and my breath among this really loud thunder and it just made me really, really happy to be alive. And sometimes it does take that element of risk or danger to coalesce all that. Otherwise, going about my life, I can forget what life can be like. I forget how we live life without being immersed in it.'

CHAPTER 6

PUDDLES AND COKE

In New South Wales, the Australian Alps are usually called the Snowy Mountains or Snowies. In Victoria, they use the term High Country. The Snowy Mountains are also sometimes called the High Country, but the Victorian High Country is never called the Snowy Mountains. Meanwhile, the bits of the Australian Alps in the Australian Capital Territory are generally just called the Brindabellas – even though there are other ranges – but never the Snowies or High Country. Would you like fries with your confusion?

Up north in New South Wales and the ACT, the Alps are a large, mostly contiguous clump of mountains. In a good snow year, you can cross-country ski long distances in all directions without dipping below the snowline. Victoria is different. Seen from space in winter, the Victorian High Country looks more like a skeleton with dark spaces between the white bones. If that skeleton has a spine, it's the 124 kilometres of AAWT that stretch ahead of me now. This is widely regarded as the track's most spectacular section. Gone are the river valley crossings. The trail stays high on knife-edged ridges for much of the way between Mt Skene and Mt Hotham. I'm blessed that there are seven fine days ahead in the long-range forecast. It'll be hot but you'd take that over Simone and Ferg's blizzard.

Coffee. Muesli bar. De-camp. It's a short walk down to a grassy clearing called Rumpff Saddle on the protected eastern side of Mt Skene, where Simone and Ferg arrived wet, frigid and exhausted to meet Ferg's uncle with his roaring fire and craft beer. My arrival at Rumpff is less welcoming. There are vehicle tracks. These are not the faint, incidental tracks of a passing off-road enthusiast. They're donut marks. Someone in a big off-roader has done circles on the snow grass for kicks, mutilating a meadow into a mudheap. There are also beer cans in the bushes. That's another key difference between the Snowy Mountains of New South Wales and the Victorian High Country. While virtually all of the snow country in New South Wales and the ACT is national park, large parts of Victoria's High Country are not. Rumpff Saddle has the car scars to prove it.

The Bible says there's water a kilometre or so from Rumpff down a jeep track. There and back is a half-hour detour, so I roll the dice. My local map says there's a minor creek near a logging track a little further on. Bingo. Above the track, the creek is little more than moist ground, but it funnels under the logging track in a pipe, and the end of that pipe is a dribble of pure, clear water. I fill both bottles. Half-empty one. Refill it. By mid-afternoon, they're both nearly empty. My energy is low too. There are no major climbs today and only one serious descent at a point where the trail cuts around a cliff. But overall, this ridgeline terrain with its constant little ups and downs is like endless flights of stairs. It's incredibly sapping and nothing picks me up. Not energy bars, not Hydralyte, not jerky, nothing. What's that noise? Is that a chainsaw? It's definitely a chainsaw. Who's operating a chainsaw out here? Daryl and Adrian, that's who. They're four-wheel drivers who've come up from I don't know where and there's a tree blocking their path. Oh, the things I could have done with that beautiful buzzing blade on Baw Baw.

Daryl and Adrian are as surprised to see me as I am to see them. They say they've never seen a hiker up here, which is probably not a thing anyone ever said on El Camino. They give me Tim Tams – real ones. Then they fill my bottles from the water drum in their ute. I've never been a fan of recreational off-road drivers. I get furious watching TV ads where shiny oversized monsters roar along the beds of gorgeous clear rivers. Always along the riverbed, not across it.

How many clear rivers do you think we'll have if everyone behaves like that? And look at that mess back at Rumpff Saddle. But there are good and bad everything. Daryl and Adrian are two fellas who love the bush and are enjoying it their way. Their vehicle creates a small amount of noise and air pollution in an otherwise pristine environment but it's not like they're trashing anything. Indeed, they're doing a service by clearing a track which authorities don't have the time or resources to maintain. As a hiker, you gravitate to open spaces, sleep in the open air, slurp water from open creeks, open yourself to experiences. You might as well bring an open mind too. Right now, Daryl and Adrian seem like kindred spirits.

Have you ever noticed what a weird word 'kindred' is? This is starting to happen a lot on this walk. Words sound funny. Kindred. Alp. Fuel. Mosquito. Tranquillity. Sometimes I catch myself saying random words out loud, rolling them over my tongue like I'm sucking a mint.

Onwards. There's Mt McKinty, there's the unnamed hump after Mt McKinty and then there's Mt Sunday. 'It's actually Monday today,' the sophisticated Dad-joke artiste in me tells it. Mt Sunday is too dignified to reply. Like people called Shirley, it has heard it all before. A few days ahead is Mt Buggery. I can't wait to tell it to bugger off. In truth, it's me who's buggered. Feels like the first week is catching up. Just got no energy at all. I sit down for a rest on some snow grass, which is still enticingly green and soft despite no moisture for weeks before the blizzard and nothing since.

Ants! *Eek!*

There are an estimated ten quadrillion ants in the world, which is ten million billion, and pretty much every one of them, give or take the odd quadrillion, is crawling on me while I eat a packet of Smooshed Wholefood Balls. Get off! Off! I'm slapping my thighs like I'm doing a Bavarian Schuhplattler. If you don't know, Schuhplattler is the thigh-slapping dance performed at Oktoberfests and such. Which makes me a Schuhplattlerer. I am Schuhplattlering. There's a word to keep me amused on the trail for the next week.

The ants encountered thus far on the AAWT can be loosely grouped into three types. There are these little bastards swarming me now like I'm made of melted Skittles. Occasionally one bites or stings or whatever it does, delivering a mild pang of discomfort, but it's the swarming that's annoying. Days after an encounter like this, you're still finding them in your underwear. The middle-sized ants are the really painful ones. They bite so hard it feels like they're taking chunks of flesh. Then there are the enormous bull ants, which are just disturbing. The other night, there was one in the tent. I squashed it but it kept wriggling. Squashed it some more until head, thorax and abdomen were well separated. The severed bits were still wriggling in the morning. Shudder.

Late afternoon. The odd ant is still crawling around my shrinking waistline. Bored of saying 'Schuhplattlerer'. Haven't gotten far enough today. Still lethargic. Every kilometre feels like two. Steep descent from Mt Sunday. Long scrub bash off the track to get water from a gully. Fill bottles from half-hearted creek. Continue descent to a low saddle between two mountains with the imaginative name of Low Saddle. Set up camp. No appetite. Doldrumsy sleep. Morning. Ugh.

Low Saddle is at about 900 metres. That means a 720-metre ascent up to 1620-metre Mt McDonald, the day's first objective. I realise these numbers don't mean much to some people, so try looking at it this way: a 720-metre vertical climb is basically two Empire State Buildings. As in, it's a lot. Then of course there's the linear distance. And I've got to do this by mid-morning otherwise I'm no chance of reaching today's planned campsite 26 kilometres down the track. McDonald is the first treeless summit on the AAWT. I'm looking forward to the uninterrupted views up there. But like I said, ugh. Also, blah. Just not feeling it today. Worried about whether I'll be feeling it anytime soon. Feel like I need a day off. But what is there to do around here except walk?

In 2009, an American self-described 'climber, writer and margarita specialist' called Kelly Cordes wrote an article about a thing called the Fun Scale. Cordes doesn't claim to have invented the scale, but his story seems to be the only reference to it online, and it is often pointed to by people in outdoorsy forums. What's the Fun Scale? It's about the three types of outdoorsy fun. There's Type I Fun, which is fun which is enjoyable while it's actually happening. Hiking on a fine day, surfing great waves, skiing powder snow – that sort of thing. There's Type II Fun, which is fun in retrospect. It's not fun while it's happening but afterwards you're glad you experienced it, glad you got through it. I'd file a fair portion of my first week under Type II Fun. And then there's Type III Fun.

Type III Fun is not fun at all. When an Everest expedition turns bad on the Lhotse Face, that's Type III Fun. When you're solo-sailing around the world in the Southern Ocean and a southern right whale upends your flimsy 37-foot yacht, that's Type III Fun. Simone and Ferg had their share of Type III Fun on this very section of the AAWT.

'I guess you never really know what sort of fun you're getting yourself into once you leave the couch, which is fine, because it doesn't always have to be "fun" to be fun,' Cordes wrote.

True. Fun is not always fun. And fun that is not fun is often good for you. But how much unfun fun can you tolerate? If you're not in a life-or-death situation, then at some stage, too much unfun fun means you're out here proving a point instead of walking for pleasure. This I ponder while trudging up the long, rocky ridge that leads to Mt McDonald. There is no water up here. Not even a chance. No chance of a Daryl or Adrian either on this skinny, occasionally vague foot track. There's water at Chesters Yard, a former cattle mustering spot which is tonight's campsite, but that's still at least 20 kilometres ahead. Ugh squared.

Time for a stocktake. The weather's good and my gear is working. I have food. I'm fit enough for what's ahead. I spent half a year training for this hike, walking a 22-kilometre there-and-back circuit in Sydney's Royal National Park with full pack each weekend. But there's a huge difference between 22 kilometres with ample water and a bed at the end of the day and another 100 kilometres of dry, ridgetop walking over five days with no comfort and no certainty of water. Water really is a huge worry. You can get through one day on minimal rations, fighting every urge to neck the remaining water in your bottles like a shearer in a beer ad. But what about the next day, and the one after that?

There's another serious issue. The AAWT is still technically closed in the notoriously dry Barry Mountains at the end of this leg, due to one of those dry-lightning fires in November. The fire was extinguished by last week's blizzard so there's no danger of being burned or smoked out or anything like that. But after fires, burnt eucalypts – and especially snow gums – always have sharp overhanging branches that can fall without warning. They call them widowmakers. Sexist term, but there it is. My favourite American punk band The Butthole Surfers released an EP back in the late 80s called *Widowermaker.* I always thought that was funny.

Now, it so happens that Simone and Ferg walked through the closed section, so it's doable. But I don't know. In the Summer of Fires, it feels wrong to walk through a trail closed by fire. What if something happens? What if an ant crawls down my pants and I slap my finger on my belt buckle while frantically brushing it off and cut my finger so badly I have to set off my emergency beacon? Point is, if I have to be rescued in that section for any reason, nobody will read the fine print. 'Idiot hiker plucked from trail closed by fire' is all anyone would hear. The trail ahead feels like it's warning me off. You should listen to the trail.

Or should you? Everything in life is geared around a no-quit narrative. You do not quit. That's the rule. Quitting is weakness. Quitting is anti-Australian slash whatever your nationality is. The biggest mistake I ever made in my sports-writing career was writing a story where I boldly declared I was planning to divorce my hopeless football team. I thought it was an idea worth exploring. If a marriage or friendship is faltering badly, you end it. Why not divorce a football team which has been terribly administered and poorly performed for a decade? Because you don't, the entire world told me with great indignation as the discussion spilled over to social media. Yeah, but why not? Because you just don't. But what if team management has been manifestly inept for more than a decade? How do you send a message that you're not happy? Not by quitting the team. Then how? You just *don't do it*. Is this the lesson that sport teaches us? That we are all passive victims of someone else's stupid decisions and there's nothing we can or should do about it? Not when it's your football team. And with that, the internet more or less divorced me.

I still believe that article had at least theoretical merit, but I know what I did wrong. It was to declare the divorce underway rather than as an abstract revenge fantasy I'd never really follow through with. People would've gone, 'Yeah, I feel your pain.' That's what being a fan is all about. Collective joy, collective pain. That's why 'You'll Never Walk Alone' is the club anthem and official motto of Liverpool Football

Club. Never walk alone. It's a very powerful image. And here I am on a high remote ridge of the Australian Alps Walking Track, walking alone.

Here's the thing about that. Since I actually am walking alone, my decisions are my decisions. Society's rules do not apply. The no-quit narrative is not a narrative I must adhere to unquestioningly. This whole trip is all about my choices, my decisions. And what I choose is as follows: I will return to Mt Skene. When I get there, I'll hitch a ride down to Licola at the Gippsland end of the road. I have two mates in Gippsland – right-wing Steve and left-wing Steve. Either will do. Either would be absolutely lovely. I've never actually met right-wing Steve or left-wing Steve, but they're social media buddies who I've bantered with for years. I can't tell you how important it is to cultivate friends and followers from across the political spectrum on social media. Get out of your hall of mirrors, people. It really is distorting your perspective. Congregate in a broad church. There's no point championing diversity if you can't at least listen to diverse perspectives.

My one exception to this rule is climate change deniers. No time or emotional energy for them at all. I once interviewed Michael Mann, the American climate scientist famous for his 'hockey stick' graph – the chart that first showed in elegant simplicity the effect of warming since the industrial revolution. Forget Mann's data for a moment. Forget the plain fact that without any carbon dioxide, the earth would be an uninhabitable snowdome, so it kind of stands to reason that the more CO_2 you add, the more heat you trap. The thing

Mann said that really stuck with me was that there's no grant money for academics who discover what other researchers are discovering too, namely, that we are warming the world. And he's right. No one ever got rich inventing a drug that's already been invented. For the record, I've also interviewed John Cook, author of the oft-cited study that said 97 per cent of the world's climate scientists are in furious agreement that humans are causing and accelerating climate change. Let's just say that was a conservative figure.

Rant over. I'm going off track here. But am I going off *this* track? I think so. Just for a quick break. The one consolation about this endless, mostly shadeless ridge up to Mt McDonald is the phone reception. I contact left-wing Steve and right-wing Steve. Both reply quickly, saying they'll drive me to Bairnsdale or even Omeo, from where I can get a bus to my next food drop at Mt Hotham. How good are people? My next contact is with the crew in the forum of snow industry website ski.com.au. I've been a semi-regular on the site for nearly 20 years, talking everything from snow and weather to politics and sport with a broad assortment of outdoors enthusiasts. They've started a thread on my hike, and when I tell them I've hit a bit of a mental and physical brick wall, they're incredibly supportive and urge me to do what feels right. One of them says the tank in the Barry Mountains is reportedly rancid and undrinkable and may even be totally dry. Right, that does it. No way I'm walking through desperately dry terrain over ground closed by fire only to find a tank with no drinkable water. I'm getting out of the mountains for a couple of days. Did Cheryl Strayed do this? Don't care. Did Bill Bryson? Well, he was never going to do the whole Appalachian Trail anyway. I'll say it again: the trail seems to be warning me off. I will listen to the trail. I will embrace my decision and the randomness that follows.

Decision made, I am immediately rewarded with trail magic. Sweet trail magic, benevolent and bounteous. First, there is energy. The minute I walk south instead of north, it's like I'm turbocharged. Perhaps that's because I'm walking downhill, but the energy boost lasts. When I reach Low Saddle again and snake back up the long incline to Mt Sunday, my progress remains swift and steady even as I sweat like an ice cube in a sauna. Though soon out of water, my dry throat is scarcely more annoying than the ubiquitous flies. On that long, steep cliff bypass that Daryl and Adrian may well have had to winch their vehicle up, I ascend without pausing. And then I find the puddle. That Australia-shaped puddle with the forest reflection back in Nowhere Country was opaque and unenticing. This puddle is transparent, even though Daryl and Adrian's wheels must have splashed through it recently. It's clear due to the shallow trickle of water running into it from a moss soak beside the trail. Moss is nature's water filter. This pothole puddle is as good as creek water. With the help of snap-lock bags, I fill my bottles. A fair bit of mud seeps in but no matter. A couple of purification pills and all will be good within the hour.

Backtracking is weird. Everything is unrecognisable. It'd be interesting to backtrack your entire life. Or I don't know, maybe it would be tortuous and nonsensical like a song played backwards, or like the Butthole Surfers' *Widowermaker* EP played forwards. Mid-afternoon. My old mate Mt Skene appears on the scene again, maybe 15 kilometres away. I'll make it up there this evening and maybe even catch a ride down the hill before dark. Ten kilometres to go. Five. Those tyre tracks, that rutted meadow. Now I think about it, Rumpff Saddle sounds like a good place for a Schuhplattler. Maybe another time. I don't exactly have the inclination or energy for a thigh-slapping dance right now. Up. Sheesh. Tough climb. I breezed down this part of the trail yesterday. Trail magic must be wearing off. No, it's not. Trail magic is just rebooting.

'Hello.'

Oh, hi. How you going?

Tom and Sue are two AAWT hikers heading northwards. They are fit and fresh faced, with matching floppy hats with sunglasses on top, and will probably make it all the way to Canberra in about five minutes. We share trail stories. They're worried about the detour to the water source down near Rumpff and I tell them about the creek with the pipe a bit further on, and the puddle after that. It's a good feeling being able to offer advice. Maybe one day my trail angel wings will be fully fledged. Then Sue sees the Coke. Yes, the Coke. Behind me in the bushes are five faded red cans.

I have three very precise thoughts at this point. In the spirit of backtracking, here they are in reverse order. My third thought is that Sue would never have spotted those cans if we hadn't run into each other right at this very spot. What are the odds? This trail magic is some crazy powerful stuff.

My second thought is that a party of skiers or 4WD campers must have left the cans outside the tent one winter night and they were buried in a snowfall. Because, seriously, who leaves Coke in the bushes? What other explanation could there be?

My first thought is Coke! Yes! Actual Coke! Should we check the expiry date? Does Coke even expire? Does anyone care? We do not, and we clink our cans and drink while thoughts two and three fizz through my mind. Oh boy. Oh wowee. Though not cold, this is very, *very* good Coke. We are teenagers playing volleyball on a beach in bikinis and boardshorts. We are sultry bespectacled students in plaid shirts in a university library having a beverage break from the study and sexual tension. We are hippies on top of a hill in the Coke ad from 1971, which for a long time was considered the world's most famous ad. And then we are gone.

Tom and Sue need to crack onwards. I have to set up camp. They share the fourth can and give me the fifth. Dinner is aloo matar with a side of Coke. My tent is in a little grove of alpine mint and the world tastes and smells good. In the morning, I'll pack up early and try to hitch off this hill.

In the morning, dawn brings a very different world.

CHAPTER 7

HUNTING FOR HAPPINESS

Peter and Melinda Smith run the biodynamic organic farm for Jalna Yoghurt, whose distinctive round plastic pots you've probably seen in the supermarket. Their dairy farm is near Echuca, the historic Victorian paddle-steamer town on the Murray River. It's a family business. The Smiths arrived 20 years ago as farm labourers. Within six months they were running the place, and now manage it with their three grown-up children and their families, milking a herd of 500 or so cows twice a day. The Smiths use no weed sprays, no pest sprays, no chemicals and no artificial fertilisers.

On weekends, they become killers.

Peter and Melinda are recreational deer hunters. Like feral horses, deer are major pests whose numbers are growing exponentially in the Australian Alps. Walking through the country north of Baw Baw, I heard their telltale honk several times. Last snow season, I was checking the snow cams at Thredbo one morning to see if there'd been overnight snow. One of the cams showed deer picking at exposed bushes on the edge of a ski run. They really are everywhere. No one has counted how many there are, but estimates are in the hundreds of thousands Australia wide, and nowhere are they more highly concentrated than in the Alps and nearby lower ranges.

'When I first came over to Victoria, you never saw a real lot of deer,' Peter says. 'I used to be excited if I saw one. But nowadays, if you don't see half a dozen or a dozen in a weekend, you're disappointed. They just keep breedin' and feedin'.'

The Smiths grew up on King Island, the 1100-square-kilometre shard of land off Tasmania's north-west coast which is famous for its dairy industry. Peter dabbled in dairy farming for a brief time but was a cray fisherman for most of his time on the island. It was far from inevitable he'd end up as a dairy farmer again, but he did know he'd leave King Island one day.

Peter used to go pheasant shooting on King Island with his mates. Another mate from Victoria would come over and join them. That particular fellow was into deer hunting, and Peter soon found himself heading over to the mainland several times a year to join him hunting sambar deer, a breed imported from south Asia in the 1860s which became a popular food source for gold miners, and which is one of the world's largest deer species.

'We were over cray fishing but didn't know what the hell to do,' Peter recalls. 'But we had eyes for southern Victoria because I fell in love with deer hunting. I just wanted to be amongst it.'

They ended up in northern Victoria instead of southern Victoria. Close enough. It's only a three-hour drive from Echuca to the High Country near Mt Hotham, where Peter and Melinda sit in fold-out chairs enjoying a cold can or two and lunch of warmed-up chicken fettuccine, looking resplendent on this warm December Friday in their matching orange 'don't shoot me!' outfits, as Peter calls them. Their set-up is impressive. Their truck has a fridge and freezer, a camp oven, a shower, long-range fuel tanks, a rooftop tent, fishing gear for trout fishing and, of course, a rack for their guns. But the cherry on top is the numberplate: O DEER.

'When the weekend's over, I'm already looking forward to the next weekend,' Peter says. 'When I start hunting, the only thing I'm thinking about is trying to find that deer. Everything else goes away, any problems, any issues, they completely go away, and I'm just homed in on hunting a deer. If I find his marks, I think of nothing else but finding that deer. Then later that night, I just love being around that fire with my wife. We're a well-oiled machine. Each of us has got our little jobs to do and it just takes our minds off the farm, off everything.'

Some people hunt deer with dogs. The Smiths mostly do it by stalking, often walking hours through mountainous country carrying everything in their backpacks like hikers and setting up camp wherever it suits them. 'It's hard work and really good exercise,' Melinda says.

When they shoot a deer, they take the back legs, the back straps and eye fillets and carry them out. The rest is eaten by dingoes, other wild dogs, feral cats and 'wedgies', as they call wedge-tailed eagles. Peter says some hunters take three or four hundred deer a 'season'. There's no prescribed limit and no specific hunting season; deer hunting with a permit is allowed all year but many hunters favour winter, when stalking is easier in the lower areas of the Alps below the snowline, with fewer noisy dry leaves underfoot to alert the deer to your presence.

Yet the deer numbers keep growing. This is a problem, especially in the sensitive High Country. Deer eat plants that native marsupials won't touch, reduce grassy earth to bare ground when they rut, and turn precious alpine wetlands to mudheaps when they wallow. Peter and Melinda are a long way from card-carrying environmentalists, but they're doing the High Country a massive ecological service.

'We're trying to,' Melinda says.

City Boy here has never held any form of gun so I ask if I can hold one of theirs.

'Two hands, it's heavy, don't f--ken drop it!' Peter says, half joking, half not.

Not planning to, don't worry.

The scope is amazing. I feel like I can read the label on the backpacks of two hikers up on The Twins, a 1700-metre double-summited peak which must be two kilometres north. Then it's my turn in the sights. Peter and Melinda want to know about my walk. I tell them I'm loving it, though the first week was a bit tough. They ask if it's lonely out there by myself. The answer's mostly no, but occasionally yes.

'It's easier with somebody else 'cos you've got somebody to whinge to,' Melinda says.

Ha! She's probably right. I should have brought a long-suffering sidekick who I could complain to. Unfortunately, all my long-suffering sidekicks were busy this summer. My short-suffering ones too.

I've got to get going. Need to be a long way north of here by this evening. But before I leave, there's a nagging question. Quite simply, is there any way to stop the deer explosion? Is there an antidote to these antlered animals? Peter says Parks Victoria have been doing aerial culls, which he doesn't particularly like because they can be inhumane. Most hunters are pretty good shots — when they shoot an animal, it dies quickly and relatively painlessly. Parks Victoria hire professional shooters, but when you shoot an animal from the air, accuracy is always compromised. The carcass also goes to waste instead of being taken home for meat. Even with the culls, Peter fears that deer numbers will keep increasing in national parks because hunters like him are not allowed in there. 'There's so much locked-up area where you're not allowed to hunt,' he says.

It's the classic national parks dilemma. Hunters like Peter and Melinda would undoubtedly help keep deer numbers down if they could venture into the parks, but hikers like me don't want people with loaded guns anywhere near us. Rangers will tell you that everybody has a different vision of what national parks should be, and how they should be managed. Their job is one of the most delicate balancing acts imaginable. Deer shooting is but one divisive topic. Don't get a ranger started on the passions aroused by wild horses and fires.

Meanwhile, back on the organic dairy farm at Echuca, Peter and Melinda have a new arrival due any day now. Molly, one of their pets, is pregnant. Molly is a sambar deer.

Let me explain how I got to chatting with two deer shooters who keep deer as pets. It all started the day before at Mt Skene. Let's return there now. It's morning and a thick pillow of misty cloud dampens everything except my spirits. I've slept well and am feeling good. I've finally worked out my sleeping mat. I was blowing it up until it was rubbery and hard, but a little less air made all the difference. Last night, I had no awareness at all that I was in a tent. Anyone who's ever slept fitfully while camping will know exactly how sweet that is.

I'm packed up by 7 a.m., muesli bar in my mouth, brewing coffee beside the road. I figure if anyone's going to come over this hill, they'll likely be travelling on farmer's time – early. And I'm right. I'm pouring the coffee when a car approaches. He stops. Coffee for two, then.

Kevin McGennan is a retired teacher who lives just outside Wangaratta. He's up here leaving supplies at Rumpff Saddle for some hikers doing a section of the AAWT. Afterwards he's heading back down to Wang, on the northern side of the mountains. I'd planned to get to Hotham via Omeo on the southern side courtesy of left-wing Steve or right-wing Steve, but there are buses from Wang, so it'll do nicely. But wait. Who needs buses when you've got trail magic? Tomorrow, Kevin is driving straight back up to the mountains to deposit another drop at Hotham. As in, the exact place where my next food drop is. The trail magic is strong in this one.

Kevin knows the High Country well. He's been on the board of Mittagundi – the outdoors centre where Ferg worked – for over 30 years. Indeed, he knows Ferg. Kevin believes that all young people should have the opportunity to learn to love the outdoors. It's a view shared by all who run Mittagundi, including its founder, Ian Stapleton. There's a famous outdoors facility called Timbertop near Mt Buller in the Victorian High Country, where students from the elite Geelong Grammar School spend Year Nine. Stapleton worked as Timbertop's first full-time hike master in the 1970s and thought it was wrong that only private school students got the outdoors experience. Mittagundi has helped address that inequity for generations of students at public schools like Wangaratta High, where Kevin taught.

As we drive over the range, something magical happens. We pierce the clouds. All those peaks I saw from Mt Skene a couple of nights ago are visible again as islands in a vast sea of clouds. One of them is Mt McDonald. A pang of regret. Oh well, decision's made now. If you're going to get off a spectacular trail on a day when angled peaks are jutting out from the clouds like inverted ice cream cones, get a lift with a good guy like Kevin.

Turns out he once walked with Bible author John Chapman. More info please, Kev. Who is he? Well, at one point, Chapman was the guy who graded people who want to be outdoors guides. I've met such people before and they're the level above next level. When I left school, I ski instructed for a couple of seasons. While earning my instructing stripes in Canada, I was taught for a couple of days by an instructor called Mike Fidork, who was the guy who graded Canada's best instructors. Fidork skied like an eagle, all fluidity and effortlessness, while we flapped around like fledglings. He skied through windblown crud like it was powder. If you're not a snow person, windblown crud is a firm layer of snow atop a softer layer. The combination is incredibly tricky. Imagine you had to swim through creamed corn with a layer of baked beans on top. Fidork would glide through the whole canned mess like it was water. I've got a strong hunch Chapman is the hiking equivalent. Love to hike with him one day. Probably couldn't keep up but it'd be fun to try. Type II Fun, no doubt.

We talk about whether Chapman is explicit enough in describing the difficulty of the AAWT in The Bible.

The book's intro clearly warns not to attempt it as a first time through-hike, yet the track's difficulty is very much understated in the page-by-page track notes. My key question: did Chapman deliberately do this because he knew he was writing for advanced hikers, or is he such an accomplished outdoorsman that he didn't find the track particularly hard and just wrote about it as he experienced it? He's a former civil engineer so I imagine his thinking is reasonably precise.

I get the chance to ask the man himself, ringing him from my shed in Sydney after my AAWT trip while mosquitoes enthusiastically use my uncovered legs as their personal blood bank. O-positive if it helps, guys. I frame my question about the understated tone of Chapman's AAWT book with a skiing analogy. In skiing, runs are classified according to difficulty as green, blue, black or double-black, with green being the easiest. Chapman is well familiar with the concept and runs with it.

'The book is written for black and double-black run hikers,' he says. 'Our south-west Tasmania book is the same. If you read the south-west Tasmania book, you'll see we note the basics and any major obstacles, but you're supposed to figure the rest out for yourself.'

South-west Tasmania is widely regarded as Australia's toughest hiking terrain, a land of craggy peaks and deep muddy bogs with virtually no easy walking in between. If you go there, you know what you're in for. Why should Chapman spend half his book warning people about every scree slope and fen? He's taken a similar approach to the AAWT book, and fair enough.

'I know I can be understated but I'm *consistently* understated!' he says.

Chapman hikes like soul surfers surf and back-country skiers ski. He's always seeking a challenge beyond the beaten path. He has come to love the Sierras in California. On a recent trip there, he created his own high route, sticking mostly to ridges and spending just four of 44 days on track. That's his happy place, away from the hordes, away from the blazed trail. Not that every trekking book he writes is directed towards experts. 'You write things according to your target audience,' he says. 'There are very detailed notes aimed at beginners in some of our books. You have to give people enough information so that they won't kill themselves. They might come out and say, "That was a bit tough" but that's okay.'

It's refreshing to speak to someone with such self-awareness. It's an underrated human trait.

Back in the car on the descent from Mt Skene to Jamieson, Kevin and I discuss the state of the AAWT. 'If a track's on the map, there should be one on the ground,' he says firmly.

Agreed.

Chapman has a different view on whether the AAWT should, or indeed could, be better marked and cleared across its entirety. 'It's never, ever going to be a completely clear trail, not with the type of vegetation that's there,' he says. 'The Bibbulmun Track in Western Australia is modelled on the Appalachian Trail. They've got a user group that does the maintenance. The problem with the alpine track is it's too far from population centres for someone to clear it with their secateurs. And the government can't do it because Parks have been stripped of staff. They take staff out of Parks because no one complains, and if they can't staff Parks, how the hell will there be money left over to maintain a track as long and remote as the AAWT?'

Chapman is part of a stakeholder committee that meets every two years to discuss various aspects of the AAWT. The committee defers to him for almost all track-related matters, including annual through-hiker numbers, which Chapman seems to have a better handle on than anyone. He believes the AAWT will improve slowly over time as its profile increases. Meanwhile, he's out there doing his part to maintain it. Chapman and his wife, Monica, have been on several track-clearing weekends in their home state of Victoria. Here is a man who quite literally talks the talk and walks the walk.

Before I let Chapman go, I ask why he walks. You don't get Australia's most respected hiking book publisher on the phone without drilling into his soul a little.

'It's a simple activity,' he says. 'Everything you have, you carry with you. Things are simplified, but you have to be flexible and versatile about how you use things. You have to make your own decisions and live by them.'

It's a familiar refrain.

We're back down in farmland now, Kev and me. There's Jamieson, a pretty little town on the opposite side of Lake Eildon to Bonnie Doon but with just as much serenity. And then there's Mansfield, where the Ned Kelly breakfast pie (eggs, bacon, chunky beef) is all the delicious armour you need against hunger for a day and a healthy heart for a lifetime.

I spent a strange night in Mansfield once with the jockey Greg Hall, who rode 1992 Melbourne Cup winner Subzero. I was writing a retrospective magazine feature on the 1997 Melbourne Cup, in which Hall waved his whip in triumph after passing the winning post aboard Doriemus, only to be denied by a pixel in the photo finish by Might and Power, which led all the way. Hall was newly retired when I visited. He'd moved to a big farmhouse for a fresh start but wasn't yet sure what that entailed. He thought maybe he'd open a café or something. That gave me an idea. Mansfield is just below Mt Buller, and businesses near ski areas are often called Frosty's Ski Hire or Yeti's Takeaway Pizza or something connoting snow or ice or cold. I told him he should open the Subzero Café, named after his Melbourne Cup winner. Hall's eyes lit up. He was mentally waving that whip in triumph before he'd passed the winning post again. 'And we could get old Subbie up here to open it,' he said. Old Subbie is a beloved equine celebrity in Victoria, travelling around the state doing countless charity events, nursing home visits, you name it. He's 32 and still neighing as I write this. But for whatever reason the Subzero Café never happened. I don't think the High Country was Hall's happy place.

Kev and I make Wangaratta well before lunchtime. It's a well-heeled, well-coffee'd provincial city on the Ovens River which is home to around 20,000 people.

McDonald's? No thanks. KFC? Blech. On previous shorter hikes, I've gravitated straight to junk food outlets on my return to civilisation. Not feeling it here. Abundance is a blessing that should be savoured in style. Not hungry anyway after eating half a barnyard in Mansfield. I feel like walking. It feels like my natural state now. So I walk. I dump my stuff in the second-cheapest motel I can find – because never buy the cheapest anything – and hike a lap of greater Wangaratta in the shimmering lowland heat. Feels like mini Melbourne. The trees, the road markings, the style of houses, the flatness. The food too. Lunch is an outstanding capricciosa pizza from Hollywoods Café. The mafia could bury bodies in that generous slurry of cheese. Coffee up the road is good too. Strong but not bitter. Creamy texture. I buy a wicking shirt at the outdoors store because my policy of not looking like a hiker has proven a bit of a failure. Too much sweat on my cotton shirts, and they're just not practical when the weather turns cool overnight as it did up at Skene. Hikers look like hikers for a reason. I send a shirt home in the mail along with three maps I no longer need. Dinner is an excellent burrito by the Ovens River, which is in no mood to hasten its inevitable rendezvous with the Murray. Then it's time for a beer. Doesn't hit the spot. My second drink is a Coke.

The bloke in the office of my motel is having heated words on the phone. Sounds like a money thing. Seems like somebody has let him down. I leave him to it. I need a power plug to charge my phone with Simone's cord, but it can wait.

Old mate from the office turns up outside my room a couple of minutes later, which is decent of him. He says sorry about the phone call. Family thing. Money, family, you know how it is. Says that's more than he should say. Anyway Phuket, he's going to Thailand. Okay, he didn't actually say the name of the famous Thai tourist island.

Off to Thailand?

'Yeah, gonna go sit on a beach for two weeks,' he says.

In the morning, I get coffee from the same place as yesterday. The barista is South African. He lived in Melbourne but came up here because it's more affordable and the lifestyle's great. But he's moving on. His café is going on the market today – he says the ad should be live any minute – and he's moving his family to Scotland.

Why?

'Always loved Scotland,' he says.

Kev picks me up at 9 a.m. to take me up to Hotham. We talk about his small rural acreage. He says he can see Victoria's highest peak, Mt Bogong, from his bathroom, which never ceases to give him a thrill. I'm glad for him. Reminds me of when I was a kid in Canberra staring out that window at the Tidbinbilla Range. I'll give him a wave from the summit of Bogong in two or three days, all going well.

We all have our dream landscapes, our happy places. Are they illusory? A substitute for meaning or the keenest expression of it? The point is to go there and find out. My happy place is the mountains and I can't wait to get back up there again. Can't wait to rip into this thing and get it right.

114

A day off the trail was like a lifetime of recharging. Personal battery level two thousand per cent. Let me at it. AAWT, look out. In skiing and snowboarding these days, the kids use the verb 'stomp' to mean they've nailed a difficult jump or other manoeuvre. I want to stomp the rest of this track. I'm so supercharged, I almost mean it literally. I feel like stomping my feet so hard upon the earth that it'll be the Australian Plains Walking Track by the time I'm through with it.

Kev turns onto a jeep track called Twins Road high in the mountains just before Hotham. We drive south into some of the AAWT country I missed. Crazy country. Mountains with rounded summits and faces that are almost cliffs. Accessible water sources nowhere to be seen. We park in a grassy saddle between The Twins and the unnamed mountain to its south. That's where we bump into Peter and Melinda, who I chat to between trips stashing water drums in nearby bushes. Then it's up to Hotham, where I buy Kev fish and chips at the local pub, The General. Least I can do. We're a long way from the sea but the fish is great. Light tempura-style batter with loads of tartare sauce. Bet you want some of that right now. Sorry. We eat at an outdoor table that had 50 centimetres of snow on it when I left my food drop here ten days ago. Snow's all gone now. Fish and every last chip too. I empty the food compartment of my backpack, give a bunch of uneaten food to Kev along with hand sanitiser and batteries that only saw a couple of days' use on the last leg, stuff the fresh supplies in my pack, and I'm off. To my happy place. In my happy place. The walking is fantastic. Everything I love about the mountains is here. All of it.

CHAPTER 8

THE REVELATION
OF POLE 214

There is nowhere else in Australia like Mt Hotham. Go there
if you've never been. Doesn't matter if it's summer or winter.
You don't have to stay long either. Just drive up and over
the aptly named Great Alpine Road, stop for a coffee and
soak it all in. This message was brought to you by the
Mount Hotham Alpine Resort Management Board, proudly
boosting visitor numbers through advertorials in hiking
books since 2020. No, not true. It's me talking. Hotham
really is spectacular.

Most ski resorts in the world, and indeed most towns in mountainous areas, nestle in valleys. Hotham's village sits almost atop its eponymous mountain with the ski runs extending downwards. The view is dominated by Victoria's second-highest peak, 1922-metre Mt Feathertop. The greatest compliment you can pay Feathertop is that it looks like an alp of the European variety, with its knife-edged ridgeline, rocky couloirs, overhanging cornices of ice and velvety flanks, yellow with summer snow grass or gleaming under winter snow. But it's not just the backdrop of Feathertop. This whole area is beautiful. It's an artful, almost sensual landscape of hollows and humps, of spurs and U-shaped gullies which in winter become natural halfpipes where you swoop and dive on skis like a surfer doing cutbacks on the face of a wave.

At the edge of Hotham village, a line of timber poles begins. They run nearly 50 kilometres to the summit of Mt Bogong, where they culminate in pole 1285. The pole line skirts the boundary of Hotham's ski area, where comically tall ski run marker signs stand like depth gauges in a dry river. On a famously steep double-black run called Mary's Slide, snow patches cling to life, their mix of dirty granular snow and softer white slush a sign that they're remnants both of winter and last week's early summer blizzard. Just beyond the resort boundary is Derrick Hut, a pale blue single-room timber structure. Charles Derrick was a champion skier who died in a blizzard in 1965 while attempting to cross-country ski from Mt Bogong to Mt Hotham. Built by the Wangaratta Ski Club in 1967, the hut is a memorial to Derrick and a refuge for modern-day ski tourers facing similar weather conditions.

There are hundreds of huts across the Australian Alps. A few, like Derrick Hut, were specifically constructed as emergency shelters. Some were built by miners and loggers. Most were erected by cattlemen in the grazing days – an era which ended across most of the Alps in the 1950s and 1960s as authorities finally realised the damage that hooved animals wreak upon alpine flora and waterways. That so many huts remain is thanks largely to organisations like the Victorian High Country Huts Association and the Kosciuszko Huts Association. These groups tirelessly maintain huts, and even rebuild them completely after fires, often with minimal logistical and financial help from government land management agencies.

The huts weren't always so treasured. Up until the early 1980s, the prevailing view among National Parks staff was that they were ugly intrusions on the pristine alpine landscape. Most were in severe disrepair and held little appeal for cross-country skiers and hikers. In the Kosciuszko National Park, authorities were drawing up plans to remove at least half of the huts. A landmark book helped shelve those plans. Published in 1982, the book was *Huts of the High Country* by Klaus Hueneke AM, a Canberra-based author, publisher, photographer, hiker and the father of the girl I was in love with in Year Nine. If you really must know, she fell for my best friend and I endured the most tormented, pitiful year of my young life.

Hueneke grew up in northern Germany. His dad would journey south to the Alps to go ski touring in winter, staying in basic huts and mountain refuges. On his return, he'd show his family movies of his trips on standard 8-mm film stock. Young Klaus was entranced. When he was ten, his family moved to Australia, and as he grew into a young man he inevitably gravitated to the mountains. There, he fell in love with the huts and began interviewing old cattlemen and other mountain types who built them. Very little had been documented about the huts at the time, and because no one knew much about them, few people valued them. Hueneke had already helped to campaign to save the huts in his role as president of the Kosciuszko Huts Association. His book accelerated the movement to save them.

Huts of the High Country hit an extremely sweet spot. It sold 5000 copies in its first year, which is an enormous number in niche publishing. Today, it has sold more than 14,000 copies, many of them hardback. From the day it was published, people's eyes opened to the cultural heritage of the huts. They became celebrated rather than viewed as piles of timber and tin to be bulldozed at the first opportunity. Today, ahead of bushfires, huts across the Alps are routinely wrapped in a foil-like fire-retardant material called FireStop. It's a painstaking process which illustrates how highly they are valued. The huts are like the piece of old junk in Grandpa's shed that turns out to be an antique worth thousands. Except in this case, the valuable antique was actually Grandpa's shed.

After Derrick Hut, the AAWT meanders down Swindlers Spur through natural glades of beautiful old snow gums. This would be amazing back-country skiing terrain. There's nothing like skiing through snow gums. Lower down, they're usually too tightly bunched but in glades like this, around 1700 or 1800 metres above sea level, they're spaced like nature's slalom poles. They're just as good to walk through. This is Type I Fun. My pack is heavy but my mood light. Three young women approach. They've walked from the nearby ski resort of Falls Creek on their first overnight hike and are intrigued by my solar charger and the size of my pack. They ask where I'm going. 'Canberra,' I tell them. It feels a little cocky saying that. Here's hoping I get close.

The crossing from Hotham to Falls Creek is almost certainly the most popular overnight walk in the entire Australian Alps. Hardcore hikers do the 37-kilometre crossing in a day, but for most people it's a two- to three-day undertaking. Commercial operators already guide a handful of walkers between the two ski resorts, but Parks Victoria has big plans to ramp up the commercial opportunities. It plans a 57-kilometre route to include the summit of Feathertop. The proposed walk's glossy 116-page master plan is littered with phrases like 'world-class trail infrastructure' and 'cultural magnets' and speaks of incorporating the crossing into 'a branded portfolio of four long-distance walks' called 'Walk Victoria's Icons'. I love the smell of a branded portfolio in the morning.

To make the new trail enticing to the slightly less adventurous, Parks Victoria proposes building 'new shelters to enable weather-protected social engagement after the day's walk'. Because who doesn't love weather-protected social engagement? It also proposes 'low-impact operated huts tailored for those who desire an added level of comfort'. Parks Victoria basically envisages its own 57-kilometre version of New Zealand's Milford Track or Tasmania's Overland Track, which are 53 kilometres and 65 kilometres in length respectively. Similar plans are well underway in New South Wales, where construction has begun on a new multi-day trek called the Snowies Iconic Walk, a 44-kilometre trek which crosses the summit of Mt Kosciuszko and links the villages of Thredbo, Charlotte Pass, Guthega, Perisher and Lake Crackenback.

The Snowies Iconic Walk will use existing commercial accommodation for those who don't want to camp overnight. But, as mentioned, the Falls to Hotham crossing would require 'low-impact operated huts' to be built. These, presumably, would be huts in the style of European 'refuges' which offer basic accommodation and hearty food to hikers and climbers in summer. My family hiked up to one called the Refuge des Bans in France. It was a bleak, drizzly day and the path was rocky and steep. The caretaker cooked us crepes with lemon and sugar and the kids just about cried with joy. My wife and I just about cried watching them just about crying. It's the one experience on our three-month long service leave trip we all still talk about. Currently, there is nothing like a European refuge hut operating anywhere in the Australian Alps. Should there be?

Bushwalking Victoria is one of many groups strongly opposed to any sort of new hut being constructed along the Falls to Hotham crossing. It says the alpine environment would be severely disrupted. It also argues that other trails are falling into disrepair or even closing due to lack of funding. 'The regional economic benefits of maintaining bushwalking tracks for visitors should be spread across Victoria rather than most funds being directed to only a few Icon Walks,' Bushwalking Victoria president Peter Campbell said in a media statement.

It's an interesting debate. To me, it makes sense to funnel the majority of hikers into the good bits of the Alps in a way that can be managed, but if that involves an extra hut or two, well, not sure. As for the issue of trail funding, it's not like the lesser-travelled sections of the AAWT have been getting much money anyway. My guess is that the AAWT in its entirety may never be well marked or maintained. Maybe the creation of two iconic sections will inspire a new generation of hikers to look further afield, and maybe that in turn will help the whole 660-kilometre track get the attention it deserves.

Meanwhile, back here on the undeniably charming but not quite world-class infrastructure of the snow pole line, I am passing pole 187 and emerging from the forest at Dibbins Hut in the valley of the Cobungra River in the late afternoon sunlight. Nice. Very nice. I'd planned to press on towards Falls Creek but this is where I'm staying the night. You've got to spend time in the beautiful places. Why walk if you don't?

Dibbins is a log cabin the size of a barn in the corner of a wonderfully sheltered snow plain with steep valley walls all around. This is so different to the wooded valleys back in Nowhere Country. There were no open grassy river flats there and you always felt hemmed in. This is like being down on the playing pitch of a vast stadium like Wembley or the Melbourne Cricket Ground. So many sports fans see those great stadiums as shrines, as holy places. They even make pilgrimages to them. I guess I've done that too. In my only visit to the city of London as an adult, I dragged my kids to a cricket match at Lord's. I get it. But I'd rather come to a vast natural arena like this any day.

In many ways, that sums up my attitude to sport. I love it but don't live for it. Many fans would die for their team, but that's not me. That'll never be me. I've never really thought about it, but I'm the sports writer who doesn't love sport as much as my audience. Bloody mountains. They're like truth serum. What should I do next then, mountains? Should I get out of the game? And if so, what should I actually do with the rest of my life? Remember when I talked to a sign north of Baw Baw? Now I'm interrogating an entire bioregion. Feels good, too. But I have to stop because two hikers are approaching. Looks like I'm sharing the campsite at Dibbins tonight. Fine. Pleasant change. G'day Gary. How're you doing, Marnie. First campfire of my trip. It's not cold but why not? I shave in the twilight and donate the plastic razor to the Dibbins medicine cabinet. Hygienically questionable, but someone might appreciate it one day. Dinner is miso soup with noodles and Vita-Weats. Bedtime is early. Big day tomorrow. There's a major heatwave forecast in three or four days and I need to put serious miles behind me before it arrives.

* * *

When you camp in a deep valley, the unfortunate topographical reality is that you must climb out of it. The snow pole line is kind. It winds its way up the hill instead of blazing straight up. It's still a pretty sharp ascent, though, and I take a quick breather in the clearing beside pole 214. You should be here. Everyone should come to a place like this once in a while. A grassy patch between the snow gums. Mint green alpine butterflies flitting between flowering alpine mint bushes. Feathertop tall, sleek and roguishly handsome from this unfamiliar angle. Yoghurt-topped muesli bar. Clear, cold water in my bottles from the Cobungra River. Wispy high clouds. The sun out but not too hot.

This I contemplate while looking down at a matchbox-sized Dibbins Hut: that the best stories in my sports-writing career have been about people and places. They were about humanity and geography as much as sport. There was the story about the local rugby club in the New South Wales town of Forbes which tragically lost three members in the 2002 Bali bombings on their end-of-season trip. I spent a day driving around the countryside with two team members. One was distracted and not yet back in spirit, while the other seemed almost too determined to put the horror behind him.

Each in his own way was trying to cope. The whole town was trying to cope, to process what had happened, to move on without moving too fast.

There have been other good stories. There were the young men in the Los Angeles gangland suburb of Compton who formed a cricket team to escape a culture of bravado and violence. There was the sprinter from Sierra Leone who ran right out the front gate of the MCG after his race at the 2006 Commonwealth Games so he wouldn't face persecution, and likely execution, for his anti-government views when he returned home. There was the bookie in the sports betting tax haven of Alice Springs who invented betting on elections and reality TV shows, and who pioneered online betting but who was never compensated for his foresight. Maybe you're saying, 'Who cares about a sports bookie?' Point is, he was (and still is) a clever, generous-spirited person who was never adequately financially rewarded for his hard work and creative thinking. His was a human story set in a big red desert. People plus geography. That's been the formula for my best work. That's why the highlight of my career has been covering three Olympic Games. The stories I filed from Athens, Sochi and Rio were mostly about cyclists, snowboarders and swimmers, but they were infused with the essence of Greece, Russia and Brazil.

People plus geography. I've been gravitating towards that formula without acknowledging it for 20 years. Walking towards it and away from it. Maybe that's why I blew up at work. I was genuinely dismayed at certain decisions made by my colleagues, but maybe I was angrier at decisions I've made over the years. Maybe I reached a point, with this trip in sight, where I dared myself to turn it into something bigger than a long hike, into a bridge to something different. Follow your true passions. Let the trail magic of life do its thing. This, you might imagine, is the revelation of pole 214. Well, it's half of it.

I have never read *Eat Pray Love*, though I'm aware of the basic premise, and I'll take a wild guess it contains food, worship and a level of emotional bonding beyond friendship. It is also my understanding that there's a complete narrative arc. Elizabeth Gilbert was lost, now she's found. She was a lowly caterpillar, now she's metamorphosed into a mint green alpine butterfly. But must all travellers' tales work out that way?

Here's what I'm thinking at this grassy clearing among the snow gums beside pole 214. I'm thinking that's real for some people, and good luck to them, but it doesn't happen every time. All those images of people standing ecstatically with outstretched arms on the edge of a cliff overlooking a Norwegian fjord. That big moment they're having? It's definitely *a* moment, but statistically it's unlikely to be *the* moment. Complete spiritual transformation is not guaranteed on the trail. You may realise some things about yourself, but that doesn't mean a solution automatically presents itself. Realisation does not equate to resolution. There is still work to do.

There is cubed wombat poo beside me. Wombats do cubed poos, every other animal doesn't. In the real world, I reckon lasting transformation is about as statistically likely as square poo. The other half of the revelation here at pole 214 is to stop expecting revelations. It doesn't always work out that way. There is rarely an easy fix in life.

Upwards. Pole 215. Poles 216, 17, 18 and 19. A new range is coming into view. It's the Jaithmathangs, but they weren't always called that. The Jaithmathangs are a high range running north–south along the east bank of the West Kiewa River. And that, ladies and gentlemen and small children, is all four cardinal compass points in one sentence. For my next trick, I'll eat my compass. Couldn't taste worse than freeze-dried meals.

The Jaithmathangs have no particularly prominent summits, but numerous sub-peaks crowned in clusters of dark boulders. From this distance, I guess you could say that the boulder clusters look a little like the close-cropped hair of an African person, and it's no doubt for this reason that they were known as the N--gerheads for well over 100 years before the name was changed in 2009 after the state government consulted with the local Indigenous community. Outrage predictably ensued.

The *Border Mail*, the newspaper of the nearby Albury–Wodonga region, published an opinion piece that began:

Who gave Gavin Jennings, the Victorian Environmental Minister, the authority to change the name of the mountain range, The N--gerheads, to some unpronounceable name?

The rest of the story is behind a paywall, but you get the drift. The *Border Mail* published no piece, or at least none readily searchable online, that asked, 'Who gave someone the authority to use a vile racist slur to name a mountain range in the first place?'

The *Border Mail* opinion columnist was not alone. Some less incendiary types also didn't like the change. The solid folk of the ski.com.au forum were divided. One forum member wrote:

I cannot abide people seriously considering renaming features to fit with their current political and cultural sensibilities. Why can we not accept our past, warts and all? Are we that insecure and politically correct and sensitive that we must rename every last feature which offends?

Forum member Cam Walker, a volunteer firefighter who owns property at Dinner Plain near Hotham, put forward the opposite view.

This has been a long time coming so it's hardly like some sudden flush of 'PC madness' and I can't see how anyone can really get upset about the loss of a name that's clearly racist.

That was the polite part of the discussion. It got a little heated after that, as these things do. Meanwhile, Indigenous groups were also at loggerheads. Members of the Dhudhuroa people argued that the range falls in their territory, not that of the Jaithmathang people, and that the new name was therefore linguistically and culturally inappropriate.

Seems like we're all fighting to shape our happy places in a manner that pleases us. This is the struggle of our recreational lives, our working lives, our personal lives. We don't often get happy, and it seems like resolution is elusive or ephemeral at best. Pole 214 might have been onto something. Wise pole, that one.

* * *

The track is at last levelling out. The valley of the Cobungra River is far below. Now we are on the Bogong High Plains proper. If the ranges of the Victorian High Country are bones in a skeleton, this area is the pelvis – the state's largest unbroken area of land well above the winter snowline. It's an area both bleak and beautiful. Bleak because it's wind-scoured, virtually treeless and the colour of toast. Beautiful because when viewed up close, there are flowers and speckled black-and-yellow grasshoppers that jump as far as you can put a shot, and fluorescent green-backed beetles which look like busy little sequins on legs, and flowing creeks lined with sphagnum moss as neat as irrigation canals.

You can really cover ground on this terrain. Pole 283 becomes pole 316 becomes pole 409 becomes pole 471. Elsewhere on the AAWT thus far, a mountain once viewed becomes a companion for days. But Mt Jim, then Mt Cope, slide past in what seems like minutes. It's like train travel. The track veers towards the eastern flank of the High Plains. Trees return, snow gum woodland flourishing in the lee of winter's howling westerlies. And then there's Wallaces Hut, an absolute cracker of a place. Built in 1889 by Irish cattlemen, Wallaces is widely believed to be the oldest surviving hut on the High Plains and the only one dating back to the nineteenth century. The heritage-listed refuge has never burned, and all renovation works have maintained its original rustic style. Good-looking outhouse too.

After Wallaces, the trail follows an aqueduct which was built to channel water into the Kiewa Hydroelectric Scheme, which is like a mini version of the Snowy Scheme in New South Wales. It's good level walking along the aqueduct, and should I? Yep, screw it, I'm going in. I haven't swum often enough on this trip. It's a serious time commitment taking boots and gaiters and everything else off and putting it all on again. But I am now standing waist deep in clear water, looking east to where the High Plains fall away to a lowland valley, and I'm half shivering with cold and half trembling with exhilaration and I swear, I am going to extend my arms in ecstasy like one of those sunset people on Instagram. Actually, I'm just washing my armpits. You're not supposed to soap yourself up in a stream, but I figure an aqueduct doesn't count although, hmm, I think I just saw a healthy young trout fingerling in here. Anyway, it's done now. Maybe I can catch it and have fish fingerlings for dinner. Sorry. Hasn't been a Dad joke since chapter five so I thought I might get away with it. I bet Elizabeth Gilbert didn't make Dad jokes in *Eat Pray Love*. Probably why it sold 73 gazillion copies.

Back along the aqueduct, a pair of mountain bikers just overtook me. We chatted briefly before they rode on past. They'd never heard of the AAWT. I've seen a few parties today, mostly day hikers. Nice change. But now the trail is branching off into the woods, crossing the aqueduct via an extravagant bridge with a roof. Must have been constructed for hydrographers so they can measure water flow without getting wet.

The trail heads up an 1819-metre hill called Marums Point. I'm feeling refreshed by the swim and could walk till dark, but I've covered 22 or 23 kilometres since Dibbins, which will do for the day. I'll camp here on Marums. But where? I'm in an area of heathy bushes with no clear ground. I'm confident there'll be snow grass meadows aplenty higher up, ideal for camping. When the snow gum trunks are as slender as they are down here, there's rarely clear ground. As the trunks widen, so do the gaps between them. And so it proves. Higher on Marums Point, there are countless open meadows, all of them ideal campsites. I pick a spot overlooking Rocky Valley Dam, with the ski slopes of Falls Creek in the middle distance. Dinner is chicken makhani with rice, which is basically Pakistani butter chicken.

It's satisfying to understand how the country works. Knowledge is power, as they say.

CHAPTER 9

BRUTAL AND BENIGN

If you want to know whether a mountain will be a tough hike, forget its elevation. Worry about its prominence. Its what? Elevation is self-explanatory: it's the height above sea level. But prominence, in simple terms, means a mountain's height above its immediate surrounds. By that measure, Victoria's highest peak, Mt Bogong, has no peer in the Australian Alps. Australia's highest peak, Mt Kosciuszko, is little more than a big lump on the forehead of the Snowy Mountains, but Bogong towers above the surrounding countryside with steep drop-offs on all sides. I can't wait to climb it. Kind of dreading it too. Anyway, that's this afternoon's or tomorrow's challenge.

Right now, the walking is easy and uplifting. The descent from Marums Point threads through gorgeous old snow gums, upended arboreal octopuses with a jumble of grey trunks. Then the track strikes true alpine terrain. The term 'alpine' in the High Country usually refers to anywhere prone to regular winter snow, above or below the tree line. In the strict botanical sense, the alpine zone only includes the area above the tree line where vegetation consists of low shrubs, grasses and wildflowers. The snow daisies are out in force today. The ubiquitous silver-stemmed beauties carpet the rounded western flank of Victoria's third-highest mountain, the 1884-metre Mt Nelse North. They're cheerful. I'm cheerful. Flowers and meadows and little green bugs. Be very, very careful or I'll break out in Wordsworth. Here it comes. Unstoppable urge. Apologies in advance.

> I wandered lonely as a cloud
> That floats on high o'er vales and hills,
> When all at once I saw a crowd,
> A host, of golden daffodils

Golden daffodils, silver snow daisies. What's the diff? They're all flowers waving in the breeze and flowers waving in the breeze make you feel good. Just ask old Wordsie. The best bit of that Wordsworth poem – which people usually call 'The Daffodils' but which is actually called 'I Wandered Lonely as a Cloud' – is the end bit, where Wordsie is back home potatoing on the couch and his 'heart with pleasure fills and dances with the daffodils'. It's true. A trip to the natural world is partly about filling your memory bank with fodder for future consumption. Wordsworth wrote a lot about flowers, all of it truth. The last two lines of his 'Ode: Intimations of Immortality from Recollections of Early Childhood', reads:

To me the meanest flower that blows can give
Thoughts that do often lie too deep for tears.

True that. The snow daisies up here just do it to me. And the billy buttons and the hoary sunrays and okay, now I'm just naming alpine flowers with silly names which I can't actually see right now and whoa, check that out. I've just topped a rise and there it is. Bogong. Deep valley between here and there. That's going to be quite the challenge.

Below, the land slopes away gently to a narrow, wooded plateau, after which it drops dramatically to the deep valley of Big River. Australia is famed for its unimaginative names: Great Barrier Reef, Snowy Mountains and all that. But whoever named Big River was clearly eating a particularly large, sticky donut and did not want a single brain cell devoted to any other task. Mind you, Mt Bogong itself is not much better. Bogong is an Indigenous word for 'mountain' or 'high plains', depending on your interpretation. So the Bogong High Plains are the High Plains High Plains and Mt Bogong is Mt Mountain.

In 1939, a hut on the flat timbered area below burned to the ground in the Black Friday bushfires. A new hut was built by a cattleman, Jack Roper, and bore his name thereafter. In 2002, the dilapidated Ropers Hut was extensively renovated by volunteer freemasons. It burned down again just months later in the terrible fires of 2003. Once more it was rebuilt, and Ropers Hut now has a strong claim as the prettiest and cleanest hut in the Alps.

I've made it down there from the open terrain above the tree line. Dappled sunlight filters through the snow gums. Duane Creek babbles. The grass in front of the hut is soft like lawn. It's an excellent place for an early lunch of Vita-Weats, sundried tomatoes, a pouch of salmon and a crispy apple from Wangaratta Aldi. Then the descent to Big River.

When my dad drove me to the start of this hike, criss-crossing the mountains on back roads and helping me hide food drops, he argued that descending on foot is as hard as climbing because it's so hard on the thighs. I suggested he walk 20 floors up and down the fire stairs of an office building and report back with his findings.

It's true that descending can be unpleasant. This descent is unpleasant – steep, dusty and slippery and, yes, hard on the thighs. The forest is dense too. Couldn't be more different from this morning's high alpine terrain. Reminds me of Nowhere Country. Not in the mood for that. But the worst part of this descent is that every step down means two steps up the other side. And there are lots of steps down. Lots, all the way down to pole 1037 at the river.

Oh, for god's sake. Big River isn't even that big. Maybe it was named during the spring melt or something. It's a good-looking river, though. Golden like honey. Handy chain to help you cross it, too. A quick swim and wash, and then the climb. The section I just descended was called Duane Spur. The track ahead climbs T Spur. *Huts of the High Country* author Klaus Hueneke attempted to climb T Spur once and failed. He got about halfway up, then had a bit of a moment which he wrote about in his book of meditations on hiking, *One Step at a Time*:

> The blood suddenly drained from my head and I felt a force pulling me down to the ground. I dropped my leaden pack, slithered down on to a log, sucked in some air, gulped some water and had a good think about what the hell I was doing on my own, on one of Australia's steepest mountains, at least two days walk from the nearest road ... I decided that Mt Bogong wanted to be left in solitude and that I would head back.

When a mountain tells you to leave it alone, you leave it alone. Mountains know who should climb them. You should listen to mountains. Besides, Hueneke sounds like he had health issues that day, so he had his excuses. Not that you need an excuse to give up on T Spur. Climbing from the river, you can just about reach out and grab handfuls of dirt from the trail in front of your face. Then the gradient relents briefly. Then it becomes cruelly, mockingly steep again. Then it settles into a long, steady rise as the subalpine mountain ash forest turns to snow gum.

Naturally, I rest numerous times. Energy bars and Hydralyte help. So does counting 500 steps at a time. Get through the 500 then slump on the ground hoping the ants don't get me. Five hundred steps. A breather. Another 500. Another quick break. No, I do not sing that song by The Proclaimers. These are steps, not miles, even if they feel like miles. Sheesh.

But do you know what? I'm getting this thing done. As any athlete will tell you, there's fitness and there's match fitness. Might be getting my trail fitness here. It's a good feeling. And, pretty soon, the track levels out in the most delightful valley. Bogong, as mentioned, is both a high mountain in terms of elevation (in the Australian context) and a tall mountain in terms of prominence, and it's also a great big wide mountain. There is so much more to Bogong than slopes and summit. The gargantuan body of this alpine behemoth has broad shoulders and muscular arms. Bogong is almost an entire mountain range in its own right, and in the upper reaches of its hulking frame, small valleys nestle with creeks running as swiftly as though it rained yesterday.

The AAWT actually bypasses the summit of Bogong by five kilometres, veering off east towards a lone peak called Mt Wills and beyond to the valley of the Mitta Mitta River. But there's no way I'm missing the summit. So I turn left onto the summit track and grind onwards. This small high valley of Camp Creek is delightful. Rich cushions of sphagnum moss line the banks, the spongey yellow tufts drip-feeding the creek. There are small pools cut off from the main flow, also lined with sphagnum, but one of them is ruined. It's a terrible sight. Where there should be moss and heath and a clear pool, there is mud and fouled water. It's either deer or brumbies who have destroyed this alpine pond. Either way, it's something with hooves that has no business being here. Horses trample the delicate vegetation when they drink at creeks, but a mudheap like this is more likely the work of deer, which like to wallow. To see such damage up here in the highest of the Victorian High Country is shocking. It's like graffiti on the Sistine Chapel.

Speaking of majestic structures, I am now approaching Cleve Cole Hut. Incredible place. It's a large, welcoming stone edifice with a cheerful green door and window frames. Such a sturdy structure. The Big Bad Wolf couldn't blow Cleve Cole over no matter how hard he huffed and puffed. Old Wolfy might grab himself a good feed, though. The most extravagantly large rabbits chomp grass around the hut. They're the size of wombats, these bunnies. Turn them into chocolate and that'd be Easter sorted for every kid in Victoria.

Cleve Cole the man was an advocate for snow pole lines in the mountains. He wanted people to be able to access places like Bogong safely. Tragically, he perished on a 1936 trip to Bogong. Cole was skiing from Hotham with two companions when a blizzard overcame them near the summit. They descended to Big River, where Cole was in poor condition after suffering extreme exposure. One of his mates left for help while the other stayed to care for him. Assistance arrived within three days. They carried Cole out along the valley of Big River which must have been an excruciatingly painstaking and exhausting task. Cole died anyway. The Ski Club of Victoria built and named this hut in his honour.

Maybe you're wondering why so many experienced skiers seem to end up dead around here. It's because Australian blizzards have a unique ferocity. There are countless snowier, colder, higher ranges in the world, but our blizzards originate in the Southern Ocean, about halfway between Australia's southern coastline and Antarctica. Sailors used to call this area the Roaring Forties and Furious Fifties, a reference to the latitude and constant gales. Several times each winter, the Southern Ocean storms lunge northwards, intensifying as they sweep up and over the physical barrier of the Alps. When it snows in Australia, it absolutely howls.

The exposed, rounded summits of our Alps amplify the fury of storms. Above the tree line, there is no shelter, no refuge. Weather stations at the top of ski resorts like Thredbo and Hotham often record hurricane-strength gusts well in excess of 100 kilometres per hour in winter, and those storms can last a week or longer. Under such conditions, air temperatures of minus five feel like minus 25. Exposed flesh freezes within minutes and places like Bogong become merciless death traps, even for skiers with modern gear, with airborne ice chunks like bullets, and barely enough visibility to navigate between snow poles. It's a wild, savage landscape on the wrong day.

Cleve Cole was far from the only person who paid the ultimate price in Bogong's early days. In August 1943, a party of three – two men and a woman – perished after they'd climbed the mountain from the opposite side to my approach. They were aiming for the old summit hut, after which they planned to head to Cleve Cole Hut. Searchers found their bodies 80 metres from the summit. No one knows exactly what happened. But the mountain knows.

The mountain remains potentially lethal to this day. Dr David Blair was a forest scientist who died in a skiing accident on Bogong in August 2019. It was reported that he hit ice and crashed into trees. A father and keen outdoorsman, Blair, 48, was greatly admired by the scientific community. 'Like many other forest ecologists, he worked in the mountains because he loved them,' Dr Tom Fairman told me.

As I ascend Mt Bogong after a restful night in Cleve Cole Hut, the main danger is sunburn. It is an absolute cracker of a morning. A belter. A pearler. An absolute bloody ripsnorter. You've got to say this about sport: it has the best words and they're just as good out of context.

The snow pole line follows the full moon all the way to the summit, where I arrive within the hour. But not before a quick sit-down beside the track to take a phone call. It's someone from work. We talk. Work a thing or two out. I'm happy. They're happy. It's official: I'm leaving. I wasn't sure things were going to pan out this way but sometimes you've got to let the trail decide for you. It would've been a tough decision to make at home. We have a lot of comforts in our western lives, but the greatest luxury is not cars, fridges, ski holidays or a tray of Pepsi Max in the shed. The greatest luxury is certainty. The knowledge that, at the end of the day, you can come home and feed people and pay the bills. Give that up and you give up your membership as a stable member of society. You become something wilder, something a middle-aged dad from the suburbs is generally not supposed to be.

I don't know. I've worked hard and paid taxes for 25 years. But if the trail says go, I go. We'll work something out, the trail and me.

The summit of Bogong is a long ridge the shape of two boomerangs or half the ABC logo. From the summit cairn – an impressive rock pile nearly three metres high – you can see almost the entire Australian Alps. What a view. I should probably be a little more expressive, but the geographical part of my brain is currently overriding the awe centre. I am processing the scene, scanning it, assimilating it into my mind map of the Australian Alps. To the north-west is the Main Range and Mt Kosciuszko. North of that is Mt Jagungal, the distinctive standalone 2062-metre peak in the north of Kosciuszko National Park. To the south is Feathertop, and beyond it, the high spine I skipped between Hotham and Mt McDonald. To the west is the Buffalo Plateau. And to the east, beyond Bogong's nearest neighbour Mt Wills, there is cloud and smoke. Could be valley fog, could be bushfire smoke, probably a whole lot of both. Either way, it's a reminder that not everywhere is as clear and benign as Bogong on this absolute humdinger of a Monday morning.

It's decision time again. Salmon pouch or tuna pouch to accompany my Vita-Weats? There's also a more important decision: where do I go next? The AAWT departs the eastern flank of Bogong in the direction of Mt Wills, traversing a long spur with the exquisitely exotic name of Long Spur. It's a two-to-three-day walk down Long Spur, over Mt Wills and on to my next food drop on the Mitta Mitta River near the small town of Benambra.

But Long Spur is closed. That November dry lightning storm is again the culprit, as it was south of Hotham. While the fire that raged here is out, the trail is still closed. I'd hoped it would open today as Monday seems to be the day when the relevant website updates. But no. Still closed. Could I walk Long Spur? Sure. Should I? Almost certainly not. What to do? The obvious play is to backtrack to a point near Falls Creek where the AAWT crosses the Bogong High Plains Road, then hitch to Benambra. But that's easier said than done. There are three turn-offs, which could mean three hitches and plenty of hot, lonely road walking in between. All part of the adventure, but not necessarily enjoyable, especially with a hot spell approaching.

I use the excellent phone reception at the top of Bogong to share my dilemma with the gang on the ski.com.au forum while munching my Vita-Weats and salmon. Salmon won. Tuna should have won because salmon is a mood, and the mood is not now. Salmon mood can be difficult to predict.

Words to live by, especially if you're a salmon. The forum crew offers all sorts of suggestions. Then one of them makes an incredible offer to pick me up near Falls Creek and drop me in Benambra. Who is this unexpected trail angel?

He is Dave from Tawonga, that's who. Dave from Tawonga is not actually from Tawonga. He's from Melbourne but is visiting his sister in Tawonga, a small town in the Kiewa Valley, 45 minutes below Falls Creek. Dave has been kicking round for a few days and is in the mood for a drive over the mountains, which is a far more reliable mood than salmon mood. I have no hesitation. Absolutely no need to think this one through. It's a yes please from me. We'll meet at the parking lot where the Big River Track meets the Bogong High Plains Road at midday tomorrow. Done deal.

There is one more important task to attend to as I descend to Cleve Cole. I must boot-ski on a summer snow patch. 'This could result in a broken leg, days from help,' sensible brain says. Objection overruled. *Yeeeeeeeeeeeeewwwwwwwwww wwhhhhoooooaaaaaaaaaaaaah!*

No, my keyboard has not malfunctioned. That's the joyous exclamation 'yew!' turning into a cautious 'whoa!' as the slope steepens then a slightly desperate 'aaaaaaaaaah' as it looks like I'll tumble into a pile of boulders. Which I do not. That was great fun.

The snow patch is actually really interesting. Or should I say, snow patches. There are two, one directly below the other, separated by a cricket pitch width of snow grass. One patch is pink, the other white. It's like a scene from Dr Seuss's

The Cat in the Hat Comes Back, where the cat tries to clean the snow after it has turned pink from the spot he left in the bath. The pink snow here is remnant winter snow coated by the dust storms of spring. The white snow is the last of the December blizzard and is thinner and softer. The pink patch is a lot deeper and has the same granular snow as the highest slopes of Hotham.

Back down at Cleve Cole, I Jetboil a coffee inside the hut. It's a layer of psychological insulation as much as a caffeine hit. Got a strong feeling that T Spur and Duane Spur won't be any easier than yesterday. It's also nice to spend a few more minutes in the hut. It really is a great place. They've piped water from the creek into it, and there's a functional sink and even a shower which can be made to run hot, thanks to the solar panels. There's also a locked section reserved for members of the Bogong Alpine Club, which was formed in 1965 to promote the environmentally sensitive and safe recreational use of Mt Bogong for the wider community, as well as maintaining Cleve Cole and Michell Refuge, a smaller hut on the opposite side of the mountain. A sign on the door of the members section asks for donations. Request approved. Last night was the first time I've slept in a High Country hut rather than camping beside it. The experience was fantastic. Had a clean mattress and everything. A friend of mine once camped at Cleve Cole in high summer and tried to count the tents. He lost count somewhere near 200, which explains why the drop toilet 100 metres behind the hut has four cubicles. My friend couldn't get near the interior of the hut on that trip, and I've had the place to myself. Maybe people are avoiding the outdoors as the bushfires increasingly dominate the headlines this summer, or maybe I just picked the right week before the school holidays. Anyway, it's been great. Some days the solo trail is lonely. Up here it's been bliss.

Down. Feet getting sore. This descent might actually be giving me the first blisters of this trip. The knobbly, flippery assemblages of bone and flesh otherwise known as my feet have held up spectacularly well so far. A big part of that is my Vasque boots, an American brand, but the real podiatrical hero of this story is not my shoes but my socks. I have a dual sock system, as recommended by the friendly, knowledgeable and extremely good-looking staff at Trek & Travel in Sydney. How many stores these days offer really good advice from people who actually care about the reason you're buying their product? The simple tip I got from Trek & Travel was to wear two layers of socks – a wicking under-layer and a thicker outer layer. Most blisters are caused not by ill-fitting boots but by sweaty feet. Wick the sweat away and hey, presto! Your feet stay dry and unblistered. Or they have done until now. These descents have been so steep, the soles of my feet are being rubbed raw, right under the arch. It's the strangest place to have chaffing, but there it is. At least the pain is a companion, taking my mind off the strain and monotony of climbing. The three hours up to Ropers seem like much less.

HONK!

What was that? Actually I know, but when you're startled by an extravagantly loud deer honk on an afternoon when the only noise is the wind and your own footsteps, a rhetorical question helps you process the moment. Bloody deer. Bet you anything that's who ruined that pond up on Bogong. Would love to eat some venison tonight as revenge. Lahori cholay will do. They're curried Pakistani giant chickpeas. I can pretend they're deer eyeballs. Delicious.

An empty Ropers Hut makes it two nights in a row I don't have to pitch my tent. Excellent. Boots off. Ouch. Bit of cream on my soles. Much better. Inflate the sleeping mat and lay it out on a bench. Crawl into sleeping bag well before dark. Need a nice early start tomorrow to ensure I meet Dave from Tawonga at our appointed spot on time.

It's an amazing feeling lying inside Ropers waiting for sleep to come while the night outside fades from deep purple to black. The hut is squeaky clean, as in, both squeaky and clean. The squeaks come from the bush rats scuttling around the rafters. I find their presence comforting. There are definitely two of them. I name them George and Mildred. Fans of British sitcoms of the late 1970s will understand. If that's not you, then know that there was a TV show called *George and Mildred* about a dysfunctional married couple, but the important thing in this context is that their surname was Roper.

As to the hut's cleanliness, that's thanks mostly to the goodwill of hikers. Klaus Hueneke says the huts in the worst condition in the High Country are the ones you can drive to. Most hikers wouldn't dream of leaving a hut without sweeping the floor, much less trashing it. Walk through a landscape and you feel a sense of ownership. You become a caretaker of everything in it. You can only join the Bogong Alpine Club if you've climbed Mt Bogong, because only people who have climbed it truly understand why the mountain is worth protecting.

CHAPTER 10

THE KINDNESS
OF STRANGERS

Dave from Tawonga is waiting by his sleek silver Subaru. He has brought a blue energy drink. Dave from Tawonga is a god. No, he's higher than that. He is a trail angel. Dave is a bearded semi-retired air traffic controller with an assured, friendly manner. If you wanted a person to prevent your plane hitting another plane, you'd definitely choose Dave.

The Bogong High Plains Road drops quickly over the eastern edge of the High Plains as he talks about skiing in Japan, and how hordes of Australians have turned large parts of the island of Honshu into Bali with skis. Within half an hour, we've lost a thousand vertical metres and are following Big River, the stream I crossed en route to Bogong, which is at last beginning to justify its name with broad deep pools between boulders the size of garbage trucks. The country is as dry as cardboard, the air smudged with heat haze. We take a short cut on a minor dirt road, open and close two farm gates, and then we're in Benambra, population 150, a map speck as hot and shadeless on this December Wednesday as any outback outpost.

We walk into the store, which is also the post office, the petrol station and the café. The burgers are excellent. They actually taste like beef, not the sausagey deal you sometimes get at small-town burger joints that have stopped caring or never did. The coffee is also well above average. Christine is sitting at the table beside us. Who is Christine? Christine is Christine from Gibbo River, about 20 kilometres north of town on the Benambra–Corryong Road. Benambra is the sort of town where locals introduce themselves to strangers if the strangers smile and say hello. They also give you their leftover chips, because Benambra is definitely not the sort of town where perfectly good chips go to waste. Great chips, too. Fat like thumbs, the way chips used to be.

Dave is loving the vibe as flannel-shirted locals fill their utes with petrol and are greeted by name. Over on his side of the mountains in towns like Mount Beauty and Bright, chips uneaten by tourists stay uneaten by other tourists, and gift stores are stocked with twee this and quaint that and frilly the other thing, and the bakeries sell sausage rolls with fennel seeds in them. No one ever put a fennel seed in anything in Benambra.

This is the plan. After lunch, Dave will run me out to my food drop at Taylors Crossing on the Mitta Mitta River, about 15 minutes out of town. I'll wait out the heatwave for two or three days, swim, write up my journal, lounge around like a teenager, then get on the trail again. There's just one complication. After Taylors Crossing, the AAWT crosses dry country to a 1570-metre peak called Johnnies Top. There's a tank up there which my online spies say is probably empty. Not good. Not willing to risk that. Does Christine know someone who can drive me out on back roads to the other side of Johnnies Top for a modest fee? Of course she does, because that's the sort of town Benambra is. Her partner, Brett, will do it. There's no phone reception at the river, but if I climb the big hill behind it in the morning, I'll get a bar or two and can confirm an arrangement. Perfect.

We drive north out of town over a range of low hills into countryside with giant cotton reels of hay and cows contentedly swishing their tails. The farmland soon drops away to a steep-sloped valley, at the bottom of which is the Mitta Mitta, the largest river anywhere on the AAWT. It's actually the rebadged Big River again, so good they named it twice, as the old Wagga Wagga joke goes. Genuinely big now too, even in this desiccated December.

Taylors Crossing is an open grassy campsite encircled by tall, swaying gum trees. Spanning the river is an extravagantly large, hospital-green suspension bridge which replaced two previous bridges that washed away in floods. I retrieve my food drop in the scrub. A bottle of Coke left beside the drum has been shredded by something with sharp teeth or claws. My guess is a goanna, but it could have been anything. No matter. The food is intact, and I got my caffeine fix in Benambra. Sixteen days ago, it was cool and drizzly here. Now the cicadas are auditioning for the world's loudest a cappella group. I bid farewell and thanks to Dave, offer petrol money which he refuses because trail angels have no need for anything so inconsequential as cash, scope out a tent spot that's shady but not underneath large branches, and introduce myself to the sole camper in the campground.

Did you know that Tiger Woods's real given name is Eldrick? Sometimes a name just doesn't suit a person and my companion at the river is one such man. His given name seems far too bookish for the figure sitting beside me on a deckchair, shirtless and shoeless, with faded yellow boardshorts and a floppy brown bush hat with the feathers of an eagle or hawk at the back. His body is uniformly tanned a deep bronze, his upper arms and shoulders tattooed, and the only item on his person which even faintly evokes the formality of his name is his glasses. I put old Rivermate in his mid-fifties, give or take half a decade.

Rivermate's plan for the rest of this sweaty Mitta Mitta afternoon involves drinking bootleg bourbon and chain-smoking black-market cigarettes while running through every entry in the Oxford Dictionary of Expletives from asshole to wanker – and if we stay here long enough, I'm sure he'll come up with one for x, y and z too. I decline his offer of a drink but accept a cigarette. The first drag is like death. Somewhere in Australia right now, firefighters just inhaled acrid bushfire smoke and didn't sear their lungs half as badly.

Rivermate has no plans to go anywhere anytime soon, that much is clear. It's apparent that he is of no fixed address and has been that way for a while. His modified ute is part vehicle, part mobile home, with a fridge and a freezer, solar panels, a bed, water drums, petrol drums, drawers full of tools and crockery, and 100 other things both ornamental and practical. Hanging off the front mirror is a large, menacing set of shark jaws that announce he is not a man to be screwed with, not least if you're a shark. In another age, jolly swagmen camped by billabongs with tea, flour, a billy, a bedroll and the odd stolen jumbuck. Rivermate camps by the Mitta Mitta with three aisles of a supermarket and half a hardware store.

We sit in his fold-out chairs, him drinking bourbon, me drinking lemonade that I just bought in Benambra. It doesn't take long to learn who Rivermate despises. The short answer is everyone but the long list includes Aboriginal people, women, his late father, the media, celebrities, cops and anyone in a uniform except the local park ranger Yakka who may or may not pop down tonight for a beer.

He asks what I do, and I tell him I work in sports media. 'They're just c--ts that can play football,' he says, which is an accurate assessment of at least some sportspeople I've met. It was a mistake to tell him my profession because now he thinks

I'm one of the wankers, not one of the workers. I should've said I do something technical behind the scenes. Sound technician or something. Anyway, it's done. Rivermate pours himself another bourbon.

As late afternoon softens to early evening, I excuse myself to go pitch my tent. Then I swim. The Mitta Mitta is the most wonderful temperature. I sit on rounded river stones, submerged to my shoulders in the half-hearted flow, washing the trail out of my toes and face. I drift with the current to a deeper spot, ducking underwater with my eyes open. The river is translucent and golden, not muddy and opaque like the Murrumbidgee, which is where I swam growing up. It is cool and silky and cleansing to the touch. I've always preferred swimming in rivers to the ocean. All those crashing waves and sharks. All that salt. What's the point of a swim if you need a shower after it?

Afterwards, I rejoin old Rivermate in his fold-out chairs. He's getting hungry, and enthusiastically so. 'I don't know what to have for tea tonight,' he says. 'I can't decide between Dagwood dogs or sausages.'

The choice between battered and unbattered sausages. We all have our dilemmas in life.

'Maybe I'll have dim sims,' he muses. 'I love me Chien Wah dimmies. I know a place down in Gippsland where you get sixty for thirteen dollars.' Rivermate loves both a bargain and the sort of cuisine that keeps the kids of heart surgeons in elite private schools. 'The bloke I buy 'em off, he's been a Marathon dim sim man his whole life. I said, "What are ya f--ken doing?" He's a Chien Wah man now. They're good on a barbie hotplate too. Cut em in half, my kids love 'em. Yummy!'

Wait, dim sims cooked on a hotplate? This, like the dim sims themselves, could take a while to digest. Wait some more. Rivermate has kids?

In the end, he settles on a Mrs Mac's pastie. He asks if I want one. The answer is yes please, that'd be lovely, mostly because it feels like the right thing to say. My belly's still full of Christine's chips.

Half an hour later, the most perfect Mrs Mac's beef and vegetable pastie emerges from whatever contraption he uses to heat things up. The pastry is crispy, the filling steaming but not mouth-burning. It's an art to heat up a frozen pie or pastie just right. How many times have you chomped down on hot pastry and found the interior still tepid? Rivermate nails it and hits a spot I didn't realise needed hitting.

After dinner, Rivermate settles down to the serious business of finishing the last two-thirds of his bottle of bourbon, because the pre-dinner session was apparently just a light aperitif. He's in the mood to talk about himself, which is fine because I need an extended break from the relentless internal monologue of the trail. Besides, I'm curious to know more about him.

Rivermate grew up in a large town in Victoria where he is no longer welcome. He was married once but is no longer welcome near his wife either. They had two kids who are both now young adults and who he still sees, although it's not clear how often. Fuelled by bourbon, he begins reeling off stories one after another, in no particular chronological order, rat-a-tat-a-tat. The stories share a common theme in that they all culminate in violence. There's the one about the bingo night brawl in the local club, there's the bloody tale of the staghound that went totally feral on a kangaroo shoot and had to be shot itself, and there's the sad story of the bloke who blew his brains out in a shipping container for reasons that Rivermate never quite made clear.

He says he's on a disability pension which is how he affords essential supplies like petrol and dim sims and bourbon and a brand of cigarettes you've never heard of. He travels from river spot to river spot in summer then in winter camps down by the Gippsland Lakes where the fishing is good and it's warmer than the High Country valleys. He used to be a commercial fisherman and reckons nobody could steer a boat through the infamously treacherous Lakes Entrance sandbar like he could. Says he still likes to wet a line and might even try a little trout fishing tomorrow, and that I'd be welcome to join him. He tells me how much he loves his kids. And then he recounts the day when he was 15 and he knocked his father out cold in the bathtub because he was sick of being hit himself.

Rivermate says there are still a lot of c--ts he'd like to smash and if he sees them, he'll do it, don't worry about that. He says his back hurts so badly, he can hardly sit up straight and says it's because of all the fighting he did when he was young. He says the painkillers he takes are no good and that drinking is all that helps, and that no matter how rotten he feels in the morning, it's better than the back pain. He says he doesn't really know why he goes on. He says maybe he won't go on. He wonders why his park ranger mate Yakka hasn't come down to the river to say hello. He wonders again what some journalist from the city is doing here. I remind him about the hike and tell him I've wanted to do it for years. 'I respect that,' he says. 'You're livin' your dream.'

I tell him it's good to see the parts of the High Country I've never seen before and that I love my kids too. He asks if I'm sure I don't want a bourbon. I say yeah, I'm sure.

In the morning, it's hot like the desert. It's just gone eight but sweat drenches my shirt as I trudge up the hill. Later, I'll learn that this will be, on average, the hottest day ever recorded in Australia. All I know on this Mitta Mitta Thursday is that it's definitely the hottest day of the trip so far. Cicadas are reminding everybody about it too. After a 45-minute slog, I call my family from the top of the hill and check the fires app. All is good and all is good. Home fires burning, still no fires near me. I get through to Christine and sort out the lift with Brett. He'll pick me up at the river on Saturday morning. That means two more days sitting out the heatwave with old Rivermate. Maybe I can escape him for a few hours and go for a long swim downstream and walk back along the bank dodging the snakes. Maybe I'll write up my journal in the shade. Maybe is an excellent way to start a day. There are not enough maybe days in our lives. For Rivermate, every day is a maybe day. Maybe you can have too much maybe.

Rivermate is up and about with the car radio blaring when I get back. It's an FM station out of Albury, at least three hours over the mountains, and the announcer sounds like every FM radio announcer anywhere ever, with his slightly-too-chirpy tone which makes you want to slap his face.

The station plays 'Don't Change' by INXS. Okay, I won't. Just like you haven't changed your playlist for 30 years.

'Want an icy pole?' Rivermate asks.

Is he kidding? I'll have a hundred.

Rivermate hands over a blue Zooper Dooper. 'Only thing I'll tell ya is you're not getting my blackcurrant ones, I f--ken love 'em. Yummy!'

Rivermate says 'yummy' a lot. He's always going, 'smoked oysters, yummy!' and 'Chien Wah dim sims, yummy!' and 'icy poles, yummy!' It's a word totally out of step with the rest of his vocabulary, yet somehow it fits.

Now the radio's playing 'Vogue' by Madonna and oh, you'd better believe we're voguing by the Mitta Mitta in our fold-out chairs, me with my blue Zooper Dooper, him with his blackcurrant one, sucking and slurping like newborns.

Zooper Doopers sponsored the cricket a couple of summers back, which got me wondering: how much money can you really recoup on a major sports sponsorship when your product is frozen ice treats that sell for $5 per packet of 24 at Coles – in other words, a very similar price per unit as Chien Wah dim sims? Lots, it turned out. This I know because I wrote a story about it. Lion Dairy & Drinks told me that sales were up 23 per cent that summer. They also shared a bunch of other Zooper Dooper facts, including that raspberry is the most popular flavour. I would've thought cola for sure, but there you have it. Any Zooper Dooper is a good Zooper Dooper on a 40-degree day on the Mitta Mitta River, I know that much.

In the afternoon, a woman comes down to the river to paddle in the shallows with her three boys. Her husband drives down later to join them. We get talking. They are Ashleigh and Stuart Pendergast, and I'm intrigued because Pendergast is a famous High Country surname which bobs up in many of the history books I've read about the mountains.

'Benambra was settled before Melbourne. It's the oldest continuously established town in Victoria,' Stuart tells me. Melbourne was founded in 1835 so Benambra must've been settled in the early 1830s. The first Pendergasts made their way over the divide from southern New South Wales in the mid-1800s and the three boys paddling in the Mitta Mitta shallows are seventh generation. Stuart and Ashleigh married at 20 and lived in Bairnsdale for eight years before coming to Benambra four years ago to help Stuart's father with his farm. They haven't regretted it for a day.

'Up until four or five years ago, I had no plan to come back to Benambra ever. I thought, "No way, not a way in hell". We liked our town life in Bairnsdale, we had a nice house down there, I had a good job and Ashleigh's family was there. But why wouldn't you come back to the country? Look how nice it is. We've got a 1950s house in the middle of a paddock, and it's flat all around it, hills in the background.

The kids can come home and jump on a motorbike. We love it, don't we? We talked about moving to Melbourne for a long time, didn't we? I was never that keen, but I would've done it. I'm glad we didn't, though. There's actually pretty good money to be made in farming if you can do it efficiently.'

There's another reason why the Pendergasts returned to Benambra. They describe themselves as 'pretty conservative' and say there's lots of stuff talked about in schools these days that they'd rather expose their kids to in their own time, using their own language. They say they like the conservative tone of the area and say that increasing numbers of people like them are moving to the bush. It's a claim not reflected in Australian Bureau of Statistics data, which show declining population overall in the bush, with only a small spike here and there in some larger regional towns. But maybe that'll change. Maybe the progressive politics of the inner city really are driving conservative young Australians to the bush, forging a new kind of urban–rural divide. Anyway, the Pendergasts are happy. And, seriously, who wouldn't be feeling both tip and top with their toes in the Mitta Mitta and a beer in their hand on a summer evening like this?

At dusk, the Pendergasts head home, signing off with a double dust cloud up the hill. They leave me with a packet of salt and vinegar chips, enhancing my growing reputation as the finest junk food freeloader in the Benambra district.

Then another ute comes down the hill. It's peak hour out here in the middle of nowhere. Yakka the ranger has finally shown up. Yakka is a stocky man with sandy hair which is just starting to turn grey. He wears a dark green Parks uniform and a baseball cap that says *No More Mr Nice Guy*, which is ironic because being a nice guy is crucial to his job. Like a country cop, a park ranger must uphold the law while staying on good terms with as many people as possible. It's a delicate balance, and Yakka has the perfect temperament for it.

Earlier today, a couple of fishermen left a fire with coals still glowing. On a day like this. Yakka was more bemused than shocked. He's seen it all before and knows he will again. Rivermate offers him a cigarette and a beer. He refuses. I ask him about the theory that environmental activists won't allow hazard reduction burns – a theory gaining credence on the conservative side of politics as fires spread around the country. He's a good listener. He waits till you've finished your question, then pauses as though he's thinking about his response even though it seems certain he's got one in his holster. Unfortunately, I can't share his thoughts because the words of a government employee can't be reported without sign-off in triplicate. I've made that mistake before and nearly cost a good man his job. But his eyes say plenty. Then he takes off under headlights in the fading twilight.

I don't want to push my luck with Rivermate's culinary largesse this evening, so I heat myself a quick palak paneer. The spinach and cheese curry is splendidly accompanied by the salt and vinegar chips. Call it gross; I call it camp fusion cuisine. Two reddish brown wallabies come to pick at the yellow grass at the fringe of the campground while I eat, and I find myself humming Concrete Blonde's 'Joey', which was

FROM SNOW TO ASH

on the Albury radio station's playlist earlier today. And then, to paraphrase the lyrics, I stand by and let Rivermate fight his secret war.

'I nearly became a copper once,' he says. 'They were lookin' for c--ts with a bit of a criminal record who could think the way the crims think. But I knew people who became coppers and I seen it change them. Takes 'em three years and they're not the same anymore.'

He pours himself another bourbon. The kookaburras think the imminent onset of darkness is hilarious.

'My dad, he wasn't a bad bloke. But I had to hit him, you understand? You can't let people f--ken push you round, y'know? Oh Jesus, me back hurts.'

In the morning, there's a change. Rivermate is up early, dressed in jeans and a singlet. 'Walk This Way' blares from his car radio. Then it's Shania Twain's 'Man! I Feel Like a Woman!'. When I'm back down the hill from checking my phone, he has vanished. No ute, no deckchairs, no classic 80s and 90s hits, no Zooper Doopers, no goodbyes. He's just gone.

Maybe he felt a little awkward at revealing too much of himself. Perhaps he just got restless. He was getting low on bourbon, I know that much. He never even went fishing. I bet he never fishes anymore. Hobbies are how we take a break from our lives, but when you've given up on your life, what's there to take a break from? I hope I'm wrong. I hope he hasn't given up. I wish him well, wherever he is.

As I lie back under a shady tree writing my journal, backpack for a pillow, I want Coke and chips. Why didn't I buy more junk food in Benambra? I miss Rivermate's food and the way he delighted in sharing it. I'd even smoke one of those dynamite sticks that he calls cigarettes.

Old Rivermate never stood a chance. All those stories that end with him punching someone in the jaw or wanting to. He never had someone to navigate him through those parts of the world where a flying fist is no way to resolve an issue. The thing that makes me saddest is that he never had the opportunity to put his talents to use. That he could steer a fishing boat with skill I have no doubt, but I feel he would have been best deployed in a job serving people. He would have made a great nurse or youth worker. He would have been an absolutely fantastic cook at a bistro somewhere in a small or medium-sized town. I can see old Rivermate in the kitchen of a local sports club, swearily deconstructing the problems of the world with the kitchen hand while the radio blares 'Bad Medicine' by Bon Jovi. I can smell the steaks he's cooked just right, the chips crispy but not burnt, the salad bathed in just the right amount of Kraft salad dressing. It's too late now. He's been the outsider his whole life, especially, it seems, in his own family.

This is all speculation, of course. I really don't know anything about the guy except his pasties were piping hot, his Zooper Doopers icy cold, his bourbon smelled like kerosene from two metres away and his cigarettes would give cancer cancer. But I do know I'm no better than him. I've gotten angry at people before too. Before I left to do the AAWT, I lost my cool at work and told someone what I really thought of them. It was the verbal equivalent of a punch to the jaw.

In my world, the consequences are a trip to HR. In his, it's a trip to the police station. The world's not fair.

* * *

Two weed sprayers come down to the river. The sound of their buzzing machines is soothing. It is purposeful, industrious. They don't last long, though, soon retreating to the shade for lunch and drinks. Today feels almost hotter than yesterday.

Have you ever stared at the sky through a large gum tree? There's so much going on. A forest is like a bustling town. Yakka said that gum trees shed leaves when it's dry to help stay alive. They're doing that now. The tree canopy is having an extremely busy day ridding itself of itself. Leaves twirl and tumble, birds dart from branch to branch. The clouds can't make up their minds whether they want to be clouds or not. The natural state of the world is busyness, not repose.

I feel like being busy too. Busy doing what? I've run out of things to write in my journal, so I rummage around inside my tent for whatever seems interesting. Could be a snack, could be a map of the local area. Not sure. I'll know when I see it. I zip the interior door shut and the zipper self-destructs. The tent is now open to the world. It's a great big party and every mosquito and spider in Australia is invited. In my medical kit, I have a needle and thread. It's a good start. Unfortunately, I can't sew, but how hard can it be? I thread enough cotton on the needle for about six stitches, then need to change it. That's when I drop the needle in the dry grass beside the tent. I am now looking for the proverbial needle in a haystack. And yes, it's just as hard as advertised. I tilt my head to look from every angle but there is no sign of metal, no glint. How can a needle just disappear? Sigh. I zip up the waterproof exterior of the tent and decide to wait until dark to find it under torchlight.

Two women drive down to the river with a toddler. They are three generations of one family, the mother Steph, the grandmother Gwen. They seem like they'd prefer their own company, so I try my journal again. Nup, still nothing interesting to write. I doze off. Wake up thirsty. Fill my drink bottle in the river and plop a purification tablet in it.

A ute hoons down, going fast, stupidly fast. What's wrong with people? It stops at the water's edge.

'Fire! Fire!'

What?

Gwen and Steph don't think. They pack the toddler and their stuff into their ute in about five seconds.

'Should I go with them?' I ask the man.

'If you don't want to be here when the fire comes,' he says. I do not. Who knows what it would be like if a fire made it down here? The latent heat. The choking smoke. You'd survive in the river but it'd be a horror show.

My possessions are strewn inside my tent but there's no time to gather them. I heave my half-empty backpack into Steph's ute alongside her toddler and jump in while the man – who I learn is her husband – screams up the road to join the firefighting efforts. In the deep river valley, there was no sign of fire. No smoke, no smell, not a clue. As soon as we're up on the grassy tableland, there it is. A plume of smoke in the middle of a dry paddock and a low line of flame. It's a grass fire for now, but if it reaches the forest, it'll be a proper bushfire that no one could contain. We stop at Steph's farm to catch her favourite mare in the paddock. It trots in the opposite direction at first, then submits when it senses something is up. A man – not sure who he is – tells me to hitch the horse trailer to the ute while he attends to something else. Have you ever felt like someone is asking you to make a bicycle out of breadcrumbs? I've never hitched a trailer before and have no idea where to start. The man looks at me like I'm covered in horse manure. Oof, clank – he does it himself. Then we roar up to Gwen's place so she can gather her documents and drive herself into town.

'I used to think the winters were tough here because it's so cold,' she says. 'Now summer is the worst season.'

Into Benambra we go. Gwen drops me and drives off. My first stop is the Country Fire Authority shed to explain that the tent at Taylors Crossing is mine. They give me Yakka's number and I leave him a message saying I'm in town so he doesn't waste time looking for me. Then I call Christine's partner, Brett, and arrange for him to pick me up in town in the morning, not the river. I explain that we'll need to pick up my stuff from the river first, assuming it survives the fire, and that I'll happily pay extra for his trouble.

Then I go to the pub.

The Benambra Hotel is a single-storey timber building that looks like the Big Bad Wolf could blow it over with a sneeze. But there is soul in this rambling old inn. And the $50 rooms are my kind of price.

In the main bar, a crowd of about a dozen locals has gathered. The local publican, Johnno, is renowned for being reluctant to open the pub on all but the busiest nights, but this is definitely a busy night by Benambra standards. Johnno the semi-reluctant publican is even serving food. The pepper steak is magnificently peppery and the lone beer on tap is cold. And if you don't like Carlton Draught, too bad, because Benambra is the sort of town where craft means crochet.

I learn that the fire was sparked by a faulty electric fence, that it has almost certainly been contained, that there was another one nearby also on private land and that, with luck, they'll both be extinguished early tomorrow before the wind picks up ahead of a cool change. There are Pendergasts in the pub because of course there are. Vince and Di are an elderly couple who drink their scotch neat in pony glasses, and who seem like the matriarch and patriarch of the valley. Vince starts sentences which Di finishes, and between them they recount the story of the Air Force Dakota DC3, which crashed in 1954 on the New South Wales–Victoria border, about 50 kilometres from here. The pilot had engine problems and brought the plane down in a clearing called Cowombat Flat, where the Murray River has its headwaters. I'll be walking towards it tomorrow, all going well. Three of the four crew members survived, including the pilot.

Naturally, Benambra townsfolk led the rescue, four of them Pendergasts. There's a section of silvery wing mounted on the wall of the pub, and I can just imagine the Benambra search party, led by Pendergasts one generation older than Di and Vince, heading off by car and then by foot into the dark bush to search for a thin silvery sliver of plane fuselage and three cold, injured airmen. It's like my needle in the grass but on a much larger scale. Eventually, the search party found the plane and brought the men home to safety. Because that's the sort of town Benambra is.

CHAPTER 11

A WICKED PROBLEM

The country east of Benambra is rugged and misshapen, like the face of a rugby forward who's played a few seasons too many. It's dominated by 1430-metre Mt Tambo, which looks like it drank six whiskies in the Benambra Hotel and sheared off half its chassis in a crash on the way home. Eugene von Guérard – the Austrian-born artist who painted the view from the summit of Mt Kosciuszko that was actually the view from Mt Townsend – had a crack at painting Tambo on his way to Kosciuszko in 1862. On this occasion, he accurately captured not just the identity of the mountain but its personality. In the foreground of his *Mount Tambo from the Omeo Station*, contented cows drink at an abundantly full dam. In the background is Tambo, hulking and aloof. That's how the mountain looks now.

The dust is up today, whipped by a gusty wind. There's smoke about too, some of it from the local fires, some from distant blazes. Brett and I bump along the Limestone Road which winds out towards such grand metropolises as Wulgulmerang, population 11, Gelantipy, population 20, and the former town of Suggan Buggan, present-day census count zero. But we're not heading that far. Our destination is the Cowombat Flat Track, which branches north off the Limestone Road half an hour east of Benambra. The track leads to Cowombat Flat on the New South Wales–Victoria border where, with luck, I'll see one of the elusive High Country cowombats. Only kidding. There are no marsupial bovines roaming the mountains dumping enormous square cowpats for hikers to dodge. Cowombat in fact means 'woman' in the local Wolgal dialect. On this day, to me it means safety.

The worst kind of weather change is on the way. Cool air is pushing up from the south but there's no significant rainband between the hot and cold air masses. That means dry lightning strikes are a strong possibility. If that happens, the last place you want to be is this dry limestone country with its unbroken scraggly forest. Cowombat Flat is a haven – a broad, mostly treeless plain with the infant Murray River running through it. If fire breaks out in these parts, that's where you want to be.

Brett's full name is Brett Lee, just like the cricketer, and his age appears about the same as Brett Lee's famous number 58 cricket shirt. In recent years, Brett has faced a much tougher opponent than any batsman the famous fast bowler ever confronted. He's been fighting depression and mostly winning. Lord knows it's difficult. Literally. Brett found God a few years back. And what the Lord told him was to get on with life, no matter how tough things are.

'It was a little wake-up call that someone else is in control, not you,' he says as we rattle along. 'But you have to ask for Him.'

In life, Brett asks for very little. He's helping to hold his family together while his mother fights cancer, and he's trying to make ends meet on his property on the Gibbo River north of Benambra. He and Christine maintain an eight-bed cabin called Kings Flat Inn which is ideal for fishermen, hunters or anyone who wants a nature retreat with a hard roof instead of a tent. It's the sort of place I'd book in a heartbeat, but with no wi-fi and the power only running a few hours each day, it's a hard sell in today's world.

Brett actually built the house at Kings Flat himself. 'I've got pioneer skills,' he says. Lately, he's been employing those pioneer skills to celebrate an actual pioneer, or at least a legend of the mountains. He's helping build a replica of mountain stockman Jack Riley's hut for the Man from Snowy River Museum in Corryong, north of Benambra. Riley, who died in 1914, is widely held to be the horseman in Banjo Paterson's famous poem 'The Man from Snowy River'. An excellent way to get a beer bottle smashed over your head in Corryong is to suggest it was someone else. The Man from Snowy River Museum's very diplomatic official stance is that the poem was a work of fiction drawing on the stories of numerous mountain cattlemen whom Paterson met in his travels in the area. Whether Riley was the horseman or not hardly matters. He certainly had the skills for the daring horseback descent immortalised in verse, and it's beyond historical question that he shared many nights around the campfire with Paterson. So, one way or another, there's no doubt Riley helped inspire the poem.

We're nearly at the start of the Cowombat Track now and the country has closed in. Don't like it. A fire could roar over the hill on a wind change and the first you'd know about it is the wall of flame. The thought of fire makes me instinctively reach for a water bottle in my pack. Mistake. Bad mistake. I've forgotten to fill my bottles. The larger one is half full which means I've got a litre of water, but it's not nearly enough and I haven't seen a creek with a drop in it since leaving Benambra. Maybe there'll be water in one of the creeks flowing down from the Cobberas, the highest range in this area. Here's hoping.

Before Brett drops me off, I tell him my wife is religious. I want to tell him I don't think he's mad. Not sure how else to say it. When a man starts talking about the Lord, he risks being mocked. The last person I'd mock is Brett.

'Religion costs you nothing,' he says. 'But faith is costly.'

It's a subtle dig at those who believe the ritual of religion is as important as belief. I assure him my wife is both religious and a believer. I'm trying to tell him I'm spending my life with someone he'd relate to. That I relate to him. That we're two travellers on a bumpy road called Limestone and called Life. We part ways. I wish him well. Brett Lee from Gibbo River can open the bowling in my High Country Good Guys XI any day of the week.

It's easy, quick walking on the Cowombat Flat Track, a wide fire trail with twin tyre ruts and a strip of grass in the middle. I still don't like the country or the weather. It's open woodland rather than what you'd call dense forest, but it's a tease. The trees are tightly enough packed to block the horizon, and there's not enough sky to gauge the weather. This country makes me uneasy. It's like playing poker against someone you can't read. It's high enough in the mountains for the creeks to have a lining of sphagnum moss, but the cushions of moss in the first two creeks are bleached and withered and the creek beds are rocky and dirt dry. If I don't get water soon, it'll be a miserable walk to Cowombat. How far to go? Twenty kilometres, give or take. How much water left? Not much. What's the weather doing? Can't really tell. Wind's still blowing, though. Picking up, if anything. A fire in here and you'd melt like a marshmallow.

East of the track through the tree canopy and haze, a mountain range comes into view. It's good to have some perspective of the country at last. The mountains are the Cobberas. Peaking at 1825 metres, they're the wildest, most remote and least-visited high mountains in Victoria — a band of craggy summits and dark-wooded slopes which are the second of five designated wilderness areas on the AAWT. The first was the Razor–Viking Wilderness between Mt Skene and Hotham, which I missed. But now I'm in actual wilderness for the first time. In a sense, wilderness is just a word. There are plenty of wild, remote areas on this track. But if the Cobberas are any guide, wilderness is also a feel, and the Cobberas feel forbidding. John Chapman recommends a side trip to the range. He writes:

> The Cobberas are the last truly wild high mountains left in Victoria. There are few tracks, apart from brumby pads, to sully their unspoiled summits. There is little evidence of human interference and this creates a strong feeling of isolation that adds much to their charm.

That's peak Chapman, excuse the pun. I see no charm. If anything, I feel repelled. It's moments like this you realise he's a serious hiker and I'm just some guy from the suburbs impersonating one. Perhaps that's self-flagellation. I'm definitely picking up some skills on this hike. One of them is finding water. As I learned near Mt Skene, when a dry creek crosses a fire trail, find the pipe on the low side. Success. Sweet success. Well, not exactly sweet, but it's still success. The first creek tumbling down from the Cobberas has a drip. On the upper side of the trail, the creek shows no sign of flow. The soil's a little moist but that's about it. But on the lower side, a steady drip is coming through the pipe. It takes half an hour to collect four inches of rust-coloured water in my large bottle. That'll do. I plop a purification pill in. I may never drink this water but it's good to know it's there. Lunchtime. Tuna wrap. Not hungry. My only urge is to move. Got to get to Cowombat as soon as possible.

I'm always amazed at people's weather illiteracy. People seem to pay more attention to astrology than meteorology. It's insane. The constellations are hidden by day and hard to identify by night, and if you really think they affect your personality, then I have a very lovely bridge to sell you at an extremely reasonable price. The weather is right here, all around us at all hours. Yet people don't know which way the wind is blowing. They can't interpret clouds or read a synoptic chart. They take their daily forecasts from icons on weather apps. A smiley sun. A glowering grey cloud. Nothing better exemplifies the way technology has dumbed us down than the way people consume weather information. In a sense, it's a snapshot of the way all news works these days. A vibe here, an emoji there, a headline, a tweet. We base our understanding of issues on the faintest whiff of information. Without our phones in our hands, we feel neutered. In truth, we're worse off with them.

So, then. What exactly is happening weather-wise on this unsettled Saturday afternoon? The sky, or what I can see of it, is a mess. There is high cloud and middle-level cloud and it's blowing in all directions. That means the change is imminent. Cool air from the south is replacing the warm air from the north. These next few hours are crucial. If dry lightning strikes, it will be soon.

Scientists are yet to prove beyond doubt that the amount of dry lightning is increasing in southern Australia, but anecdotal evidence suggests it is. The devastating 2003 and 2006 alpine fires were both started by dry lightning. Meteorologists know that the atmosphere in southern Australia has become less moist in the last 30 years, and there is evidence that with the drier atmosphere, the base of thunder clouds is higher up, which means there's not the depth to generate as much rain. When storms form on the back of a hot, dry air mass, they're often dry. Sorry, boomers, but Fleetwood Mac lied to you when they said thunder happens only when it rains.

There's a thing I do when I'm feeling uneasy on the trail. First noticed it back on the approach to Mt McDonald. Call it a nervous tic. When I'm walking in a relaxed mood, I plant my hiking poles once every few steps. When I'm feeling edgy, I go pole, pole, pole every single step. I'm going pole, pole, pole now. I'll be going pole, pole, pole all the way to Cowombat. The last of the Benambra water is gone. No stopping now. Pole, pole, pole, pole, pole. Mouth dry. Saliva foamy. Swallowing a little difficult. Headache brewing. I wanted to make Cowombat without touching my rusty water, but it's needed to help swallow two paracetamols. Okay, that's better. It's amazing how little water it takes to satisfy you when you're really dry. You just want your mouth rinsed out. That's all you can think about. Proper hydration can wait. I'm in full Simone mode now, rattling along to Cowombat. Descending. Blinkers on. Not looking at the country or the sky. Lost track of time. Pole, pole, pole, pole, pole, pole, pole.

And then I'm there. Right at the very edge of Cowombat Flat is the plane wreckage, sheets of grey metal flapping in the wind. The physical reality is much less interesting than a bar-room discussion in Benambra. You could probably say that about lots of things.

If you've ever taken a good look at the border between Australia's two most populous states, New South Wales and Victoria, you'll notice it follows the meandering course of the Murray River for most of its length, before cutting to the coast in a straight line. That would be the Black–Allan Line, a 180-kilometre strip of geographical pragmatism named after the men who surveyed the area. The eastern point of the straight line is Cape Howe and the western point is technically the start of the Murray River, just a few kilometres up the hill from Cowombat Flat. In a wetter season, and at the end of a less arduous day, it might be tempting to visit that first trickle of Australia's longest river, but a quick walk along the river at Cowombat Flat makes it pretty clear there would be no trickle. The metre-wide Murray is virtually dry, with stagnant pools fouled by brumby poo. Need to fill my bottles. Walk downstream. Okay, here's a section where the river is flowing. The water seems to bubble out of the ground. A spring? Not sure. Anyway, it's good water. Bottles full. Three purification pills in each. Don't trust any water around here with all those brumbies. Thirsty as hell but not touching the water until the pills have kicked in.

Cowombat Flat is huge. In news stories, they often quantify area in terms of football fields, which is a nifty idea in theory because everyone knows the size of a football field, but who can imagine several hundred side by side? That's what I'd give Cowombat. Definitely a hundred or more football fields. The brumbies own this place. This is their prime territory, all the way up through the Cascades to the ironically named Dead Horse Gap near Thredbo. There seem to be several herds here, each with ten or more members. Mountain stockmen used to call this part of the Murray the Indi River. Elyne Mitchell, author of the Silver Brumby books, named her first daughter Indi. She knew Cowombat well and helped mythologise the area and its four-legged residents in her award-winning children's literature. These horses are such a powerful symbol. They represent wildness and beauty and unconstrained freedom, and when you see brumbies in the flesh they are indeed wild and beautiful and free.

But the brumbies are pests. This is vividly illustrated by a fenced plot of land at Cowombat which the volunteer group Friends of the Cobberas initiated and funded with support from Parks Victoria and other groups. Inside the exclusion plot, healthy bushes and native grasses flourish. Outside it, most of Cowombat Flat is picked so bare by the equine grazing machines it looks like a fifth-day cricket pitch. The very source of the Murray has been fouled by brumbies. Could there be a more symbolic beginning to our most contested inland waterway?

On 2 June 2015, John Barilaro, state member for the Snowy Mountains seat of Monaro, stood up on the floor of

the Legislative Assembly in the New South Wales Parliament
and delivered an impassioned speech:

> I ask the House to picture this image: a beautiful stallion
> running wild and free, his muscles bulging with strength.
> When he stands up on his back hooves one is overcome
> by his grace and power. There is nothing quite like seeing
> a brumby in the wild. It is an absolute thrill.

He went on to describe brumbies as part of the cultural fabric
and folklore of the High Country. He said they were part
of the unique environment that Kosciuszko National Park
exists to protect. He spoke of Snowy Mountains brumbies
who were captured and put to service with the Australian
Light Horse in World War I, and he concluded his speech
with the Banjo Paterson poem 'Brumby's Run'. But before
his poetic finale, Barilaro deferred to a political colleague and
well-known mountain horseman whose family runs a trail-
riding business in the Snowy Mountains.

'It is said that wild brumbies damage the environment
which is home to endangered native species,' Barilaro said.
'Peter Cochran, a former member for Monaro and avid wild
brumby supporter, suggests evidence is lacking in this area.'

Evidence is anything but lacking. In 2018, Barilaro brought
a piece of legislation to state parliament called the Kosciuszko
Wild Horse Heritage Bill. Its stated object was to recognise
the heritage value of sustainable wild horse populations
within parts of Kosciuszko National Park and to protect that

heritage. The Australian Academy of Science immediately took it on. In a letter to Barilaro which acknowledged the input and expertise of at least 14 experts, it said:

> The Heritage Bill places a priority on a single invasive species over many native species and ecosystems, some of which are found nowhere else in the world ... Leading research on the impacts of feral horses locally and from around the world provides clear scientific evidence of environmental damage done by this invasive species ... Reports from bog, stream, and dry habitats in Kosciuszko and Victoria indicate a wide range of ecosystems are degraded by feral horses. This research leads the Academy to expect substantial negative impacts on species and ecosystems within the Park arising from the provisions of the Heritage Bill.

But Barilaro's political muscles – like the stallion he eulogised in his 2015 speech to state parliament – were bulging with strength. The bill passed. Not for the first time in history, science was defeated by emotion. For many people, it was hard to swallow. David Watson, a Professor of Ecology at Charles Sturt University, immediately quit his post on the NSW Government's Threatened Species Scientific Committee, which he had held since 2015. 'The wilful disregard that you and your government colleagues have for science diminishes our collective future, relegating our precious national parks and priceless environment to political playthings,' Watson wrote in a letter to the then NSW Environment Minister Gabrielle Upton. He shared it on social media and created quite a stir.

Jindabyne father of two Rob Gibbs has spent 16 of his 30 years as a ranger in the Kosciuszko National Park. He was what they call a patch ranger for much of that time, and his patch was the Pilot Wilderness area south of Thredbo through to Cowombat Flat. Nobody in the mountains understood more about the damage brumbies do than Gibbs.

To Gibbs, the brumby issue was a classic example of what they call a 'wicked problem' in planning and policy. A wicked problem is an issue that seems almost impossible to resolve, with no easy answers or decisions. Gibbs knew that the issue was not just about horses and their management, it was about people's values. He understood that some people feel dispossessed from national parks and disenfranchised from government land management decisions. He carried this understanding to work every day like a packed lunch.

Over five years, Gibbs worked as part of the team compiling and writing the Kosciuszko National Park Wild Horse Management Plan. He did his job in the spirit of compromise, speaking to people from all sides of the debate, trying to understand their views. He shared scientific facts with those who saw only the mythology of the wild horses, and he spent time convincing Park managers, environmental scientists and conservationists to acknowledge and recognise the cultural and social values held by brumby lovers. His efforts earned him friends and enemies and everything in between. There were even threats to him and his family.

When the draft plan was published in 2016, it contained a long list of negative environmental impacts caused by brumbies, along with images of silted-up streams, their banks eroded and trampled by hooves. It also had a section on cultural and social values of the horses which acknowledged that brumbies are a drawcard for some visitors. The plan leaned towards protecting the alpine environment while retaining a small population of brumbies within Kosciuszko National Park. Horse numbers would be reduced through 'humane and cost-effective means'.

Brumby activists wouldn't have a bar of that. They campaigned against the draft plan on social media and lobbied politically. Misinformation was rampant. A false rumour about a proposed mass aerial shooting of 6000 horses spread as fast as any High Country bushfire. Meanwhile, Parks staff were unable to say a thing, constrained by public service rules against speaking out. When John Barilaro's Wild Horse bill passed in 2018, it effectively turned the 2016 draft plan to confetti. Gibbs walked away. He worries about what will be lost, but there's only so much a man can do.

Today, Gibbs is the program manager for the Australian Alps National Parks Co-operative Management Program. Formed in 1986, it coordinates management of the Australian Alps as a single bioregion of national significance by the four state, territory and Commonwealth parks management agencies. It's also responsible for the upkeep and long-term direction of the AAWT.

In his new role, the issue of brumbies inevitably landed back on Gibbs's desk. The program has been coordinating aerial surveys of feral horses across the Australian Alps since 2001. In autumn 2019, it undertook its latest survey. The results were alarming. Brumby numbers had increased from an estimated 9187 in 2014 to 25,318 in 2019. In other words, the population nearly tripled in five years. For now, the brumbies are winning.

I could walk further this evening but Cowombat Flat, like Mt Bogong, deserves to be savoured. In the pub in Benambra, Di Pendergast urged me to soak the place up. She said I'd feel something. I *do* feel something. I am soaking it up. This big open valley ringed by mountains is a place of great power. This one's for you, Di. I wonder if she'll ever get here again. You used to be able to ride a horse here back in the day. Not anymore. Feral horses everywhere and they'll lock you up if you ride a horse in.

Okay, how long has that guy been sitting there? There's another solo hiker over near the river. Must have missed him when I went over to the plot of native vegetation after gathering water. I approach. He waves. We take pictures of each other standing astride the Murray with one foot in each state, which is more or less de rigueur for anyone visiting Cowombat. He is a New Zealander who lives just out of Brisbane and is about to paddle down the Murray. His canoe is stashed nearby, about ten kilometres downriver where it becomes navigable by personal watercraft.

How far are you going to paddle?

'All the way to South Australia.'

Wow. I read a story about a couple who did that once. They started at Khancoban, which is a bit lower down from here but still close enough to the source of the Murray. It took them nine or ten weeks, as I recall, so my mate here has got a decent old paddle ahead of him. Naturally, I ask him why. He finds it hard to articulate. The trip is not a lifelong quest or spiritual journey. He is not especially fascinated by the Murray River, even though its 2500-kilometre length places it comfortably among the world's 50 longest rivers. He's just a bloke with a decent job in IT who's taking time off to paddle a bloody long way down a river.

Which I find annoying. That's not a particularly charitable reaction, but there it is. Maybe I'm dehydrated and irritable. Anyway, that's just how it feels. Aimless. Annoying. Are journeys better when they mean something? Absolutely. Must a journey have a higher purpose? No, of course not. A higher purpose is far from a prerequisite.

But I've been thinking about my conversation with Brett this morning. The quiet, uncomplaining dignity of the man. Tough life he's made for himself out there on his property on the Gibbo River, and tough battle he faces each day with the black dog of depression. And while Brett is not paddling up or down the Gibbo in a canoe, he's trying to lasso meaning like he's capturing a brumby, with old-fashioned hard work and faith. Brett feels like a real journeyer to me. Not sure what I make of Kiwi mate. Something about his journey bothers me. Maybe I'm reading him wrong. Maybe the trip has a meaning which he is incapable of expressing, or maybe he's just doing it because he's doing it, which is far from a terrible reason. Did not George Mallory live for, and die on, Everest 'because it's there'?

It's chilly now, the coldest it's been on this trip since Baw Baw. Thankfully, the cool change came without lightning, but it has brought smoke from fires in Gippsland and the orange sky is closing in. You can smell the smoke too. Kiwi mate is worried about a fire close by. I'm not. This is a classic dry summer sou'-easter and this smoke is from fires 100 kilometres or more towards the coast, somewhere down that Black–Allan line. Nothing to worry about. All the same, my companion is keen to camp on bare ground in the middle of the flat rather than somewhere a bit more protected among the olive-limbed black sallee trees. I don't want to camp in the middle of Siberia and have the wind buffet my tent all night, but there are times to compromise. Lord knows, a little give and take in this world would help us all get along.

CHAPTER 12

THE AWFUL, AWFUL THING THAT CHARLIE CARTER KNEW

Over the river into New South Wales. My home state. State with a clunky name. A name plucked from Captain Cook's diary which presumably referred to the new part of the world that looked like south Wales, not the new, south part of the world that looked like Wales. It's hard to imagine how it resembled either place.

I went to southern Wales once. Bit of a pilgrimage. It all started at my desk on a busy news website, when a major travel brand named the world's top 25 beaches and a Welsh beach called Rhossili Bay finished higher than the only Australian beach on the list, Whitehaven in Queensland. It was a quiet day in news and sport, so I put my Angry Travel Writer hat on. I felt no genuine outrage, as such surveys are rarely worth the pixels they're not printed on, but it seemed like fun to play the infuriated Aussie, so I rang the publican of the Worm's Head Hotel in the small village of Rhossili and demanded to know what made the beach below his village so special. In truth, we had a delightful conversation, but I wrote up my story in thunderously aggrieved tones. The British press took the bait. Within hours, news sites went crazy and I was doing BBC radio interviews with smug hosts delighting in my antipodean indignation. It was the most fun I'd had in ages.

A year or so later I was in the UK, so I took a day to drive out to Rhossili Bay and introduced myself to the publican, who of course remembered the whole kerfuffle. We had a good laugh followed by a great feed. His fish and chips were world class. The fish was oily, but good oily, not bad oily. The oil seemed to come from within the fish rather than the deep fryer. The chips were snappable but soft inside, just how chips should be, and the beer was malty and good. Then the important bit: the beach. Rhossili Bay is a long sweep of sand between steep green hills where woolly sheep contentedly nibbled on lush pastures. The water was cool but not cold on that July afternoon, and

I had a lovely swim in clear, bodysurfable waves in what I believe is technically called the Celtic Sea. Back home, I wrote up my glowing impressions. I was wrong, I said. Your beach is worthy. Rhossili Bay *is* a lovely beach. Wouldn't make the top ten thousand beaches in Australia, but I wasn't going to write that and break anyone's heart. The British press loved the second story even more than the first.

Would you like some irony with your cod and warm ale? To many people, this region of magnificent, often snowy, Australian mountains must sound as absurd and incongruous as an attractive British beach. We feel compelled to compartmentalise the world. Desert here, beaches there, mountains here. A whole country becomes the bit it's most famous for. There's actually a lot that people don't know about Australia. Here's a biggie: nothing is going to devour an adult hiker and spit out the bones here. Not while you're on your feet, anyway. Forget all those deadly snakes and spiders that people always talk about. They're out there, sure, but the number of snakebite and spider-bite deaths in Australia each year can barely be graphed; it's as low as one or two for snakes, and zero most years for spiders. But the really great thing about going bush in Australia is that there are no large, fearsome predators to watch out for. Australia does not have bears lurking in the bushes, waiting to shred you like lettuce. It's a much safer place to hike than the United States or Canada, for example, or pretty much anywhere.

That said, there's a brumby up ahead doing its best to freak me right out. I've just climbed a long, steep hill from

Cowombat Flat to a high ridge lined by burnt snow gums from the 2003 fires. It's unnerving up here. You just know you'd be hopelessly trapped if a fire roared up from the valley. Those scalded snow gums tell you everything you need to know. The worst part is you can't see the country below. There's still smoke wafting around and it's blocking the view on both sides, giving this long treed ridge the impression of hanging in the air. You know the floating mountains in the movie *Avatar*? Kind of like that. But the immediate concern here is the brumby. It's not a happy horsey. As I walk onwards, it gallops ahead beside the track then wheels around to face me, maybe three cricket pitches ahead, pawing the ground like a dog wanting to be let in. He's telling me to go. A stallion protecting his herd. I've heard they charge occasionally. If he charges, I charge too. My poles are my weapons and we'll have ourselves a nice jousting match. Then again, I may run away shrieking. Could go either way. Okay, a shrieking retreat is far more likely.

There are two types of brumby herds. There are harem herds, where a dominant stallion runs with several mares and their foals, and there are so-called bachelor herds, where colts and a selection of other horses run together. This, surely, is a stallion protecting his hard-won harem and their offspring. But after a while, he decides I'm no Russell Crowe. If you never saw it, the movie version of Elyne Mitchell's *The Silver Brumby* starred Crowe as The Man in one of his first film roles in the early 1990s. He was actually pretty good, though the real star of the movie was of course the Australian High

THE AWFUL, AWFUL THING THAT CHARLIE CARTER KNEW

Country. Not enough movies have showcased the beauty of this place. The film version of *The Man from Snowy River* had a great cast with Sigrid Thornton, Jack Thompson, Tom Burlinson and, improbably, the late, great Kirk Douglas. But there wasn't much action above the snowline. It was mostly set in dry valleys that could have been anywhere in Australia. That always disappointed me. Then again, if they'd churned up precious alpine flora with horses' hooves for the sake of a movie, I would have been just as upset. Just another episode in the eternally wicked problem of horses and the mountains.

Speaking of the Snowy River, you might have noticed no mention of it thus far outside the context of Paterson's poem. That's because it mostly bypasses the Alps. While the Snowy starts on the slopes of Mt Kosciuszko, it is soon tamed by Lake Jindabyne. Thereafter, it runs with a severely depleted flow, south to the Gippsland coastline through steep, dry valleys east of the Alps which are too rugged for any sort of farming. The much-mythologised Snowy is in actuality a little-visited river which few Australians could identify on a map. But mythology is often more alluring than reality. Just ask John Barilaro.

Here's the plan. Got to get to Thredbo. It's two to three days away and I'm meeting my wife and son there in three days. More or less on schedule here. Gained a couple of days bypassing closed bits of the trail, gave them back on the Mitta Mitta eating Zooper Doopers with Rivermate. Tonight's destination is Tin Mine Huts, a pair of restored huts originally built in the 1930s for the miners who worked at a nearby tin mine. The huts are on the Ingeegoodbee River. Ingeegoodbee. What a great name. I camped on the Goodradigbee in the north of the park once. Could the Ingeegoodbee be good as the Goodradigbee?

The trail descends the high ridge now. Through the orange gloom, The Pilot comes into view. It's the big mama in these parts, a dark, scrubby 1829-metre peak clearly visible from the ski slopes of Thredbo. In the two seasons I worked there, I often dreamed of hiking out to this distant peak. Seemed like a place where you'd really feel something. So here I am beside The Pilot after all those years. Should I climb it? Nah, don't feel like it. Happy just seeing it up close. We've turned mountains into binary objects. You either climb them or you've failed. Mountains don't work that way. You can enjoy them without standing on top of them. Anyway, The Pilot is an unwelcoming sort of mountain. Like the Cobberas on the Victorian side of the border, it feels like it wants to be left alone. You've got to listen to mountains.

* * *

The journey to Tin Mine Huts is easy walking. This is not a big day at all, just 17 kilometres. Weather warm but not hot. You need days like this. The AAWT is not a relaxing hike. This I can now officially report as the normal state of affairs on this track. Remember when I was talking about the sink-in moment back on day one, just out of Walhalla? Well, it has sunk in now. The psychologist I interviewed was right: it takes about three weeks. That unease I felt on the first afternoon that I've felt often since then? It's the normal state of mind on this track. The feeling comes and goes, but it's always there in the background for a hundred different reasons. Your guard is always up on this thing.

Just before the huts, the trail crosses Tin Mine Creek. Great little spot. Grassy banks and a pool just big enough for a swim. Why not? We're always rushing to get somewhere in life. It's good to obey an impulse. The creek is wonderfully refreshing. March flies, giant flies with bulbous green eyes like snooker balls, destroy me but that's okay. I'm dressed again now, which is always the best protection against marchies. And I'm now the cleanest hiker between here and Cowombat Flat, not to mention the only one. I'm also covered in shiny specks of iron pyrite, aka fool's gold. Tin turned out to be the real fool's gold in these parts, and when the mine went belly up in the late 1930s, Charlie Carter moved in and made the huts his own.

Carter was a lot of things over the course of his 81 years. He was a novelist. He ran for state parliament in New South Wales and received 33 votes. He was a self-taught lawyer and philosopher. He was a landowner and leaseholder in this area, although his ongoing feud over brumbies with powerful neighbours the Freebody brothers took him to court five times. He moved in and out of the High Country a few times in his life, but when he came to the Tin Mine Huts in 1938, he took the larger one known as The Barn and made it his home. There he lived until he died in 1952, trapping brumbies and selling their hides in Jindabyne, which was several days' travel over rough country. With the proceeds he bought supplies, supplementing his diet with vegetables he grew. He continued writing up at Tin Mine, penning pamphlets on the flaws of communism and the financial system. He tried his hand at mining. And he claimed to have found the cure for cancer with a mix of petroleum jelly, pulverised bluestone and God knows what else. Some say ingesting his own cancer 'cure' was what killed him. Some believe he died of a heart attack. Others say he was done for the day his horses got away. That seems plausible. They found him with a bridle in his hand.

On balance, it seems like Charlie Carter was three-quarters mad long before he ended up at Tin Mine. But you have to respect the man. Reading through his pamphlets in the appendix of alpine historian Klaus Hueneke's excellent book on his life, it's clear he wanted to contribute to the world and its knowledge. Here was a recluse who maintained a strong interest in the outside world. He also maintained his social manners. Carter was said to be a convivial and generous host when visitors on foot or horseback passed through his saucer-shaped valley on the Ingeegoodbee.

My belief, based on a mix of gut feel and Carter's writing, is that he knew something so awful, he dared not say or write it. I think he knew that for some people, it's impossible to live in society and just as difficult to live outside it. Some people just fall through all the cracks. Or maybe they chisel out the floorboards themselves and make the cracks impossible to miss. There's a clue to his mindset in Carter's mini treatise on the flaws of communism:

> Whatever forces contribute to the destruction of any particular form of life, that particular form of life will do more towards destroying itself than all the other forces combined.

Turn on the History Channel for proof of that one. You might also check the dictionary under 'Rivermate'. I mused earlier about the fantasy of fleeing, if you could reconcile yourself to your place in the world when you return. I'm beginning to think maybe you can't. Not if you stay out there too long, anyway. Much as I admire some aspects of their personalities, you don't want to end up like Charlie Carter or Rivermate. This trail, for me, is an escape but only a temporary one. That's becoming clear to me now. It is a bridge from one thing to another.

The Tin Mine Huts sit on the edge of a large natural clearing and are in fantastic condition. For this, the Illawarra Alpine Club and their enthusiastic volunteers deserve much praise. They've re-shingled, re-fireplaced, re-chimneyed, re-floored, re-everythinged. The small hut is neat and inviting, but with no one around, I live it up in the big one, Charlie's old house. It's a beautiful evening so dinner is outside. Mixed veg curry is good, peppermint tea on the smooth grassy lawn even better. Spot of Twinings in the twilight. A delight.

You can see why Carter loved it here. There are two streams, a small one running behind the chimney end of the hut, and the larger Ingeegoodbee, which does indeed be good. Despite the dry spell, there's still running water here on the New South Wales side of the border. Don't know if it was the geology of that crazy Victorian limestone country or if that area is in a rain shadow. Maybe both. But the Ingeegoodbee gurgles healthily as it threads the centre of a gently cambered valley, although its banks have been severely trampled by hooves. Brumbies own this place, just like they owned Cowombat, but it's a little higher here, and just above the snowline where grass tussocks flourish. Brumbies don't particularly fancy coarse tussock grass, so while Cowombat has had the number one blade at the barber shop, the valley here retains more of a bushland feel. It has native animals too. Wallabies graze near the hut and black cockatoos wheel and squeal in the trees. At night, possums come out, and in the morning as I take to the trail, out pop the emus.

Been waiting for these guys. Love emus. Didn't always love them. When I was a kid, my mum took us out to Tidbinbilla Nature Reserve for a barbecue, which every Canberran has done at least once. I was barbecue master. When you're a kid without a full-time dad on deck, you take this role seriously. Emu came up and stole a lamb chop off the barbecue. I saw it coming and was powerless. Broke my 11-year-old heart. Hated them for a while after that, but I've come to adore them. They're good company. They don't hop off into the bush like kangaroos. They're happy to walk the trail only a few metres ahead of you, only breaking into a run if you get too close. That run really is hilarious. If your feather duster was six foot tall and grew legs and took up sprinting, it would run in as ungainly a manner as an emu.

This, by the way, is an exceptionally fine trail. Its name has changed from the Cowombat to the Cascade Trail and it is lined by trees which are neither snow gum nor alpine ash but a handsome white-barked species of moderate height which I can't name. The trees frame the track perfectly, gently arching over it. I take a photo. The light is milky and dreamy like a colonial painting, due to the smoky air. It's the most magical photo. Trees and a path sound like the world's most ordinary thing, but there's something extraordinary about the image, something almost mystical. You look at that photo and you want to be walking down this track. It's like a TV ad for fried chicken at dinnertime. You just want that thing so bad it hurts. I'm lucky to be here. Sometimes you forget that. Wouldn't actually mind some fried chicken but maybe that can be arranged in Thredbo. Definitely looking forward to some Christmas leftovers. 'Yummy!' as my old mate Rivermate would say. Hope my wife remembers to bring them.

It's another perfect day of walking. Not too much distance, not too many ups or downs. The trail gains a little elevation as it bears directly northwards towards Thredbo, and then we're in alpine ash country. The forest is recovering well here from the 2003 fires. There hasn't been a fire here since then; the High Country fires of 2006 and the 2009 Black Saturday fires were Victorian events. This forest is nearing a crucial moment. The young healthy saplings are already about half as tall as the skeletons of their dead parent trees. Alpine ash flower at about 15 or 16 years. Four years after that, the seed is ready to go. If this forest were to burn now, forget it. Dead forest. Probably gone forever. That's why forest ecologists like Dr Tom Fairman of the University of Melbourne talk about a magic 20-year window.

'You don't just lose the trees when you lose a forest,' Fairman explains. 'Humans often say that big tall forests have a cathedral feeling, which is true, but there are other aspects. A lot of the fauna that live in Australian forests are hollow-dependent. Possums, gliders, birds. Then there's the aspect of carbon sequestration. A mature ash forest can store hundreds of tonnes of carbon per hectare, whereas shrubland is more like 50 or 60 tonnes.'

A few more years without fire and this forest stands a chance. Our fortunes are riding with it too. Fingers crossed the fires don't make it up here. There are so many fires in Australia at the moment. The smoke in the sky is going to be my companion for the rest of the trip, that much is clear. Except it's not clear at all. The sky is getting heavier and heavier with smoke this afternoon. Haven't had phone reception all day so I can't check the weather forecast or the fires app, but I don't recall any bad weather on the way or any fires nearby. I've been blessed with the weather on this trip. Baw Baw was the right place to have a blizzard because it's not particularly exposed and the Mitta Mitta River sorted out that hot spell. Then the dry lightning day fizzled two days ago. Very lucky. Don't like this sky though. It's going orange again. They used to say nothing rhymes with orange. That was before the AFL footballer Daniel Gorringe came along. Pole, pole, pole, pole, pole. I'm babbling and poling quickly. Both are signs of an uneasy mind. Got to get to Cascade Hut.

Cascade Hut is one of the prettiest little huts in the mountains. It's barely 50 metres off the track but you could easily miss it through the snow gums. Like the Tin Mine Huts, its pristine condition is thanks to the hard work of the Illawarra Alpine Club, and like most huts I've spent the night at so far, it's empty. Newcomers to the Alps are often unsure about the etiquette of the huts. Summer or winter, it is this: take a tent on your trip. Do not ever, ever rely on huts. They are emergency shelters. That said, you can stay in them in non-emergency situations if you are respectful and do not intrude on the privacy of groups who are already there. If you make a fire, replace the wood and then some. Sweep the hut well and wipe the table and any other surfaces you've used. Try to leave a small food sachet or useful items like batteries or matches if you no longer need them. That's about it. In short, respect the High Country huts.

* * *

Elyne Mitchell's fictional silver brumby Thowra was 'King of the Cascade Brumbies'. This was his turf. Or his snow grass, anyway. A big, bold black stallion seems to run the show these days. He's not impressed that someone is staying the night. Seriously, mate, why the long face? Sorry/not sorry. Had to say it once.

Dinnertime. Not in the mood for curry. Tough luck, curry it is. Well, sort of. Pulao. Basically Pakistani rice with vegetables. In the Jetboil it goes. Out it comes, spicy and more satisfying than expected.

Smoke comes into the valley. This is beyond spooky now, this is concerning. This is by far the densest smoke I've seen anywhere in the mountains this whole trip. It's orange and thick like pumpkin soup. Surely it's not from round here, though. Don't know. I'm not as confident as I was down at Cowombat. Don't have much of a read on the weather. Not much of a wind change or anything this evening. I just don't know. But this I do know: it's time to prepare for the worst. Got no other choice up here.

I walk down to Cascades Creek. Yes, it's Cascades Creek plural and Cascade Hut singular. No, accurate grammar will not save me if an inferno screams through the valley. Yes, thinking about trivial things helps in stressful moments. The creek is not large. Maximum water depth is shin or knee deep at best, but there are high earthen banks in several spots. I leave my yellow cap above the most protected bank so I can find the exact spot with a headtorch if required. Then I return to the hut and put all my cotton and woollen clothes on because synthetic clothes stick to skin in a fire. I pack up everything except my sleeping gear. Put my boots on and lace them up loosely so I can sleep in comfort, place both water bottles beside the slab of timber I'm sleeping on and crawl into my sleeping bag and wait.

CHAPTER 13

MAY YOUR BOULDERS BE YOUR BLESSINGS

When American adventurer and self-amputee Aron Ralston released his brilliantly titled book *Between a Rock and a Hard Place*, to which I referred earlier, he undertook a global book tour which eventually made its way to Australia. I was working in Canberra at the time and rang his publicist to arrange a phone interview. I got my ten minutes and decided to roll the dice. Instead of asking the same predictable questions everyone else would ask him that day, I decided to use the time to persuade Aron to cast his schedule aside and drive to Thredbo, where I would join him and escort him to the summit of Australia's highest mountain, Mt Kosciuszko. Imagine my surprise when he said yes.

Ralston set off from Melbourne with his dad, Larry, who was accompanying him on the Australian leg of the tour. They drove through the mountains, just like me and my dad on this trip. They had great father–son bonding time like we did too. And like us, they drove through Corryong. Larry Ralston loved Corryong. The Ralstons passed through the small Victorian town just as school was getting out and kids were walking home. Larry said that rarely happens in America anymore, even in smallish towns. He said it reminded him of the lost, more innocent America of his childhood. They both loved the steep drive up to Thredbo from Corryong through tall alpine ash. I was glad they'd had a good experience. Hopefully Thredbo would be even better.

The first morning in the mountains dawned too wet to walk. The cricket was on in Brisbane, so we turned on the TV and watched. This was back when Shane Warne was still playing. I explained Shane Warne to Aron. The scandals, the silliness, the cricketing genius, everything. Imagine if you had to describe a larger-than-life figure like Michael Jackson or Donald Trump to someone who'd never heard of them. That's what it was like. Aron had never watched cricket in his life but was a keen student. He was a really engaging sort of person. Took an interest in your interests. As a journalist, you're always asking the questions. It's rare to meet someone who asks them back.

In the afternoon, the rain turned to drizzle and the cricket turned to drivel. It was too late for Kosciuszko, so I took the Ralstons for a quick hike along the Cascade Trail, just up the valley from Thredbo. The country looked lovely. The bark on the snow gums had turned bright red and orange, mist hugged the range, and the heath glistened with tiny water droplets. It was all very Scottish Highlands. The Ralstons were thrilled to have left behind the world of publicists and radio studios and book signings and airports for this. Too bad if book sales Down Under fell a little short of expectations; this trip was exceeding them.

Aron was an energetic walker. His dad and me and my photographer Jodie could barely keep up. At one point, he turned off the track and rock-hopped up a tumbling creek. He topped a low rise and was quickly out of sight. 'Aron always had to know what was beyond the next rise,' his dad said.

I've never forgotten those words. All hikers need to know what's beyond the next rise. That's a huge part of why you hike. And here's the really beautiful part: no matter what's there, you're not disappointed. If there's an amazing view or a wombat that moos like a cow, terrific. If not, doesn't matter. If the next part of the trail looks just like the part before it, so be it. The point is to find out. Modern life is not geared this way. If a new thing is just like the old thing, we're conditioned not to value it. That's why they're always upgrading your iPhone and why Gen Z kids expect to be promoted three days into a new job.

I'm thinking about the Ralstons right now because I've reached the point where Aron scooted up his rocky creek. Was definitely this creek or the next one. I've made good time today. Left Cascade Hut early after a restless night. The old maxim was wrong. Where there was smoke there was not, in this instance, fire. Deep down, I strongly suspected as much, but it was good to have a fire drill. To grip myself firmly by the wrist and say this is no ordinary summer. Be prepared. Assume nothing. Fear the worst from here on in. Look around you. Study the sky. Read the wind. Keep one eye open, even while sleeping.

The trail this morning was gorgeous. From the hut it followed Cascades Creek through an open valley. Then it climbed up and over a high range called Bobs Ridge, the trail zigzagging at a merciful gradient. Are you listening, Victorian track makers? One job, guys. The top of Bobs Ridge was a milestone moment, with the first view of the Main Range since Mt Bogong. You could see the range more clearly from 100 kilometres away. Smoke is everywhere now. Half the east coast is ablaze and everywhere is copping it. Even New Zealand's glaciers are coated in dust and ash.

So here I am at the Ralston spot, on the other side of Bobs Ridge and only a few kilometres from Thredbo. It's Christmas Eve. I could go into town and grab a feed. I feel like ordering a family-size pizza and eating the whole thing myself. The pizza would have three ingredients and three only: cheese, tomato and anchovies. I will politely request an entire jar of anchovies and offer a dollar a fish, whatever they want.

They'll probably say two dollars, knowing ski resort prices. Way to kill a pizza fantasy. Probably won't feel like anchovy pizza by the time I get to Thredbo, anyway. Anchovies are a mood, just like salmon. Anyway, I've got somewhere better to be. A little back country mission, inspired by Aron Ralston.

On 30 December 1950, a Czech ski instructor and Olympic skier named Antonin Sponar sailed through the heads of Sydney Harbour in sparkling blue weather with his British wife, Lizi. They were aboard the SS *Nelly*, an 11,000-ton ship crammed with 1700 Eastern European refugees. Tony Sponar, as he became known, soon gravitated to the Snowy Mountains, where there was work on the Snowy Mountains Hydro-Electric Scheme. He found employment as a hydrographer and began to explore the area around Charlotte Pass and Mt Kosciuszko on foot and ski. Sponar was delighted to be on snow but was frustrated by the relatively short back-country ski runs. He craved the long runs of Austria, where he had instructed. Then one day, late in the summer of 1955, he followed a hunch and a tip. Someone had told him about a deep valley where the snow extended all the way to the river from well above the tree line. 'Maybe somewhere along here, slopes could be found where there was skiable snow over a vertical drop of 600 metres or more,' he recalled in his autobiography *Snow in Australia? That's News to Me*. Sponar hiked out to see the valley for himself. Thus, eventually, did Thredbo come into being. The first ski lift opened in 1957.

For my twelfth birthday, my dad gave me a book called the *World Ski Atlas*. I treasure that faded old hardback. Its entry for Thredbo reads, 'Thredbo is to Australian skiing what St Moritz, Gstaad, Davos, Val d'Isère and Aspen are to the rest of the world.'

It was high praise for the quality of Thredbo's skiing relative to other Australian ski resorts. And in my opinion it was warranted. Still is. No Australian ski resort rivals the length or vertical drop of Thredbo's runs. In simple terms, you get on and off the lifts less often at Thredbo. Skiing elsewhere feels like skiing interrupted. Nearby Perisher has more ski lifts, but its layout is higgledy-piggledy and its runs much shorter.

The *World Ski Atlas* on Perisher:

If ever a name fitted a location, it is Perisher. A long, virtually treeless valley, a funnel for every wind that blows, it presents an uninviting, straggly face with a long array of miscellaneous ski lifts, one next to the other, rising a bare hundred metres or so to a scrubby ledge, scoured with erosion gullies and speckled with stunted mountain gums.

Brutal. Just brutal. The author, Mark Heller, really had it in for poor old Perisher. Maybe he saw the hot chocolate prices at a certain on-mountain restaurant there. Anyway, it's safe to say Perisher withstood the blow. In 2015, American company Vail Resorts bought it for a cool $176 million. Perisher is Australia's most popular ski resort by a large margin these days. And, in fairness, there's lots of good skiing there. But it's just not my hill. Thredbo is my hill. Thredbo is beautiful.

Thredbo could use a coat of paint here and there but in many ways it's like a classic European ski resort, give or take the snow gums. It's set in a deep, V-shaped valley, with the village nestled by the river and the ski slopes on one side of the valley – the same side which connects to the Main Range and Mt Kosciuszko. The other side of the valley is almost as high but it's wild and desolate and no one ever goes there.

For years, I've skied at Thredbo and wondered about those nameless peaks on the other side of the valley. What's over there? What do Thredbo's ski slopes look like from that side? Can you see all the way up to Mt Kosciuszko? Time to climb those little-visited peaks. Time to turn off the Cascade Trail and find out what's above the next rise.

Bush-bashing through trackless terrain. No path, few landmarks. But for the first time on this trip, I relish it. Unlike in Victoria, I know the surrounding country well. If I get lost, I know I can get found again. It's a powerful feeling. John Chapman probably feels like this everywhere he hikes. These bushes, though. It's like they're spring-loaded. You have to lean into them with your shoulder to force your way through. It's an intense physical struggle for a good half-hour, real rugby stuff. Bash, shove, oof. At last I pop out on a small open knoll. Map out. And there's my knoll, a tiny round contour like the symbol for degrees of temperature. If you're a hiker, you'll get how satisfying this is.

Upwards to a rockier, higher knoll. And there they are. The ski slopes of Thredbo. Can't really see much through the haze, but you definitely get a sense of ski runs from the reverse perspective. Now for the second part of this side trip. Looking across from the ski slopes, I've often noticed a level, grassy clearing about halfway up this side of the range. What's it like there? Down we go to find out. There's more thick scrub on the descent. This time, I use it to my advantage. My confidence is high, my mood bold. Heading uphill, these bushes seemed to be pushing me back. Now I let them cushion my momentum, jogging down the steep slope and using them to slow me like the walls of a bouncy castle. I'm having a ridiculously good time out here. Now I'm setting up camp on that grassy flat. Got here in minutes. It really is a fantastic spot.

I have gone mad on this trip. Has that been made adequately clear? Talking to triangles at the back end of Baw Baw was just the first sign. Now I'm the full banana. At this moment, I'm in character as a property developer, walking around the grassy clearing halfway up this anonymous mountain and naming sections with the inane nomenclature of modern housing estates. Across the valley is South Rams Head, a huge bouldered peak whose snow patches give it a real cookies-and-cream look, so naturally my estate is South Rams Head Reflections. The elevated section where I pitch my tent is South Rams Head Heights. There is also South Rams Head Meadows, South Rams Head Heath and South Rams Head Ponds down by the creek, where my imaginary blocks start at an incredibly affordable $199,000. The widest, most open area at the western end of the estate is called the Cricket Pitch. It's reserved for community sport and other events and can be booked by any local resident.

In life, insanity is no joke. Here on the trail, it is world-class entertainment, especially when you're a shonky property developer selling off chunks of an imaginary housing estate on prime Commonwealth land. Merry Christmas, by the way. Tomorrow is Christmas Day. All I want for Christmas is a quarter-acre block of prime alpine real estate at South Rams Head Reflections and some Christmas lunch leftovers in Thredbo. With luck, my wife will pull in by dinner time.

Thredbo on Christmas Day is beer and schnitzel in the pub. It's barefoot reading by the river. It's afternoon couch time in the ski lodge my dad joined all those years ago. There are still numerous such clubs in the Australian Alps. Most are not-for-profit collectives that provide clean, affordable no-frills accommodation for snow lovers. Skiing is for the rich, they say, and that's partly true, but Australia's club lodges ensure that regular middle-class folk can afford to ski too; they're an indispensable part of our mountain culture.

It's good to see my wife and 13-year-old son. He's grown, I say. I've lost weight, they say, but not much. Makes sense. I was feeling skinny after Bogong but probably added a few kilos on the Mitta Mitta. We call my daughter, who's on student exchange in France. Briefly, we are almost together as a family. My wife has been incredible since I left. Working, parenting, Christmasing, handling all the administrivia. The best way to thank anyone for that sort of service is with booze, so we leave the boy with his rectangular mate and head down to Bernti's, a hotel with a great outdoors bar overlooking the mountain.

Bernti Hecher was an Austrian ski instructor who I remember well from my childhood. He used to ski around wearing a white beret on even the most brutally snowy days. But you didn't need that distinctive headwear to identify him on the hill. Bernti had a signature Austrian style which has long since vanished from the slopes of both Austria and Australia – ankles locked together, body as steady as a statue above the waist. He married a Melbourne girl, Tricia. Together, they built Bernti's eponymous mountain inn and lived happily for years. The Thredbo Historical Society called them 'Thredbo's legendary glamour couple', but their fortunes turned after the 1997 Thredbo landslide which destroyed two ski lodges and killed 18 people. First, business dropped off drastically after the disaster, which happened just a few doors up from the hotel. Then poor old Bernti had a severe stroke. The bank repossessed the hotel barely a year after the landslide. The Hechers later divorced. Remarkably, Tricia remained Bernti's full-time carer. Sadly they're both gone now, but Tricia must have been quite a woman. Bernti was by all accounts a charming man and gracious host. Whenever I'm riding the Kosciuszko Express Chairlift, I still expect to spot him skiing down the World Cup run trailed by a private lesson student trying but failing to imitate his immaculate turns. Bernti is like a rare bird that has disappeared. The mountain seems poorer without him.

The Sponars are long gone too. Tony Sponar used to drive around Jindabyne in a Ferrari with his pet pig in the front seat. He was quite the local eccentric. Shocking womaniser as well, so they say. I interviewed his widow Lizi once. There was a look in her eye when talking about Tony. Part distaste, part fondness. A look both sweet and sour. She's gone now too. The human geography of the mountains is ever changing. Seems the physical geography is changing pretty quickly these days too.

The next couple of days belong to leisure. My son and I chase and find mayhem on the metal track of the Thredbo bobsled. We picnic at the fantastic swimming hole at Thredbo Diggings with leftover Christmas turkey. How do you spell the Homer Simpson drooling noise? Then it's back to Thredbo and the trail. My wife and son will hike for an hour or two with me before I continue solo. Naturally, we take the chairlift up to the Main Range instead of hiking the official AAWT route from Dead Horse Gap. I believe the precise term for this is 'cheating'. 'Wimping out' may also be appropriate. But Chapman's Bible does not expressly state 'Thou shalt not avail thine self of the automated cableway'. In fact, it acknowledges that many hikers take the chairlift. It's a pretty easy decision with a freshly loaded backpack.

It's quite a scene at the top of the Kosciuszko Express. Seems like half of Australia is setting off for our highest peak. The chairlift does most of the hard work. From the top station, the terrain flattens out and it's only two hours each way to the summit of Australia. Even Kossie itself is a piece of pie. The trail wraps 360 degrees around the mountain like the swirl on a cinnamon bun.

I'll be up there soon enough. But for now, we three have other plans. I'm going to climb Australia's fourth-highest mountain, Mt Rams Head, and my family will accompany me part of the way. We hike the line of Australia's highest ski lift, Karels T-bar. There's dragon bush everywhere. Oops, watch out for that, mate. It'll rip the skin off your shins like paint stripper. The world turns, the next generation learns.

We're now way above the tree line. Huge granite tors dominate the landscape up here, like droppings from an unimaginably huge wombat. For millennia, bogong moths have congregated in the caves and crevices of this boulder country to escape the summer heat in the dry plains out west where they breed. Indigenous tribes used to come up here and feast on them, smoking the moths out and grinding them into a smooth paste which by all accounts is quite nutty. Bats, ravens, currawongs and pygmy possums are among the bogongs' modern-day predators.

The pygmy possum is one of Australia's rarest animals and the ultimate emblem of the fragility of our mountains. Once thought to be extinct, there are now a couple of thousand in the highest, rockiest parts of the Alps. Small enough to hold in your hand, pygmy possums are the only Australian animal that hibernates. To do this, they need snow. That's because snow is nature's blanket. Even if it's minus ten degrees in the still night air, it stays around zero under the snowpack. The declining snowpack in the Alps is a huge threat to the ongoing survival of the pygmy possum. In recent years, they've also been imperilled by an alarming fall in the number of bogong moths.

Scientists believe the prolonged dry spell of the last two years is to blame for the current absence of bogongs in the Alps. The caterpillars that turn into migratory moths have had their breeding cycle badly disturbed in their drought-affected homes out west. As the warming climate makes droughts both more likely and more severe, the bogongs could vanish forever from the High Country boulders. The changing climate imperils nature a million different ways.

Aron Ralston is on the speaking circuit these days. There's still a strong appetite to hear his harrowing survival tale. Ralston has taken to finishing his talks with a message of hope to his audience. 'May your boulders be your blessings,' he tells them, using his entrapment and freedom as a metaphor for overcoming hardship. For millennia, the boulders up here have been a blessing in a very literal sense for the iconic bogong moths and the people and animals that feed upon them. But for how much longer?

CHAPTER 14

DANGER, GLADLY MET

It's one of the most memorable news images of recent times and, in its way, one of the most disturbing. The queue of climbers in red jackets on the south face of Mt Everest, snaked halfway down the mountain like a trail of blood. It now happens virtually every May in the brief Everest climbing season and I've written up the story twice, both times with the headline 'Peak Hour' because recycling will help save the world, haven't you heard?

Another Everest-related story I wrote recently was a little more tangential. It concerned the review into Australia's cricket culture after the ball-tampering scandal in South Africa. Commissioned by Cricket Australia, the review was written by not-for-profit organisation The Ethics Centre, whose damning report was conducted, so it proudly explained, under the 'Everest Process', which involved 'extensive qualitative and quantitative research to determine how key stakeholders view an organisation', whatever the heck that meant.

Unfortunately, the Ethics Centre's geographical research was neither qualitative nor quantitative enough because they illustrated their Everest Process page with the wrong mountain. They chose Ama Dablam, a peak visible from the trek to Everest Base Camp, which is undeniably spectacular but barely three-quarters the height of Everest. It's a mistake many others have made. Professional photo libraries used by media companies are stacked with images of Ama Dablam labelled as Everest.

There's another well-known mountain which is extremely busy in climbing season and which has also often been mistaken for another. That would be Australia's highest peak, Mt Kosciuszko. I'll be there soon. First, Rams Head. The 2190-metre summit of Australia's fourth-highest mountain is a little out of the way, but it's worth the detour. It's a lonely sort of mountain, and if you think mountains don't have personalities, then you haven't climbed enough of them. Good spot for a packet of dried mangoes up here. Can't recommend sugary dried fruit from Asian grocers highly enough on the trail. Then it's off to join the Kosciuszko track. Need to get going. Tonight's campsite is still a long way off.

It was great seeing my wife and son. Your world is your world. That's the reality. If you go full Rivermate or Charlie Carter, you can never come home. I hope to return to my world a better man. A more contented, less frustrated man. Formulated a little change of plans in Thredbo too. The Bimberi Wilderness area in the ACT has just been closed due to the threat of fire. The high ranges near Canberra are one part of the AAWT I've walked before. They are always drier than the Snowy Mountains and haven't seen more than a speck of rain for months. So with the last three days of the official AAWT route off limits, I've drawn up a new ending. I'll still hike the six days from here to Kiandra, where my last food drop is hidden under a bridge. After that, I'll change things up with a loop around the northern end of Kosciuszko National Park, finishing at the Big Trout in Adaminaby. I like the idea of walking into town, sitting down on a bench beside the giant pink fish and slowly, methodically, removing my backpack and leaning my hiking poles against the fence. Maybe a tourist will ask where I've come from as I greedily eat a pie washed down with a chocolate milkshake. 'Upstream, where the fish are smaller,' I will deadpan. I can't believe I'm thinking about the end of this thing. I'm 25 days in already.

Trail time goes fast. Geological time goes slowly. Ten to 20 thousand years ago, in the last ice age, glaciers enshrouded vast swathes of the earth. Here on mainland Australia, they covered a mere pinprick of land – just 25 square kilometres on the very highest parts of the Main Range. But those

Pleistocene epoch ice sheets left their mark up here, gouging out five hollows that became lakes when the ice retreated. Today, those five glacial lakes are all gems, each as sparkling as the next. Lake Cootapatamba is coming into view now. It lies below Kosciuszko's south-east ridge and is Australia's highest lake. Like all five glacial lakes, its waters are bitterly cold in all seasons. It always seemed like their way of shooing people off. You know how some mountains don't want visitors? These lakes are the same. Luckily for Cootapatamba, Kosciuszko is a pretty good distraction. In the middle distance, hordes of day hikers clog the main trail to Kossie. That steady train of bodies actually does look like ants. For quite possibly the first time in the history of travel writing, the cliché seems apt. Time to join the picnic.

The flanks of Kosciuszko still hold huge patches of snow with overhanging cornices. A conspiracy of ravens perches on the ridge seeking lunch. Yes, that's the collective noun. That and an unkindness. Both would be accurate if you're a bug. They're feasting, these ravens. Beetles and other insects become trapped when they alight on the snow patches, snap frozen and powerless to move. That's when the ravens move in. They must really say 'faaaaaarrrk' when the snow patches melt.

The AAWT sidles its way around Kosciuszko before diverting northwards 900 metres from the summit. Pack and poles down at the track junction. Stuff some food in pockets. Quick jog up to the rounded, grassy rooftop of Australia. Half the country is up here. In all seriousness, there must be 200 people. Kids, oldies, everyone. On another day on another trip, the crowds might annoy me, but I've had my solo summits on this trek, Bogong to name just one. It's heartening to see so many people queuing to take selfies at the summit plinth. Some will never return, a box ticked, a moment Instagrammed and soon forgotten. Others will note that the grasshoppers up here are fatter than the ones down on the tablelands, and that the creeks run strongly despite yellow grass that crackles. They will see curves and musculature in the landscape that pleases their eye like the outline of human bodies. And they will come to call themselves lovers of the mountains.

The shape of Kosciuszko greatly pleased Polish explorer Pawel Edmund Strzelecki when, in March 1840, he became the first European to climb the mountain. His reason for naming the mountain after a compatriot is inscribed on a plaque near the summit:

> The particular configuration of this eminence struck me
> so forcibly by the similarity it bears to a tumulus elevated
> in Krakow over the tomb of the patriot Kosciuszko, that,
> although in a foreign country, on foreign ground, but
> amongst a free people who appreciate freedom and its
> votaries, I could not refrain from giving it the name of
> Mount Kosciuszko.

Tadeusz Kościuszko was a revered Polish military leader who later moved to the USA, where he befriended President

Thomas Jefferson and fought for America against Britain in the War of Independence. He was also a strong supporter of abolishing slavery. There's a huge memorial to him in Krakow called the Kościuszko Mound, which contains earth from the battlefields upon which he fought. Australians should know more about him.

There's a fair-sized memorial to Strzelecki these days on the lakefront at Jindabyne, in the form of a large bronze statue. Strzelecki is depicted as tall and purposeful, his right arm boldly outstretched. 'That's where we're headed, fellas,' old Strezza seems to be saying. 'Yep, that one there. The really high one.'

But which high peak did Strzelecki actually reach and bestow with the name Kosciuszko? Many believe he summited Australia's second-highest mountain, Mt Townsend, a craggier summit which stands just 19 metres lower than Kosciuszko at 2209 metres above sea level. The peaks are about five kilometres apart. Climb either peak and it's impossible to discern which is higher with the naked eye. Strzelecki would have had no chance without the aid of twentieth-century instruments or technology.

For years, historians, cartographers and High Country folk have debated this issue with the passion of JFK conspiracists. There's even a grassy knoll at the centre of the squabble, in the form of Mt Kosciuszko itself, which, as stated, is an unremarkable grassy mound that just happens to be fractionally higher than its more jagged neighbours.

The fact that Strzelecki was reminded of the Kosciuszko Mound in Krakow seems like a compelling piece of evidence that Strzelecki got it right. The author, artist and back country skier Alan EJ Andrews is a staunch believer. In his 1991 book *Kosciuszko: The Mountain in History*, he wrote:

> There seems sufficient reason to conclude that the present Mt Kosciuszko is more likely than any other protuberance to have been given the name of the great Polish patriot by Strzelecki, and to have been ascended by him on 12 March 1840.

Many others swear he got it wrong. Strzelecki set off in early 1840 from Sydney with a party that included an Aboriginal guide, Charley Tarra. They skirted their way north around the mountains in a long loop. Having reached the Murray on the western side, they employed the services of a local Aboriginal guide, a Djilamatang man called Jackey who had climbed the high peaks many times in search of bogong moths. Up they went. It's tough climbing the Main Range from the west. In fact, it's the longest vertical ascent in Australia, a climb of roughly 1700 metres. By any standards, that's serious vertical. It's rough country until you reach the tree line too.

'The steepness of the numberless ridges, intersected by gullies and torrents, rendered this ascent a matter of no small difficulty,' Strzelecki later wrote in understated, almost John Chapmanesque tones. 'Once on the crest of the range, the remainder of the ascent to its highest pinnacle was accomplished with comparative ease.'

Strzelecki described the mountain he climbed as a 'pinnacle, rocky and naked, predominant over several others'. This description fits Townsend, not Kosciuszko. The plot thickened in the 1860s when Eugene von Guérard labelled his view from Townsend as the view from Kosciuszko, and again in the 1870s when mapping authorities assigned the name Kosciuszko to the peak we now know as Townsend.

It's confusing. Strzelecki climbed a rounded peak and named it Kosciuszko because the Polish hero Kosciuszko is buried beneath a mound. But he also described the mountain as a rocky pinnacle. What actually happened? Which one did he climb?

On balance, the evidence appears to show that he climbed both. Reading through sections of Strzelecki's writings and those of a travelling companion, James Macarthur, it seems likely that the party first climbed Townsend, whose rocky summit Strzelecki proclaimed as the highest in the land. Then he had a rethink upon observing Kosciuszko to the south-east and went and climbed and named it. But it's not clear and may never be. Personally, I believe he was determined to name Australia's highest mountain after his hero Kosciuszko no matter what it looked like, but that's pure speculation.

What we know for sure is that Strzelecki made it all the way through to Melbourne after Kosciuszko. It was quite the ordeal. His Aboriginal guides escorted his party over the mountains to Omeo and then through Gippsland. In a sense, they did an 1840 version of the AAWT, only instead of eating curries, tuna pouches and Vita-Weats, they shot possums and bandicoots and even koalas for food. Fire-roasted koala couldn't have been too much worse than my salmon pouches. Eating one now with Vita-Weats on the summit of Kossie. Salmon mood continues to prove elusive. Not sure why I didn't donate the pouches to my wife in Thredbo.

Whichever peak or peaks Strzelecki climbed, the rooftop of Australia would have looked very different than it looks today, and not just because of the lack of crowds. A report of his journey in the *Port Phillip Herald* noted that the area around Australia's highest peaks was 'beyond the reach of vegetation, surrounded by perpetual snows'. Remember, Strzelecki summited in early autumn. You never see 'perpetual snows' up here now, even after the snowiest winter. The snowpack is undeniably diminishing in the Alps.

The statistics back up the anecdotal evidence. Since Snowy Hydro first started measuring snow at Spencers Creek in 1954, peak season depth has declined by around 18 per cent and the season has shortened by about 20 per cent. 'Perpetual snows' are a thing of the past. Summer snow patches rarely last beyond mid-January these days, but on this late December day they're still looking pretty resilient. Mostly the patches linger on the eastern faces of the range, sculpted by snow blown by winter's wild westerlies. To call them mere 'patches' is to underplay their size, their beauty, their depth, their form. They are embankments. They are frozen waves. They are the white eyebrows of the range. Often they are still five or six metres deep. Many have deep fissures where chunks have subsided, undercut by creeks. The mini crevasses are frightening to the eye, treacherous to the unwary summer snow slider.

But mostly the summer snow patches are great fun to walk across. As I rejoin the AAWT and head northwards along the Main Range towards Townsend and other peaks, the trail crosses numerous broad patches stained reddish pink with spring dust. Tramping across these ephemeral icefields, you can imagine you're nearing the summit of Elbrus or Aconcagua. Kudos if you knew that they're the highest peaks in Europe and South America respectively. Bonus points if you knew that Elbrus in Russia's Caucasus Mountains, not Mont Blanc in the French Alps, is in fact Europe's highest peak. A free set of imaginary steak knives if you knew that both Elbrus and Aconcagua can be ascended on foot without ropes or technical climbing equipment. Of course, you've got a long future as a human popsicle if you catch either mountain on the wrong day with inadequate gear, but that's another story.

For ecologist Brodie Verrall, these summer snow patches are an outdoors laboratory. The Gold Coast native spent his youth camping in the rainforests and surfing on the beaches of south-east Queensland. Like many surfers, he became a snowboarder and was drawn to Canada, where he briefly trained to become a mountain guide and developed an interested in retreating glaciers. On his return to Australia, he fell in with ecologists at Griffith University who were researching the impacts of climate change on alpine ecology in the Australian Alps. 'Here is a way I can still spend time in the mountains doing things I love,' he thought to himself.

Verrall is currently undertaking a PhD on how climate change is affecting tiny alpine arthropods. He's also an expert on delicate high alpine plant communities. If you're up beside a Main Range snow patch and you see a long-haired dude intently studying the ground like he's lost a contact lens, you've probably found Brodie. And if you're lucky enough to get chatting to him, he might just tell you about the feldmark.

Feldmark is a type of sparse vegetation found in alpine areas around the world as well as in high-latitude tundra landscapes. In Australia, it exists only on the most inhospitable parts of the Main Range. There are two types: windswept feldmark and snow patch feldmark. Some of the plants are uninspiring brown mosses. Others are improbably delicate and beautiful, like the ranunculus anemone, a tiny buttercup with white petals and bright green stems, which grows by snow patches and seems almost too pretty for its surrounds. Then there are cushion plants, bright green pillows of tiny leaf clusters that sit on stony ground like tropical islands in a grey sea.

Verrall is seeing these cold-hardy little plant communities vanish before his eyes. Based on 15 years of data from projects established by Griffith University and NSW National Parks and Wildlife Service scientists in the early 2000s, he and his colleagues have found plants from neighbouring communities invading both types of feldmark. Even a degree of warming has injected enough warmth and energy into the ecosystem to allow for the increased growth and germination of grasses and shrubs high on the range. This in turn increases the landscape's flammability. Once, it was unthinkable that fires could reach the highest, most windswept parts of the Main Range. Not anymore. The 2003 fires burned small tracts of precious windswept feldmark. Meanwhile, as snow patches diminish in the face of the lighter winter snowpack and quicker melting, grasses and shrubs are muscling in on the snow patch feldmark too.

'The Great Barrier Reef gets a lot of attention and media, but it's the same scenario in the Australian Alps,' Verrall says. 'Besides the Reef, this is one of the ecosystems that is the most threatened from climate change.'

Verrall speaks of 'zombie plants', which are species living on borrowed time, slowly being overtaken by plants more tolerant of a warming climate. Grazing was stopped in the mid–twentieth century to protect the plants up here. Now, the zombies march again.

Heading northwards as Lake Albina comes into view, I feel glad that people like Brodie Verrall are out here documenting the changes to alpine ecology. Verrall is active on social media and is fluent in both the language of the academy and the language of the internet. The world needs bilingual scientists like him.

A landscape's appeal exists on both the micro and macro scale. Putting aside the microscope and taking a hiker's eye view, these next few kilometres might just be the most spectacular section of the entire AAWT. Technically the AAWT descends from Mt Kosciuszko along the old gravel summit road to Charlotte Pass (see the map facing page 1), then follows the bitumen road through Perisher Valley before eventually swinging northwards up the Munyang River valley towards Mt Jagungal. But Chapman recommends the scenic route across the Main Range in all but terrible weather. On this occasion, I'm definitely with Chapman. Why walk roads when you can walk ridges and peaks? Lake Albina, the second of the glacial lakes, is a narrow tarn in a basin hemmed in by steep, boulder-strewn slopes interspersed with meadows of silver snow daisies. High above the lake, snow patches line the ridges like smears of sunscreen. The lake's waters are a bluey-beige reflection of a sky hazed with bushfire smoke. At its northern extremity, the land drops away dramatically into Lady Northcote Canyon and the timbered country far below, giving the whole scene the appearance of a natural infinity pool.

This section of the AAWT is part of the existing Kosciuszko Main Range Walk and will soon be incorporated into the Snowies Iconic Walk, as it should be. The Australian Alps don't get more iconic than this. But there's another section of the AAWT up ahead which is jaw-droppingly, face-slappingly dramatic. It's the high ridge overlooking Watsons Crags, which is part of an area known as the western faces. This is the one place in Australia where back-country skiers and snowboarders shoot videos on slopes as hair raising as any in the world. But don't take my word for it. Go to YouTube or Instagram and search for 'Little Austria' or 'Watsons Crags'. You might also take the word of the first woman to ski these slopes. That woman was Elyne Mitchell.

Before her signature *The Silver Brumby* went to print in 1958, Mitchell wrote several non-fiction books on the Alps. Her first book was called *Australia's Alps*. Published in 1942, it chronicles her journeys on foot, ski and horseback high in the mountains. Some of those journeys were in the lonely years when her husband, Tom, was interned at the infamous prisoner-of-war camp in Changi, Singapore. Other journeys took place in the 1930s, when Tom taught Elyne to ski in the Kosciuszko back country. She was a natural on skis. Indeed, she became a champion racer, winning the Canadian Downhill Championship in Banff in 1938. The skills acquired in competitive racing provided the perfect technical base for the western faces. Together, she and Tom skied them before anyone. It was an incredibly adventurous undertaking in the days before modern ski equipment and emergency beacons. Tom and Elyne Mitchell were Australia's original extreme skiers. Elyne wrote about her thrilling descents in *Australia's Alps*:

Skiing at Kosciusko has earned itself a name for being like that of Norway – on gentle, rounded hills rolling endlessly onwards. The very name 'Monaro', being Aboriginal for 'breasts', indicates the unrugged contours of the side of the Alps that is best known. But for those who seek them, on the other side, are slopes comparable to those of the European alps, to the gullies of Chile, and steeper than many of the mountains at Sun Valley in the United States of America.

Walking past the lone peak called The Sentinel and looking over to the furrows and cliffs of Watsons Crags, it's surreal and exciting to contemplate the Mitchells arcing their way down the couloirs and knife-edged ridges in their antiquated gear. You can be assured they didn't pick their way down the slopes. They were not surveying the country. These two were in it for the adrenaline. Here's Elyne again from *Australia's Alps*:

Finally, after the steepest schuss, we swung south off a deep saddle in the spur, and down a steadily dropping ridge, tearing down it, throwing one stupendous christie on the edge of a chasm which seemed to fall uninterruptedly to the Geehi, and then flying down towards the trees.

'Schuss' and 'christie' are skiing terms from the language of yesteryear. In the language of today, they absolutely ripped it up. Stomped the gnar. Yes, modern extreme skiers have actually taken 'gnar' from the word 'gnarly' and turned it into a noun. But few would have ever stomped the gnar like the Mitchells. They were fully sick, those two. And they did it without the protection of brain buckets.

Mitchell saw adventure as the healthiest kind of irresistible urge, and as a panacea for life's ills. Her phrase 'danger, gladly met' feels like the heart that all adventurers wear on their sleeve:

From the start of time, adventure has sent up rockets that call people away from civilized things into odd corners of the world, where danger glitters, fascinating, like a jewel; where danger, gladly met, is glorious ...

But Mitchell was a spiritual traveller in these mountains as much as an adventurer, a woman as prone to reflection as action. There's a tone of reverence, of veneration in her writing. At times it becomes almost liturgical.

In a mountain evening, or dawn, or a moonlit night, entity is almost lost in a transcending feeling, deeper even than love, for the Mystery of the world and the universe. Body and soul dissolve into something all-embracing. If truth lies in a man's heart, each to seek it and learn for themselves, then, on the High Hills, thrust out from the earth into the atmosphere, the Way and The Light shine ahead.

In a nutshell, it sounds like up here, she felt close to God.

* * *

I'm feeling close to the angry God, the one with thunder and lightning bolts, I'll tell you that much.

I'm on a rough, disused vehicle track on Australia's third-highest peak, Mt Twynam, and a storm is brewing to the west. There was nothing in the forecast, but the Main Range makes its own weather. Clouds explode out of nothing. Often, you don't see storms on the weather radar either because the mountains block the beam. But that rumble. That's some serious atmospheric indigestion. Need shelter here. Got to pitch the tent. It really is about to pelt down.

There's a small patch of snow grass squeezed between two boulders on the western side of the mountain. It's directly facing the weather, but the boulders are a shield from the worst of the wind. This'll do. I get the tent up just in time. Rain is steady but not torrential. Got a new tent by the way. I rang the store in Sydney about the broken zip and they gave my wife a new tent, which she brought to Thredbo. Good form. New tent is good. Dinner, not so much. For the first time on this trip, I don't cook at the end of the day. A few Vita-Weats, some cheese, a handful of sun-dried tomatoes, a fresh apple from Thredbo. Could be worse – could be salmon. The rain eases off a little now. Twilight. It's beautiful up here. The earth smells earthy and the air metallic. Through the rain and smoke haze, you can see range after range after range. Another storm is on the horizon. More lightning in this one. Go on, nature, give us your best shot. For this camper it'll be danger, gladly met.

rrrrr! A brisk start to summer on the flanks of Mt Hotham

magical AAWT section favoured by both hobbits and hikers on the Baw Baw Plateau

Left: Reflecting on what it means to be Australian en route to Mt Skene

Below: The odd couple: my beloved hiking pole and stick

Above: There were never enough trail markers when you needed them

Right: My food supplies, give or take a few apples, Vita-Weats and food drop treats

'A scoop of caramel and a scoop of vanilla, please': snow patches on Mt Bogong

Some snow gums have slender single trunks, others are multi-trunked like this arboreal octopus on the Bogong High Plains

Ropers Hut on the Bogong High Plains: home to two delightfully well-behaved native rats, George and Mildred

Left: Even in dry times, High Country creeks flow steadily thanks to banks of sphagnum moss which release water slowly

Below: Feral horses and/or deer made a shocking mess of one of these two adjacent alpine ponds

There is no sturdier or more welcoming emergency shelter in the Australian Alps than Cleve Cole Hut on Mt Bogong

The Mitta Mitta River, so good they named it twice

A river runs through him: the author straddles the infant Murray River at Cowombat Flat with one foot in New South Wales, the other in Victoria

Colonial art? Nope, it's the sublime AAWT near Tin Mine Huts

Orange sky at night, hikers take fright: an ominou. smoky sunset at Cascade Hut

Above: Lake Albina, nature's infinity pool

Left: Bacon and egg bush with a side of snow daisies on the Main Range

Top: Twynam twilight: the calm between two storms on Australia's third-highest peak

Above: Snow patch meltwater pond on the Rolling Ground

Right: How could you not fall in love with Valentine Hut?

Top left and right: Jagungal, mirror to the sky, issues its warning

Left: Menacing smoke plume in southern Kosciuszko National Park, viewed from near Jagungal

Mackeys Hut and outhouse snapped hastily from the departing helicopter

CHAPTER 15

THE ROLLING GROUND

Morning on the western side of Mt Twynam. Rain cleared away, sky only moderately hazy, nowhere you'd rather be. To the west is Australia's deepest valley, or bits of it anyway. To the north, maybe 40 kilometres away, is Mt Jagungal, the only peak over 2000 metres that lies well beyond the Main Range. I'll be there late tomorrow, all going well. They call Jagungal the crouching lion. It's a solemn, monolithic mountain which towers over the surrounding snow plains. Jagungal is a place of great power.

I climbed it once from the north and can't wait to approach from the south. Imagine if you could get to know a familiar person all over again. That's what it's like approaching a mountain from a new angle.

Twynam is a broad hump of a thing in the mould of Mt Kosciuszko which dominates the view from Guthega ski resort. Indeed, it's often mistaken for Kossie by skiers who take selfies from the top of Guthega's Freedom Quad Chairlift. Guthega is said to have gotten its unusual name from a bloke named Guthrie from Bega who built the road into the resort. It was always the most charming of the Australian ski hills. Back in the day it was a standalone resort, an overlooked gem with runs weaving between some of the healthiest old snow gums in the mountains. But, inevitably, Perisher spread the tentacles of its lift network and subsumed it. Just as surely, many of those snow gums burned in the 2003 fires. But Guthega is still beautiful. And on a quiet August weekday, you can still feel the old vibe.

Cresting the shoulder of Twynam, I'm now seeing the reverse view of Guthega's ski runs for the first time. Know what it looks like? Like Guthega. You've got to laugh at yourself sometimes. Not every new perspective is a revelation. Got to laugh at the word Guthega too. Guthega, Guthega, Guthega. It's as satisfying to enunciate as the most vulgar expletive. A word like that might come in handy later this afternoon.

I've been dreading today's walk as much as I've been looking forward to it. The part I'm dreading is the Rolling Ground. It's a long, high, featureless plateau north-east of the

Main Range where every hump and rocky outcrop looks the same. John Chapman strongly recommends bypassing it in foggy weather. He says get off the range and go walk some roads instead. I'm lucky. Visibility is relatively good today.

The challenge on the Rolling Ground is to navigate northwards until you find an old jeep track that leads down to Whites River Hut. The jeep track is notoriously difficult to locate, and Chapman's Bible doesn't instil much confidence. It says find a small saddle between two rock outcrops. That's like telling you to turn left at the sand dune in the Sahara.

But that's this afternoon's objective. This morning's task is to bear north-east along the crest of the Main Range towards 2068-metre Mt Tate. There's a track from Twynam and then there's not. You can feel it petering out. First, the foot pad becomes faint and noncommittal. Then it just fades from view, like an actor no one casts anymore. Happily, no track is required for the time being. The approach to Tate is great walking. Better than great, it's exhilarating. I'm walking through a large natural amphitheatre carpeted by snow grass and snow daisies with the occasional snow patch for texture. To one side is an enormous messy cluster of boulders called Mann Bluff. On the other side is a ridge dotted with intermittent outcrops called Gills Knobs. Gone are yesterday's crowds. Gone for the moment is my apprehension about this afternoon. This bowl-shaped meadow feels like a sanctuary. Like a special part of the mountains that belongs just to me.

It feels like I've reached a personal place, an intimate place. Not this specific snow grass meadow between Gills Knobs and Mann Bluff on the approach to Mt Tate, but an internal place. A mood. A transcendence. It feels like I've reached the place the boy staring out the window at the last blue range of Australian Alps yearned for.

This is hard to explain. Thankfully, there's always Wordsworth. In the Opening to his 'Ode: Intimations of Immortality from Recollections of Early Childhood', he wrote:

> There was a time when meadow, grove, and stream,
> The earth, and every common sight,
> To me did seem
> Apparelled in celestial light,
> The glory and the freshness of a dream.
> It is not now as it hath been of yore;—
> Turn wheresoe'er I may,
> By night or day.
> The things which I have seen I now can see no more.

Wordsworth knew that, as you age, you lose the intensity of feeling you had as a child. I guess I'm just trying to say that as a child I sensed that deep feelings could be felt here in the mountains. I'm feeling them now, raw and undiluted. My adult experience and childhood longing have briefly fused. In the prelude to the 'Ode', Wordsworth said, 'The Child is father of the man'. In this moment, I am both the child and the man. I am the dream and its fulfilment.

It's a fleeting feeling. Gone now. Now I'm just standing in a snow grass meadow again. Wow. That was like a flash. Like a reverse déjà vu.

What, you never had a major existential moment on a mountainside before?

Onwards.

Mt Tate is a conman. Grass all the way to the summit on the eastern side, a sheer cliff on the west. You could get into all sorts of trouble here on a foggy day. From the summit, there's the semblance of a trail down to a saddle called Consett Stephen Pass. Climb the hill on the far side of the pass and you're there. The Rolling Ground. Wakey-wakey, compass. You've been dangling around my neck for a reason.

The goal here, per The Bible, is as follows. Walk northwards through the guts of this stark, windy plateau until you reach the three Granite Peaks. Find a small pond below the first peak. Bear east from the pond across a shallow valley. On the far side of that valley, look for a gap between two boulder outcrops. Walk through that gap and find the old jeep track leading to Whites River Hut. Easy-peasy. Tap your heels three times and you'll be in Kansas.

First problem: there are literally dozens of rocky protuberances ahead which look like they could be the Granite Peaks. Protuberance. Outstanding word. I stole it from *Kosciuszko: The Mountain in History* author Alan EJ Andrews. It's still not the word of the day, though. That word is still Guthega. Guthega you, Rolling Ground, and the brumby you rode in on.

Rambling across the Rolling Ground is actually quite a pleasant experience even as it's tempered by navigational dread. Is not life exactly like this? Today seems to be philosophy day, so let's work with this idea. In life, you rarely have more than a vague idea of where you're headed. The landmarks up ahead: are they false markers? Can we trust them? Most of us stumble through life with uncertainty. With haze, not clarity. We don't know if the pile of rocks ahead is the first Granite Peak or just a pile of rocks. Never trust people striding too purposefully in life, too certain of their aim, too confident in their ability. It's all a veneer. This I believe like I believe snow is cold.

I often envy sportspeople. Sure, their road is tough. There's competition for scarce spots, ruthless fitness regimes, health issues and the fear of being tossed on life's scrap heap when their career is over. But for all that, sportspeople have coaches, teams, clubs, whole sporting bodies willing them on, guiding them, laying down an unambiguous path to success. I once shared a taxi with a former international athlete after a TV panel show. He couldn't believe how hard life after sport was. He was struggling like hell with having to plan his every move. I sympathised with him, but I also felt like saying, 'Welcome to real life'.

Real life is like the Rolling Ground. The landmarks are indistinct. Navigation is not easy. Okay, is this pile of rocks the first Granite Peak? Don't know. Maybe it's that next one a few hundred metres ahead? Not sure. The map says the first peak is three kilometres from where I first ascended the plateau. Have I walked three kilometres? Don't know. You walk a kilometre every 15 minutes or so on terrain like this. Has it been 45 minutes? No idea. Big mistake not to check the time on my phone earlier. Rookie error there. Back to the minor leagues for me.

Planting my hiking poles with urgency now. Pole, pole, pole, pole, pole. This assemblage of granite boulders is the highest yet. There's a larger one up ahead but I'm guessing that's the second Granite Peak, and this is the first. But where's the pond? Chapman says there's a pond next to the first Granite Peak. Where is it?

There are a few depressions which are stony and vegetation-free. Maybe the pond dried up? That rain last night was the first rain in weeks. The pond could easily still be dry. Reckon this large depression might be it. I'll veer east and cross this shallow valley. Nope, this isn't it. Retrace my steps. Let's take five here. Vita-Weats with Laughing Cow cheese. Satay jerky from my local Asian grocer. Rip into it like a Neanderthal. Big energy boost. Guthega!

Heading north again. Another granite outcrop. Pretty high, this one. This, surely, is the first Granite Peak. I can see another peak ahead of it too. Can't see the third because the view is obscured, but this must be it. Now to find that pond. Where is this thing? Sidling around the base of the peak, there's a snow patch with a large pool of meltwater below it. Is this the pond? Guthega this for a joke.

Might as well call it the pond. There's a shallow valley beside it, so what's to lose? I cross the valley. There's more of a dip this time. For the first time on Rolling Ground, I'm out of the tussocky snow grass and into the wet heath zone. There's no creek but it's damp underfoot, with dragon bush growing out of wide, springy sphagnum pillows. Gaiters and compass both earning their keep today. Okay, valley crossed. On a low ridge now. I think I'm in the right spot. Looking back across the shallow valley to the west, I can definitely see the three Granite Peaks. One, two, three. To the east is a new view.

It's the deep valley of the Munyang River. That's where Whites River Hut is. If I can find that jeep track, it'll take me straight to the hut. If not, I'll have to scrub bash down to the Munyang River and follow it upstream to the hut. Not an attractive option. I can tell by the bright green bushes that the scrub down there is neck deep. Really don't want to do this the hard way.

Have you ever considered what separates the great sportspeople from the very good? It's all about winning the big moments. I could watch Roger Federer's artful single-handed backhand all day – there are geometry professors who can't foresee the angles he creates on a tennis court – but what really makes champions like Federer special is that when it really counts, they nail it. When it's deuce at 4–5 in the fifth, they reel off consecutive aces. I mention this now because I just found the jeep track. Yes, I really did. Please be clear that I am not comparing myself with a champion tennis player or a champion anything, least of all a champion hiker. If my hiking skills translated to tennis, I'd be Johnny Struggler slugging it out on the back courts of the Shymkent Challenger event in Kazakhstan on the second tier of the ATP tour. But even journeymen like Johnny Struggler occasionally blaze a sizzling forehand winner down the line when they're down a break point.

Thwok. The 17 Kazakhs in the crowd go wild! Well, I go wild, anyway. Guthega! That's excited, fist-pumping Guthega, not angry Guthega.

I really don't know how I found this track. From my vantage point over the Munyang Valley, there were numerous rocky outcrops. But with map and compass and a large dose of intuition, I chose the two which looked most likely. Aced it. So now I'm on the jeep track and it's pretty indistinct, but who cares? This is the AAWT, after all, not the Hume Highway. The track even disappears for a bit, because of course it does, but within half an hour I'm down at Whites River Hut boiling a sachet of flavoured rice which tastes like the floor sweepings at the chicken salt factory.

Whites River Hut is a beauty. It's wedged between two creeks which converge just below it and is nice and clean inside. Busy here, though. This is one of the most popular and accessible huts in the Alps, just eight kilometres' walk from Guthega Power Station on a relatively easy trail. The holiday crowds haven't missed it, and they can have it. There are still a few hours of light and I've got an early dinner in my belly. It'd be a waste not to move on.

Relaxed again. In a terrific mood. The high plateau of the Rolling Ground is to my left, dark now with the sun sliding behind it. A few kilometres on, the next hut appears. It's Schlink Hut, known as the Schlink Hilton on account of its exorbitant size. Most High Country huts have one or two windows on either side; Schlink has six. It looks like a big dormitory, which is pretty much what it was. Schlink was built in 1961 to house Hydro-Electric Scheme employees working on transmission line maintenance and other jobs. Inside, a party of three hikers is looking nice and relaxed, air mats blown up, books in hand. Classic bushwalking types, this lot. In their sixties or seventies and lean like jerky. We chat briefly. I consider staying. Quick freshen-up in the creek, then I'll decide. Oh man, that water is chilly. G-g-g-g-guthega.

The next hut is Valentine Hut, six kilometres ahead. I could make it easily by nightfall. Good wide trails in these parts. But Schlink will do after a long day. Last night's campsite on Twynam was only 19 kilometres back, but there was a fair amount of mental energy burned on the Rolling Ground. There's a whole spare room here too. Means I don't have to pitch the tent. Easy decision.

In the dawn of popular online culture in the early 1990s, an American called Mike Godwin put forward a theory which stated that any online discussion will inevitably reach a point where someone invokes Hitler or Nazis as a way of putting someone down. It is now called Godwin's Law and is listed in the Oxford Dictionary. Why is this on my mind? Because a disturbing discussion is underway here in the hut. Seems these hikers are members of a particular bushwalking club, but they used to be members of a rival club and they're saying terrible things about that club and its culture. The discussion is not going the full Godwin, but it's lurching in that direction. Could the other club really be that bad? Do its members not lace their hiking boots in the morning and seek beauty among the snow gums? All I know is I wish I hadn't unlaced my boots and unpacked my gear. My mood is shot to pieces listening to this. Feel like moving on. Hot miso soup with noodles improves things. Nice crunchy apple helps. Early bed and my own room help even more.

* * *

After the success of *Huts of the High Country* in 1982, Klaus Hueneke wrote *Kiandra to Kosciuszko*. It's my favourite of his works. Among other things, the book documents famous journeys between the Kosciuszko area and Kiandra, the former gold mining town where my next food drop is located. The 100-kilometre journey is a six-day walk, give or take, but can be done much quicker in winter over the longest stretch of reliably skiable snow on the entire continent. It's the classic Australian alpine crossing and I've always wanted to do it. There are no deep subalpine valleys like there were in Victoria. It's genuine High Country all the way. Regular huts. Good streams. Undulating country. Snow gums with creamy bark dappled with patches of olive and chocolate. Couldn't ask for anything better.

Feeling chipper on the walk from Schlink to Valentine Hut. Never felt chipperer. No brumbies in this part of the park.

Just a pretty little stream called Duck Creek for company. Over my left shoulder, the Main Range is shrinking. No sign of Jagungal up ahead yet but it's bound to pop its head over the horizon soon enough. Turn right onto Valentine Trail. Up and down a hill or two. And there it is, the little red gingerbread house.

Valentine Hut is exquisite, with red timber walls, fresh white door, white awning with a row of five red love hearts and matching red and white outhouse. Inside, even the broom and dustpan are painted red and white with love heart motifs.

There's no romantic story behind the hut's name. No tryst between lovestruck cattlemen à la *Brokeback Mountain*. The hut's just up the hill from the Valentine River, hence its name. But let the record show, this would be an outstanding place to bring that special cowboy or cowgirl for a night or two, especially in winter. Just remember to bring a tent. You know the drill. The huts are emergency shelters and all that. The Valentine River has a great swimming hole, with a high waterfall just downstream. No time, sadly. Want to make some serious ground today. Aiming for 30 kilometres or thereabouts. Onwards.

The trail takes a long 180-degree loop to the south. It crosses the Geehi River, one of the largest tributaries of the upper Murray. Killer hill up from the river, but nothing a few peanut butter Vita-Weats and a sachet of Hydralyte won't fix. The trail turns north again through the open, heathy wetlands of Back Flat Creek. This really is stunning walking. It's not the majestic, high alpine terrain of the Main Range.

This is the guts of Kosciuszko National Park, its very essence. Wooded slopes with old snow gums. Open valleys scoured by frost and wind. For the last two days, everything was on a grand scale. Here, it's on a manageable, human scale. The Main Range is sublime. Up there, you feel humbled. You can also feel toyed with, belittled, brutalised when the weather turns. Here, you feel encouraged, empowered. This is now the Jagungal Wilderness, and it's the first time I've felt comfortable in a designated wilderness area. Might be turning into a real hiker after all.

Twelve kilometres into the day. Thirteen. Need a proper feed now. The next hut, Grey Mare, is just up ahead. It's 500 annoyingly steep metres off the trail on what's becoming a super-hot day. Worth the diversion, though. I'll get out of the sun and cook a curry inside for lunch. Grey Mare is tucked into the eastern side of a moderately high hill, sheltered from the westerlies among the snow gums. There's a grey horseshoe motif on the door. Nice touch. Elyne Mitchell stayed here on one of her High Country journeys. She wrote in *Australia's Alps* about some stockmen who stayed here trying to catch a beautiful grey mare:

I could imagine them thundering after her over the grassy hilltops till she vanished, a grey streak into the friendly timber; or hiding herself in the ghostly gullies thick with dead snow-gums, where her colour would blend with the colour of the trees. I thought of the talk in the hut at nights of the splendid mare so long pursued.

Eventually she was caught by one rider, more intrepid than his 'cobbers', and he tamed her wildness enough to put a halter on her and tied her to the horse-yard fence near the hut. When he returned from his work he found that the mare, fighting her captivity, had leapt the fence to escape and hung herself. This is how the Grey Mare got its name.

Mitchell's fictional silver brumby was a stallion called Thowra who leapt over a cliff rather than be captured by the character known as The Man. Did Thowra commit equine suicide or escape to run free evermore? No spoilers from me. Whatever the case, you can't help thinking the inspiration for a classic Australian story started right here in this modest seven by 3.5 metre iron and timber hut.

On the shelves of Grey Mare Hut is a small tome of considerably less renown than *The Silver Brumby*, and perhaps any book ever. It's a book called *Scheisse*, which is German for you-undoubtedly-know-what. This lewd and surprisingly loquacious latrine literature features images of German soldiers in World War II doing the business. 'It was a war raged from behind,' it begins. 'Gas was a popular weapon.' You get the idea.

Need something uplifting to read after that. There are a few copies of the Kosciuszko Huts Association newsletter lying around. Those will do nicely. I lie down on the floor of the hut with my pack as a pillow. An hour later, I'm still there. What? It's 3 p.m.? How did that happen? Had me a little sleep here. You know that murderously grumpy feeling when you awaken from an afternoon nap? When the nap was on a hard timber floor and your mouth tastes like dust and matar paneer from a foil pouch, the feeling multiplies by a factor of ten. You know that really terrific feeling when the grumpiness wears off? Got that now. Got it big time. I'm back on the trail, baby. Down the hill from Grey Mare to fill bottles in the creek. North now on the Grey Mare Trail. Crest a hill, and there she is. Jagungal. What an absolute beauty. And what a beast in the other direction.

The fires are closing in. The whole summer feels like it's closing in. My time on the AAWT has been mercifully fire free, give or take that grass fire near Benambra. Said it before and I'll say it again, I've been lucky. But there's definitely a major blaze to the south now. It's a fair way off – probably well south of Thredbo, down near Tin Mines or that part of the world – but it has generated a high anvil of smoke, like a thunderhead. It could actually be a thunderhead formed by the hot updraft. Whatever caused it, I don't like it at all. Conceivably, lightning from the storms two nights ago sparked fires. Don't know. Haven't had phone reception for 48 hours, so no way of telling for now. But as I approach Jagungal, the mountain looks ominous. Like Uluru at sunset, it's changing colour. It's not yet evening, but the crouched lion is turning from its usual greeny-grey to a greyish-orange colour. Now it's dark brown. Jagungal looks worried, and if you think mountains don't have moods, you haven't climbed enough of them.

Can I squeeze another week out of this summer? Doubt shrouds me as I press northwards. I should be enjoying the sparkling Tooma River, which I've just crossed, and the wail of black cockatoos and the glorious open space of the plains west of Jagungal. Instead, I'm feeling cheerless. This isn't like the situation at Mt Sunday, where I felt vulnerable inside. Now the world around me feels threatened, defenceless, and me with it. As afternoon turns to dusk, smoke-tinged sepia clouds over Jagungal intensify the feeling.

You go through a lot in a day on the trail. If a positive mood lasts a couple of hours, that's a pretty good run. But apprehensive moods can disappear quickly too, and as I reach O'Keefes Hut in the twilight, I'm in high spirits again. A clean, empty hut and 28 comfortably walked kilometres will do that.

But there's more to it than that. You build resilience after a long stretch in your own company. You watch chaos building around you and realise you're powerless to stop it. There's nothing you can do about that menacing sky over Mt Jagungal. Kick the dirt, snap a dead snow gum branch, nothing's going to change. People throw the word resilience around these days like stale bread to pigeons, to the point where it has become meaningless. Isolation on the trail recharges your resilience. It gives you composure and perspective. It crystallises the things you can change, the things you can't. And one thing you can always change is your outlook.

* * *

No High Country hut is like the next. They're as individual as people, these huts. But after a while, it becomes difficult to convey how one slab-walled, tin-roofed hut is different from the next. O'Keefes does not present that problem. Where to start? In 1939, obviously. The interior walls of O'Keefes are papered with sheets of newspaper from the World War II era, dating back to 1939. All huts in the snow country have ghosts. O'Keefes has ghosts you can see and read behind a thin layer of Perspex.

'Anti-Semitism Rising Behind Iron Curtain' warns one headline. 'Britain Rejects Nazi Peace Offer' blares another, with a subhead of 'Mr Chamberlain Sees Deep World Changes'.

Nineteen thirty-nine was indeed a year of terrible change and upheaval, as the world erupted into an orgy of killing on the battlefield and beyond. Here in Australia, the Alps suffered their own fiery hell, burning more fiercely and extensively than anyone alive had ever known. It was the once-in-a-century megafire that devastates the sensitive alpine environment, but from which it can and did recover. O'Keefes was built in 1934, then rebuilt after it was levelled in the 2003 fires. The silvery snow gums around the hut say all you need to know about the severity of that fire. This landscape is not ready for another blaze.

CHAPTER 16

HITTING THE FAN

At 5 a.m. on 31 December 2019, Ian Dicker wakes to his alarm in the Abbotsleigh Motor Inn, a clean, well-appointed motel opposite a Caltex in the northern New South Wales town of Armidale. A call came through last night. He is needed back home immediately.

Dicker is Team Leader Fire, Southern Ranges Branch, in the NSW National Parks and Wildlife Service. Based in Jindabyne, his patch runs from Albury to well north of Canberra, all the way down to Bombala and the Victorian border. At the heart of that zone is Kosciuszko National Park.

That's the area Dicker knows best. Nobody understands how fires run in Kosciuszko like Ian Dicker.

But Dicker hasn't spent much time in Kosciuszko of late. For much of spring and the first month of summer, he's been flying up north to help fight fires in the vicinity of Narrabri, Glen Innes, Armidale, Casino and Grafton. This is his seventh deployment as an air attack supervisor for the season, but this one will end a day early.

On the way to Armidale Airport, Dicker picks up two helicopter fire crew who are heading south on the same flight. He's got a rental car. Might as well save them a taxi fare. At 6.30 a.m., their Qantas flight departs for Sydney. It's a tense flight. One of the fire crew lives directly in the path of a huge fire that swept through his valley near Tumbarumba overnight. Communication is down and he has no idea if his house is still standing. The other bloke is from a small town south of Albury where a young volunteer was tragically killed when his fire truck flipped over in a freak fire tornado. The victim hasn't been identified yet, but whoever it was, he's certain he'll know him.

Dicker's connecting flight from Sydney touches down in Canberra sometime between 10 a.m. and 11 a.m. A colleague is there to meet him. They drive to Jindabyne without stopping for food. On arrival in Jindabyne around 12.30 p.m., Dicker can see smoke starting to brew up over the ranges he knows so well. He goes straight to the office. There is no time for pleasantries. All he hears is, 'Thank goodness you're here, put your flight gear on, go!'

At 6 a.m. on the same morning, Kate Pearcy, a holidaymaker in the tiny New South Wales south coast hamlet of Rosedale, wakes up after an uneasy sleep. Her son, Leo, and three-year-old whippet, Pepper, are still sleeping; neither of them are morning people.

Pearcy tiptoes downstairs to hose the perimeter of the ageing tin-roofed A-frame home set among the spotted gums, high on a hill overlooking the ocean. She knows that if fire comes, this will be the day. What she doesn't know is whether she'll seek safety on Rosedale beach or in a nearby large town like Batemans Bay or Moruya.

At 7.11 a.m., she receives a text from her absent husband. It's a screenshot of a message from the New South Wales Rural Fire Service, which reads:

> There are a number of large and dangerous fires burning across NSW, in particular along the south coast. Strong westerly winds are expected to increase very early tomorrow morning. People in bushfire prone areas between Batemans Bay and Bega should move towards a larger town away from bushland areas, such as Narooma, Moruya, Bega and Batemans Bay, before 8 am.

'I am very worried about you at Rosedale,' her husband adds.

'I have watered the house and we will head to the beach,' Pearcy replies.

'OK, but maybe you should go to town in the car just in case. I'd head south to Moruya. Anyway I'll leave it with you. Not much charge or reception here so you may not hear from me for a while. Good luck and happy New Year!'

Pearcy has been visiting the Rosedale house since she was a teenager. It belongs to a schoolfriend's family, and she's never found a beach house she'd rather park herself in with a good book and good company. It doesn't bother her at all that on windy nights it creaks like an eighteenth-century sailing ship, or that there's no privacy because the bedroom walls stop short of the vaulted ceiling. The house has charm and it has memories. Barbecues on the back deck. Monopoly in the sunroom when the fickle south coast weather turned wet and miserable. They never made a jigsaw puzzle too large to finish in a south coast summer rainy spell. But this has not been one of those weeks. No jigsaws this year. Each day has been hotter than the last. Now the wind is picking up and the air has that furnace feel.

Leo and Pepper awaken and shake off their fleas. They accompany Pearcy to the beach on a reconnaissance mission. Pearcy is expecting a crowd, people setting up for the day with food and water and sun tents. But nothing. There's no one there. Leo doesn't like it. He tells his mother he wants to leave Rosedale. They climb the steep path from the beach, quickly pack essentials and valuables, and drive off.

'We are going to Moruya,' Pearcy texts her husband just before 8.30. He has slipped out of phone range and misses the message.

* * *

At 8 a.m., light ash is falling at O'Keefes Hut. It sounds strange but I don't think much of it. Feels like someone else's problem. Like when you're driving in the city and the radio says there's a breakdown and backed-up traffic on a freeway on the other side of town. All the same, it's clear this trek is a day-by-day, hour-by-hour proposition now. The sky delivered its warning last night. This morning's ash is the latest update.

Two muesli bars and a coffee on the steps of O'Keefes, then it's time to hit the trail. It's 25 kilometres till Happys Hut, and I want to get there by late afternoon, settle in and survey the scene. Got to memorise every kilometre of terrain now. If the worst happens, you need open ground and a good creek. Happys has that. So does Mackeys Hut, which is ten kilometres from here. Got to walk valley to valley, hut to hut, with eyes open and mind alert. All going well, I can reassess at my food drop in Kiandra in two days. If I'm spooked, I can always hitch out of the mountains from there. Onwards.

The moment I start worrying is when charred black leaves begin twirling down from an uncertain sky, dotting the snow grass tussocks like chocolate shards on cupcakes. Where have the leaves come from? What do they mean? Are they another gentle reminder of distant danger or a sign of imminent peril?

The Grey Mare Trail is traversing the sort of country I've been dreaming about for weeks. The terrain is undulating but not steep, the trail well marked, the creeks still flowing after a month without rain. You can put a lot of miles behind you in country like this and I am doing just that. But these black leaves, crinkly and powdery to the touch. They worry me. There's more ash now too, gently floating to earth like grey summer snowflakes.

It's hard to charge my phone in these conditions. The sun is not strong enough. Been walking with the phone off to save power, but I switch it on now to check the Fires Near Me app one last time while I've still got a flickering bar or two of reception. The nearest fire is still 50 or 60 kilometres away, down near Tumbarumba on the western side of the mountains. The phone dings.

We are going to Moruya.

I'm thrilled Kate has made the decision to head to a larger town. Also relieved from a narrative point of view that the cat's out of the bag and I can stop calling her by her surname, Pearcy. Made her sound like a footballer. My wife has many talents, but football ain't one of them.

About seven kilometres north of O'Keefes, I pause for the first break of the day by a narrow unnamed creek flowing through open heathland, glugging mouthfuls of water between strips of jerky. Up the hill from the rest spot, the Grey Mare Trail meets an offshoot called the Doubtful Gap Trail. I pause again to look at the sky. I'm feeling doubtful all right as those singed leaves and ash float to earth.

These blackened leaves are not snow gum leaves, that much I know. Snow gum leaves have a distinctive grain, their veins curving along the length of the leaf in near-parallel arcs. Even in their singed state, these leaves clearly have the pattern common to most eucalypts, where the veins fan out towards the edge of the leaf from one long central strand. That means they are from a distant lowland forest to the west, and have risen on hot updrafts, travelling my way on strong upper atmospheric winds. I touch a leaf. Cold. Another. Also no warmth. These leaves couldn't possibly start a spot fire, could they? And if they're not from around here, surely there is no immediate danger, right?

I have no answers. All I know is that the day feels wrong. Gloomy and wrong. You might think it's easy to dramatise that feeling in hindsight, but I shared my mood on social media before setting out from O'Keefes Hut this morning.

Smoke from a fire near Tumbarumba has blown in. No danger up here for now, but the mountains have a very bleak feel today, which grabs hold of your mood. Onwards, and good luck to all firies and people in harm's way today.

It's beginning to feel like I might be one of those people at some point.

* * *

Around 9 a.m., Kate and Leo drive south towards Moruya. They can't get through. There's already a fire closing in near the small town of Tomakin. She swings the car around and drives back past Rosedale and on through Malua Bay. Just after Malua Bay, there's fire at Lilli Pilli. No way through to Batemans Bay now. Roads north and south blocked. That RFS message to evacuate by 8 a.m. was frighteningly accurate. This thing is closing in like a fishing net. Kate turns around again. Malua Bay is the only option.

Malua Bay is a town of 2000 whose population swells in summer. The town is ringed by bush but has a wide, mostly treeless stretch of grassy parkland fronting the surf beach. On a hot day, that expanse is the Simpson Desert. Now, it's an oasis, a perfect firebreak which is filling rapidly with parked cars, each row tighter than the next.

On the beach are hundreds of people and their pets. Dogs. Cats in cages. Ducks, geese and chickens. At least six horses, some of them with riders. The sky turns orange. Then it goes greeny-grey. Now it's purply charcoal. Then it's black. Pepper the whippet can't breathe so well. He's coughing an awful, undogly, ungodly cough. My son, Leo, is frightened. Knee deep in the water, he can see headlands stretching down the coast, all of them ablaze. He knows the house at Rosedale doesn't stand a chance. No way a fire could reach the headlands without burning right through Rosedale. He feels certain the house is already gone. He and Kate can't breathe so well either, even through shirts. The dog keeps coughing. Horses pick at mouthfuls of hay which someone thoughtfully brought, unsure why day became night. The four-hour firestorm takes a fortnight. A woman turns to my wife and says, 'Maybe we should pray?' The beach is a dark, living hell.

* * *

Midday. On the Grey Mare Trail near Mt Jagungal, two Parks staff drive north in a Toyota LandCruiser trayback with a slip-on firefighting unit on the back. They're on the lookout for a single male hiker doing the Australian Alps Walking Track. They get within five kilometres of Mackeys Hut before turning around. That smoke column to the north-west is terrifying. You see a column of smoke like that, you drive away from it, not towards it.

The men in the LandCruiser know that the smoke is from the Dunns Road fire, a blaze that originated near Tarcutta, a small town whose claim to fame is being halfway between Sydney and Melbourne on the Hume Highway. Tarcutta is a long, long way from Kosciuszko, but the fire ran through farmland, then bushland, then more farmland, then more bushland, growing all the while. As it roared up the steep western face of the mountains, fires apps were powerless to document its true size and exact location. Ian Dicker reckons it has travelled 80 kilometres in 48 hours. That's close to unprecedented. But then, the usual rules don't apply this summer. After Australia's hottest, driest year on record, there are no fire dynamics experts. The only fire prediction you can rely on now is to expect anything.

By early afternoon, Dicker is aloft with his regular pilot, Col de Pagter, in their trusty B3 Squirrel helicopter operated by Heli Surveys in Jindabyne. The single-engine six-seater with the callsign Firebird 296 is as familiar as an old couch, if not quite as comfortable. The two men have known each other for 30 years and flown together for 20. You know when your favourite sporting team just gels? Those days when the passes stick and the moves all come off and each player seems to know what the next is thinking? That's Col and Ian.

Firebird 296 is tasked with flying the western side of the mountains, then up north towards Jagungal. They fly through Tom Groggin and Geehi and confirm that the campgrounds down that way are empty. They land at Whites River Hut, where two families believe they are in no danger. Dicker politely points out the nearby dead trees from the 2003 fires. Point made and taken. While the families hurriedly pack, Col hits the siren on the helicopter. Dicker runs over to see what's up. Col says there are radio calls about a solo hiker doing the Australian Alps Walking Track. His trip is logged at the National Parks office in Jindabyne. Their next job is to find him.

* * *

Out on the trail, I've just pulled into Mackeys Hut, 510 kilometres into the AAWT. Still the falling leaves, still the ash. Still the sky that's a bit grey, a bit orangey pink, a bit can't make up its mind. It's a sky the colour and texture of salmon skin. At least someone's in salmon mood.

Mackeys is a beauty. Tin walls, tin roof, timber floor. Best verandah of any hut so far. I could happily spend an afternoon out here on a log stump stool drinking peppermint tea and watching the weather. Good creek down the valley too. Is the sky smokier now? Can't tell. I go fill my bottles in the creek. Then it's back into the hut to warm up a lovely pouch of chicken nehari, which the packet describes as 'luxuriant boneless chicken with invigorated mix spices'. We had backyard chickens for a while. After one died, the survivor scratched at the back door every night and insisted on sleeping under the kitchen table. We had to put newspaper down every night. That was a luxuriant chicken. Not sure this chicken nehari deserves describing in those terms, much less the life of the chicken that ended up in it.

I'll tell you what is luxuriant. This scene. What could be better than this beautifully restored bush hut tucked into a gentle rise overlooking Tibeaudo Creek? They really did build these huts in the best places. For all the spectacular parts of the Australian Alps, these gentle waves of snow gum woodland and heathy plains makes me happiest. Crash your cymbals, crank up the Tchaikovsky or death metal, go climb Feathertop, Bogong, Watsons Crags. You can have them all. I'll take these subtle bits, the bits that look like the rest of Australia but are so different if you know how to look closely.

Back in the hut, I tip the gear out of my pack so I can repack it in an orderly fashion. I hang up the shirt I washed in the creek, feeling the need to be organised. Definitely going to spend the afternoon here at Mackeys and see what happens weather-wise. I'd do anything for a bit of phone reception to check on Kate and the fires but that's not going to happen. Hold on, what's that noise?

* * *

In the chopper, Col and Ian have been tracking rapidly northwards along the Grey Mare Trail. Ian is worried. There's no sign of the lone hiker. If he's not at Mackeys, they'll have to search a much wider area to the east where the mountains drop off towards Lake Eucumbene. The helicopter reaches Mackeys. Hovers low. The hiker pokes his head out from under the verandah. Ian hopes like heck it's the man they've been looking for.

* * *

I poke my head out from under the verandah. It's a chopper circling the hut. No markings. Can't tell if it's National Parks, though who else would it be? I wave to the guy beside the pilot. All good here, I'm telling him. No need to land. The chopper lands anyway on the gentle uphill slope behind the hut near the outhouse. That's when I see it. The tall plume of smoke in the middle distance. Don't know how I missed it until this moment. Something about where the chopper landed, I guess. Never quite got the clear north-westerly view straight through to the smoke plume. But I see it now.

And I see something else. The symbolism is unmissable. I see the outhouse and the blades of the helicopter. In other words, the shit hitting the fan. A smoke plume reaching halfway to heaven and the main thing I see is not imminent mortal danger but a really good pun. This is what happens when you've been writing headlines too long.

A tall Parks officer in a fireproof yellow uniform emerges from the helicopter. He has a friendly face and assuring manner. He is your kind uncle, not your crazy uncle.

'You are walking the Australian Alps Walking Track, aren't you?' he says. I can see he needs me to say yes. Yes is my answer.

'Ever been for a ride in a helicopter?'

Once, a long time ago.

He tells me his name is Ian and proceeds to give me instructions about how to approach the aircraft. I nod like I'm listening intently but take not a syllable in. This does not compute. Error 404.

Two months later, I will meet Ian Dicker in Jindabyne. He will recount further details of our brief conversation beside Mackeys Hut with the rotor blades still spinning and a huge plume of smoke in the background which I somehow hadn't seen until his helicopter landed. He will tell me that one of the first things I said was, 'I'm not going to finish my hike, am I?' And he'll tell me that he responded, 'Not today.' Of this interaction I have zero recall. But if I return to the moment, I can understand why I said it.

I'm not ready for the hike to be over. This hike was never about the achievement of finishing the full 660 kilometres. After all, I've already bypassed a couple of sections. When people attempt Everest, they enter a binary universe. Either they reach the summit or they fail. The second option is so unpalatable to many people that they court death in the name of peak-bagging. But my AAWT journey was never an all-or-nothing conquest. It was a pilgrimage, and it was a pilgrimage without an end. The track itself was the destination. I just never expected the track to end here, and so suddenly. And when I say suddenly, I mean suddenly.

I request two minutes to pack up my gear. Ian gives me one. Inside the hut, I frantically squash everything inside the bag. The shirt doesn't make it. Neither do my prized hiking poles. This I realise as the helicopter is lifting off. Stick, you've got another new home, I tell it. You were a good stick. Thank you for coming all the way from Black River. I hope no one burns you in the fireplace at Mackeys. I hope Mackeys itself doesn't burn.

There's Col, Ian, me and two young women in the helicopter. The women were on a trail that intersects with Grey Mare back near O'Keefes when they got picked up. They had no idea about the fire either. Some fires are obvious, some aren't. It depends on terrain, weather, a thousand variables. But as we clear the trees, I see the smoke plume in its towering awfulness. It's an evil genie sneering over the park. It's a thousand times higher than Jagungal, than anything. How did I not notice that before? Am I the world's dopiest hiker? I realise it must be the Dunns Road fire because it's coming in from that direction. But how did it get here so quickly? Already, the north-western quadrant of the park is completely enshrouded in smoke. There's actually a pretty clear-cut line between smoke and clear sky. I must have been only seven or eight kilometres from the fire front, and that thing was roaring in like a lion to meat.

There's more. The fire has spawned evil offspring – pyro-cumulus clouds that are generating dry storms with lightning bolts. The air is charged, alive, malevolent. The beast is breeding, feeding off its own energy. Kosciuszko is under attack.

We're flying south to Jindabyne over an area called Snowy Plain, which you may have guessed is a plain that's snowy in winter. A little further on, there are dozens of brumbies taking fright from the chopper. There really is a plague of feral horses in the park. The trampled vegetation and fouled waterways of Kosciuszko send their polite thanks to you, John Barilaro. All the same, I hope the brumbies below don't get trapped by fire where the park meets fences and farmland.

The helicopter is noisy and my phone is out of charge. Could be worse. Could be the other way around. Humour helps when your world has been upended and you're being rescued and you're feeling humbled and helpless and foolish and emotional and there are two women beside you and you don't feel like being emotional in front of two women because you're a middle-aged man programmed to keep that sort of thing to yourself.

To the left of the aircraft is Lake Eucumbene and, before long, Lake Jindabyne. And then we're landing at Jindabyne Airport, which in reality is a strip of dirt in a paddock with a shed or three. The smoke has chased us here. Jindabyne is soon socked in. The helicopter plucked me and the women to safety just in time. It's grounded now. Someone drives us into town. Nice of them. Not sure who. Everything's a bit blurry and confusing at this point. For a while, I walk around town wearing my backpack, feeling naked without hiking poles. I'm neither hungry nor thirsty. Don't feel like going anywhere, don't feel like sitting still. I wander down to the lake and say hello to old Strzelecki. He looks a bit comical standing there in his robe with his hand sticking out saying, 'Over there!' Yeah, Strezza, Kosciuszko is over there somewhere through the smoke. Can't possibly miss it. Aboriginal people beat you by forty thousand years, by the way. Then again, you beat all the Europeans and I respect your curiosity and sense of adventure. I guess I just think your robe looks a bit silly or something. Who goes exploring in a robe? I don't know, maybe it was your raincoat. I really don't know anything right now.

* * *

New Year's Eve in Jindabyne is a room at the Banjo Paterson Inn, combination chow mein from Chong Yees and phone calls to family. Can't get through to Kate. Communication is down over most of the south coast. Mobile phone towers have burned and the whole region is in chaos. I'm not worried. She will have gotten herself to Moruya or somewhere safe. I'm certain of it.

Around 9 p.m., the world's most predictable cover band starts cranking out the oldies. 'Sweet Home Alabama'. Some Bryan Adams. 'Brown-Eyed Girl'. And then it's 2020.

CHAPTER 17

TOO WILD TO KEEP, TOO GOOD TO LOSE

'Klaus can't come to the phone right now. He's grieving.'

Oh, I'm sorry. I didn't realise someone had died. Please excuse me, I'll call another time.

'No, it wasn't a person. It was the hut.'

Klaus Hueneke, author of *Huts of the High Country*, is in mourning because Four Mile Hut is gone. Hueneke first stumbled upon the old timber slab and corrugated iron hut near Kiandra in 1975. It wasn't too different from a lot of huts in the area, but it always felt like his special place. He organised the first ever work party to restore it in 1978. He interviewed the elderly brother of the miner who built it. He took his daughters Anna and Abigail camping there, and for the last two years he has been writing a book about it, only to see the object of his work go up in smoke in the first week of January.

Klaus is an experienced outdoorsman with a delicate soul. His wife, Patricia, knows it. That's why she's playing phone bouncer right now, fending off callers with a kind but firm tone. She takes my message and Klaus rings back the same day. I offer condolences and tell him I'd like to meet. It's a hut thing, and an AAWT thing ... It's a few different things. Can we meet? We can meet.

It's 1 March 2020. Two months off the trail. I'm travelling south from Sydney to Kosciuszko National Park to tie up a few loose ends. I want to see the fire damage for myself and need to pick up the charred remains of my food drop under the bridge at Kiandra. Also keen to thank Ian Dicker in person for plucking me to safety on Firebird 296, and looking forward to camping among the black sallees on the Thredbo River and having one last mountain swim before the weather turns. But my first stop is the home of Klaus and Patricia Hueneke in Canberra. To get to their street, you have to turn off Kosciuszko Avenue. Because of course you do.

Over hot black tea, Klaus tells me that Four Mile Hut had a unique design. The miner who built it, Bob Hughes, cut kerosene cans into strips and nailed those strips between the timber slabs to keep out the wind, rain and wind-driven snow.

Four Mile wasn't thrown together like a humpy; it was built with the two most valuable commodities in construction: craftsmanship and love.

'You can go there and see it,' Klaus says, then he cuts himself off. 'Well, you can't go anymore.'

Klaus has put his creative hat on for his latest work. He's writing it as a novel rather than as a straight history, the story told in the first person from the perspective of the hut. He says this is easy for him because he feels he has become the hut.

'You can see why this is so traumatic for me, why being burnt has thrown me somewhat,' he says. 'It's a death in the family.'

I ask if the hut's destruction caused him to consider abandoning the project.

'Oh, yes. Since it burnt down, I've had my doubts at times. But it's gone so far and I've done so much, and I love the place so much, even though it's a figment of my imagination now. The desire to write it is greater than whether or not the hut's still there, you know what I mean? I feel I owe it to myself and I owe it to the hut, and I owe it to shelter in general. I owe it to that whole generation, I suppose. I feel I owe it to Bob Hughes, the builder.'

What will the hut say now that it has burned to the ground?

'Well, I'm still working this out a bit. But I think I – the hut – am going to have a conversation with the general public. I'm going to tell you why you should rebuild me. Sorry, I'm losing my words here. Go on, ask me another question.'

The big fires are coming more often now. Do you feel in any sense that the Alps that you love – both the human relics like the huts and the ecology – are almost irredeemably threatened now?

'It certainly looks like it now. Our High Country has never had such a frequency of fires. And we have a different kind of fire now. We have incredible evaporation, and such long periods of drying out that the bush becomes combustible much sooner. And when it burns, it burns more severely. In my gut I have fear now. I have fear for us. I have fear for the environment. I have fear for the High Country. And I have fear for the huts because the argument is that if the frequency increases, why rebuild them if they're going to burn down in ten or 15 years' time? Why bother? Why try and preserve and replenish and renew the built heritage? Why?'

Is there an answer?

'Well. That's ... that's ... I don't know.'

Klaus is struggling here. Feels like maybe this is too much of an interrogation and not enough of a chat. I'm more of a journalist than I give myself credit for sometimes. But he surprises me by saying, 'You're helping me today.'

Am I?

'You're pushing me. You just prompted me to express the things I'm finding hard to express, things I dare not think, dare not believe. I keep wishing the hut's still there, that lots of huts are still there. I keep regretting it.'

Regret is a hell of a thing. It burns almost as badly as the fire itself. Klaus wears a face that's hard to describe. It's

his 'what if?' face. What if they had back-burned around
Four Mile to save it the way they did in 2003? What if
they had wrapped it in the fire-retardant material FireStop,
the way they wrapped other huts in the New South Wales
and Victorian High Country? They wrapped the little red
gingerbread house Valentine Hut. They wrapped nineteenth-
century gem Wallaces Hut near Falls Creek in Victoria. Why
not Four Mile?

'Probably because we couldn't see it. The big restriction
in bushfires is visibility,' Ian Dicker explains when we
meet in Jindabyne the next day. 'Wind and turbulence also
play a huge part in where we can and cannot get to.'

Dicker and his team did manage to save Mackeys.
Firefighting, like a game of football, is won on strategy and
defence. In the end, it was a new blaze, the Doubtful Gap
fire, that attacked Mackeys. Dicker believes the fire was
started by a dry lightning bolt that struck at the very moment
he was descending to pluck me to safety. The fire came again
and again from all angles. Three times it attacked the hut and
three times they saved it with everything from helicopter
water drops to back-burning to old-fashioned frontline
fighting with buckets and big leafy snow gum branches. I'm
glad they saved Mackeys. Maybe my poles and shirt are still
there. Seems churlish to ask. I ask anyway. We're none of us
perfect. The answer is he's not sure but he'll let me know.

It's good to see Ian again. An exhausting spring and summer
are behind him but he's clearly still catching his breath. He
logged 63 flying days and 380 hours aloft, which is an awful

lot. He says it was mentally draining and physically taxing too. When he finally got a few days off in mid-February, he pretty much glued himself to the couch in his home at Grosses Plain, 20 kilometres south of Jindabyne. Ordinarily he doesn't mind a drop of an organic South Australian tipple called Farm Hand Cabernet Sauvignon, but he was so tired, he didn't feel like drinking. Mostly he spent time on the phone speaking with colleagues and firefighters.

'Just the "how are you doing, mate?" kind of calls,' he says. 'Fatigue is a big thing in our space at the minute. Parks staff around here started travelling in August to do northern NSW, then came home to our own fires. So we're really trying to look after people. There's a lot of really high-grade work going on. We've never had that at such a scale before.'

We order much-needed second coffees. I didn't sleep so well down at Thredbo Diggings campground last night. Got well and truly used to beds again. Ian needs a second caffeine hit too. The waitress is called Ash because of course she is.

'I'm just a broken-down old fire guy who's done thirty-something years of it,' Dicker jokes.

It's not true and he knows it. But after the Black Summer, he probably feels it.

We sit by the window in the Parc Café at Jindabyne, stirring cappuccino froth with teaspoons as a light drizzle falls outside. January's bare earth is bright green now from heavy February rains. The lake that was obscured by smoke on New Year's Eve is now cloaked in mist. Ian has explained how the distant Dunns Road fire became Kosciuszko's nightmare quicker than anyone could have imagined. He has helped me piece together the details of the day of my rescue. There are two more subjects I want to broach. The first is a little awkward. Might as well just blurt it out: was I foolish to do the AAWT this summer?

'I wouldn't be that harsh,' he says. 'But I think it was inevitable we were going to be impacted by fire this summer. As early as July last year, I was looking at the conditions and forecasting that we were going to have a significant fire event. All of the vectors were lining up. It was almost identical weather conditions to what we had at the same time in 2002 before the 2003 fires.'

What about the day you picked me up? Was it naïve of me not to sense imminent danger even though I never really saw the smoke plume until you landed?

'Again, I see the imminent danger because I've been doing it a long time,' he says. 'I've worked in Kossie for 18 years and seen how fast fire can go. I knew what the weather conditions were that day and how long the fire front was behind it. There was a heap of potential for what it could do.'

Ian Dicker is exceptionally talented at fire management, but if the Department of Foreign Affairs ever needs a diplomat, I'd recommend him any day.

My final line of inquiry is broader in nature. I'm wondering what we learned in the Black Summer, when fires killed 34 people and burned 18 million hectares, including a third of Kosciuszko, the largest national park in New South Wales.

'There are lots of lessons to learn from a year like this,' Ian says. 'Each agency is now taking the time to review, including formal inquiries. For my agency, it was just one of those years. The drought conditions meant that "normal" firefighting often didn't work. Areas like rainforest gullies or green creek beds which typically slow or stop fires didn't have their normal effect. Back-burning during cooler nights often just didn't happen. And the fire behaviour was crazy. Fire runs of 30 to 40 kilometres in a day, like the Dunns Road fire, are not common. We'll have to learn for next time.'

Next time. The problem is that next time isn't like the last time anymore. And the gap between next times keeps shrinking.

I thank Ian. Important detail: never forget to thank a person who saved your life. You have to believe they want to hear it even if saving lives is their job.

Back at my campsite on Thredbo River, I take a walk along the new mountain bike track that runs up the valley to Thredbo Village. After maybe ten minutes, there's a sandy riverbank visible through the trees. A quick scrub bash and I'm on the best river beach you've ever seen with incredibly fine sand, not the usual gritty river sand. The river is deep, clear and enticingly swimmable. So I swim. There's no sign of the bike track. Not a hint of the ugly Skitube terminal down the valley at Bullocks Flat where they paved paradise and added a car park for 3500 cars and 250 buses to serve tourists taking the railway tunnel up to Perisher. There is just mountains and river. You don't have to attempt the whole AAWT or even a small section to find somewhere magical in these mountains. Long may it remain so.

On the road again. Gear packed up. Heading to Kiandra to pick up the food drop. Down in Victoria, alpine ash grows as low as 900 metres above sea level on the southern flanks of Baw Baw. Here in northern Kosciuszko, and especially on the drier eastern side of the park, the tall, stately eucalypts don't really kick in until 1300 metres or higher. How good is arboreal navigation? Reckon I can tell my elevation within 20 metres across the entire Australian Alps based just on the trees. Utterly useless life skill. Wish I had more like it.

Between Adaminaby and Kiandra is Sawyers Hill. Its name reveals much about its history; the alpine ash here was a prized source of timber for the pubs and churches and mines of Kiandra in the nineteenth-century gold rush. The hill recovered. The ash grew tall again. Then, in 2003, Sawyers Hill was decimated by fires. Most of the trees died. The denuded ghostly forest giants looked like arm-flailing inflatable men out the front of car yards. But there was hope. New saplings were growing. As mentioned, alpine ash takes 15 years to flower and another five for the seed to be ready. Twenty years without fire and the forest should survive. Then came this summer's fires. For Sawyers, they were three or four years too soon. Now the hill is doubly dead.

Ian Dicker was a forester before he worked in fires. He reckons if Sawyers survived the era of saws, it can survive anything.

'Those hills have been flogged for a long time when you think about it from a forestry sense. So I'd like to think I'm optimistic and say Mother Nature will look after herself.'

The question is whether we're giving Mother Nature a fair chance these days. Klaus Hueneke has a poem called 'If I Was a Mountain Hut' in one of his books. The last stanza reads:

If I was a mountain hut I could
live forever
as long as people loved me and
no joker burnt me down.

Maybe the joker who burned his beloved Four Mile Hut down is all of us. Maybe it's time we focused not just on fire prevention and mitigation, but on why the fires are coming hotter and stronger each year. Maybe it's got very little to do with management or lack of it. In the drier, warmer Australian Alps, even lifelong fire managers no longer know the rules. The new megafires make their own.

Environmental custodianship can help. Helicopter seeding has regenerated ash forests in the past, especially in Victoria, but it's an expensive procedure and the problem is getting bigger every few years. Our mountains need inoculation, not hospitalisation. We need to take the 'c' word off the list of words some politicians refuse to use, because climate is a huge part of the equation. The biggest part. And if you think arsonists were the main force behind Australia's Black Summer, then you weren't in a helicopter flying out of Mackeys Hut, watching lightning bolts from a dry thunderstorm spawned by a fire so vast and hostile it had created its own weather.

* * *

Kiandra was always a bleak place. Too frosty for trees, bare hills scarified by the mining era, the wind constantly niggling, bullying. Amid all that bleakness, the elegant 1890s bluestone courthouse was a portrait of dignity and defiance. How could a building like that burn? They say its aluminium window frames melted. How could such a barren valley explode in flames like it was made of gas?

Turns out Kiandra's bleakness was its weakness. It was the wind that sealed its fate. That and the lack of trees. After the fire took out Selwyn Snow Resort, it roared through Kiandra like dragon's breath. Even the rocks burned, or at least the dry lichen on them, but it would have looked like granite boulders were ablaze. Ian Dicker said the convection column was 14 kilometres high the day Kiandra went. That's way up in the stratosphere, much higher than commercial jets fly. The thing was a monster.

Dropping my food drum in Kiandra in December, the initial idea was to hide it in bushes near the road. Couldn't quite find the right spot. Instead, I stashed it in what you might call the armpit of a bridge across a creek near the Selwyn turn-off. The fire must have ripped under that bridge as though projected by a giant flamethrower. There are new green shoots along the creek but everything else is still scorched, blackened. Yet my blue barrel tucked under the road looks untouched. On closer examination, the lid is loose. Someone has been snooping around. The chips are gone, and I'm pretty sure there's a bottle of sarsaparilla missing too. People, eh? But otherwise, everything looks untouched. Kiandra's last building, its 130-year-old courthouse, is destroyed, but my 25-litre plastic drum filled with curries, Vita-Weats, muesli bars and dried mangoes is not even singed.

Driving out of the mountains, traffic is blocked by trucks clearing fire debris. I fish a yoghurt-topped muesli bar out of my food drum and give it to the stop sign guy. Big thumbs up from him as he swallows it in two bites. Probably for the best he doesn't know its history.

In Adaminaby, I buy the pie and chocolate milkshake meal that I was going to have at the end of my rerouted trek and eat it on a bench beside the Big Trout. Old Pinkie looks like it's had a coat of paint and a general spruce-up. I find this gratifying. Is there anything sadder than a Big Thing that's fallen into disrepair? We might have to throw the Australian Alps and indeed the whole planet into that category.

* * *

Back in Sydney, Vladimir Putin is giving me dead eye like a fish. You know those Russian Matryoshka dolls where the fat ladies fit one inside the other? On a shelf in my shed, I've got novelty Russian leader dolls. There's Putin, Medvedev,

Yeltsin and old Gorbachev with his birthmark. Putin is the big one, of course. The rest of them progressively shrink beside him. So is recent Russian history written.

On another shelf is my two-litre bottle full of water from Tibeaudo Creek, the small stream near Mackeys. Don't think I'll be tipping that out any time soon. Don't think I'll be heading to the mountains for a while either. It's becoming increasingly clear that nobody will be going to the mountains, or anywhere, for months at least. Coronavirus is stopping the world in its tracks. Even the national parks are closed. This is proving much harder for some people than others.

'When they closed the parks, it was like I couldn't breathe. It's like they closed my house and told me I couldn't go home.' The words belong to Simone the trail angel. She's been texting encouragement and little nuggets of trail wisdom as I write this thing. She's also been sharing episodes from her life. She said she had this job once. She liked the job, but there were times when it really got to her and she wasn't the type to hide her frustration. One day, her boss told her she was too wild to keep, too good to lose. I love that phrase. In many ways, it's the dilemma of our most precious natural places, the mountains included. Too wild to keep, too good to lose.

Simone is full of good lines. I asked her why she hikes. What does she seek out on the trail? What does she feel? Her response blew me away.

'For me, hiking is like breathing. When I am not hiking, I feel like I am suffocating or drowning at the moment. It's the only peace I get from the chaos that is going on in my world. Through-hikes allow you the time and space to de-frag, breathe, follow thoughts for long periods of time, not be bombarded by random sensory input. I find I am most creative when I walk. No distractions of other things. I have been on the trail so long I am not sure I fit back in the real world. Perhaps the trail is my real world now. I have amazing façades and can pull off all sorts of "Simone", but the most authentic is out in the wild by myself.'

Wow. How can you not admire someone with such eloquence and self-awareness?

Simone says she feels most authentic in the wild. This I understand and respect. But her world is not my world, and her life is not my life. My authentic self is here at home, as a father and husband and more. That's where the trail has led. The trail was a wonderful escape, but it was not, in itself, the answer. This I knew after a couple of days slurping Zooper Doopers with Rivermate on the Mitta Mitta. Sometimes, escape is a prison.

The nights are getting cooler. The mosquitoes in my shed are now just a crowd, not a swarm. Old fish-eye Vlad looks like he's plotting something. The air is still. A tap drips. On my desk are a dozen or more books about the Australian Alps, as well as a pile of old ski and outdoors magazines. One of the magazines is America's most popular outdoors recreation title, *Outside*, its tagline 'Live Bravely'. In all likelihood, it means go climb that mountain you think you can't climb, or hike a whole damn trail somewhere. To be frank, I'm not inclined to read too much into it because living your life by mottos is about as nourishing as eating the plastic dinosaur in the cereal box. But there's something about those words. Live Bravely. That's what outdoors adventure is all about. And the outdoors kicks back. It empowers you. Live bravely on the trail and you live bravely back home.

So, then. Time to apply the mindset of the trail to general life. The trail has shown the way and I'm out here in my shed with my compass dangling on a hook in the breeze, doing everything I can to make changes that need making. In the short term, I'll stack supermarket shelves if I have to. Sometimes, living bravely is all about shelving your pride. Meanwhile the monthly mortgage payment is due and funds are low and there's no toilet paper or hand sanitiser in the stores.

But I've had a little win. At the bottom of my blue plastic food drum that survived the Kiandra inferno, below the batteries and Jetboil fuel and pouches of palak paneer and chicken karahi, there's a small bottle of hand sanitiser and a lone roll of toilet paper. The trail is still giving.

EQUIPMENT LIST

Everyone wants to know what you took on a long trek. My philosophy was simple. I took high quality gear which was as light as possible, but I didn't obsess over weight. There's a bit of an arms race these days to carry next to nothing. When you've attempted one or two through-hikes, then I guess you can start to triage the essentials from the non-essentials. But the AAWT was my first long hike, so I travelled fairly heavy. My base weight was about 10 or 11 kilograms, depending on what I was wearing. Add 3.5 litres of water and a week's worth of food (up to a kilogram per day), and my pack weighed in at around 20 kilograms after food drops. I trained with the pack at 17 or 18 kilograms, so I was comfortable enough.

KEY ITEMS

My portable universe was my **One Planet Larrikin 85-litre pack**, which I had professionally adjusted and fitted at Trek & Travel. It's a super waterproof pack which gave me great peace of mind. It's also very roomy, though it could use an extra external pocket or two for convenience. It also frequently toppled over which was a constant minor annoyance, though maybe I was packing it wrong.

My sleeping bag was a **One Planet Camp-Lite V2 20D** which is a lot of letters and numbers meaning I'm not sure what. It's a good size and delightfully silky to the touch, but I'd buy a warmer one next time. It's rated to minus three degrees, but I had several sub-zero nights early on and it barely did the trick. My fault. The lesson is always to buy a sleeping bag rated to much colder temperatures than you're expecting.

My sleeping mat was a **Sea to Summit Ether Light XT** and it was a joy. It comes with a special sac that you inflate before pumping the air into the mat. My family thought this system was hilarious and cruelly mocked me as I huffed and puffed into the sac. I shut them right up when I inflated the mat in 90 seconds with six good lungfuls of air. Rarely in my domestic life do such decisive moments of vindication occur.

My tent was a **Lansan Ultralight two-person tent**. It was the only major purchase I didn't make at Trek & Travel, but it met several key criteria. It was affordable, it was tunnel-shaped (an advantage in high winds), it was light enough at 1.7 kilograms and it was properly waterproof. Realistically, the tent would be very cramped with two people but it was perfect for a solo hiker. You want something with a bit of room in case you're stuck somewhere in bad weather. Unfortunately, the zip broke after only a couple of weeks (see chapter 10) and it wasn't like I'd spent my nights playing 'zip goes up, zip does down' like Homer Simpson. To their credit, the store replaced the tent.

My stove was my beloved **Jetboil Zip**. No fancy attachments, just a one-litre pot with a coffee strainer. I had 100-gram cannisters of fuel in each food drop which were more than enough for a week, though you'd need more when cooking for two, or in winter when melting snow for water.

CLOTHES AND FOOTWEAR

My boots were **Vasque Breeze GTX** and I adore them. They are so comfortable, I have no trouble at all sleeping in them. Ugly as hell, but as Red said in *The Shawshank Redemption*, 'I mean, really, how often do you look at a man's shoes?' My inner and outer socks were **Bridgedale**, and if you think socks don't matter, you either despise your feet or haven't hiked enough.

Mont is a Canberra-based company that produces quality gear, and my **Mont Austral rain jacket** did its job just fine. But when it rains (or snows) in the High Country it's generally cold too, and I found that I craved an insulated jacket. That's my fault, not the jacket's, and I probably should have carried an extra fleecy top.

My **Outdoor Research Apollo waterproof pants** did a great job of keeping the rain out while being super easy to slip on and off.

Possibly my most valuable all-round clothing item was my **neck thing**, which I believe may technically be called a neck gaiter or neck warmer. It's a tubular piece of synthetic wicking fabric which has a million purposes, from keeping the sun off your neck during the day to keeping you warm on cold days and cold nights, when you slip it over your chin, ears and head for extra warmth. It can even be a hanky or bandage, you name it. Don't even think of through-hiking without one. Just be sure to wash it often.

My **Columbia Omni-Shade hiking pants** were a good buy. They zip off at the thighs, which negated the need to carry shorts. Lots of handy extra pockets too.

My **Outdoor Research Rocky Mountain High gaiters** were well priced and did their job, which mostly was to make me feel good. In regular life, is there something you carry in your bag or wear on your person that just makes you feel ready for the day? Gaiters do that for me on the trail.

I also carried a beanie, ski gloves, a baseball cap, sunglasses, three pairs of undies, three shirts, a t-shirt, two warm layers and thermal long underwear.

On the advice of an extremely accomplished trekker, I took a **Coghlans Mosquito Head Net** and never used it once, which just goes to show: get out there and find what works for you.

I carried my clothes in an **Exped dry bag** inside my pack which doubled as my pillow at night. Worked well. Some hikers bring inflatable pillows. Waste of weight unless you're super fussy.

BITS AND PIECES

My **BioLite 5+ solar panel** worked really well when it was sunny, but not so well in the ever-present smoke haze during the second half of the hike. It stores energy so I could charge my phone to 60 or 70 per cent at night, but on balance, I think a charging brick would have been a better all-round option. Per chapter three, a spare charging cord is a must, too.

How good was my **HikersWool**? This ingenious apostrophe-free Kiwi product can be scrunched up to cushion your feet anywhere they need padding. I only used it once or twice, but knowing it was there was like having a superpower at the bottom of my pack.

Do not skimp on a headtorch. They sell them for $10 or less at some outdoors stores and they've made great birthday presents for other people's kids over the years. But you need a bright one. My **Petzl Tikka headlamp** had 200 lumens, which was more than bright enough, and the Tikka's batteries never chickened out. No, you can't escape Dad jokes in this section of the book either.

My **medical kit** had everything you'd expect including sunscreen and insect repellent, plus a small **sewing kit**. Next time I'll take a second needle plus more safety pins. I took rope and clothes pegs but didn't use them. Still think I'd carry rope again just in case. My water purification pills were **Aquatabs**. I had no water filtration system because mountain water is generally pretty clean, except in areas with large herds of feral horses.

I'm not a fan of multi-tools so took a **7-centimetre Opinel knife**. This lightweight French blade folds into its wooden casing and is a tool of great simplicity and elegance.

My eating utensils were a **Sea to Summit cutlery set**. The knife, fork and spoon live on a small carabiner which broke. This really annoyed me as I could never find the right piece of cutlery thereafter. Next time I'll just take a plastic spoon. I took no plates or cups, eating main meals from their foil pouches and drinking hot drinks or soup from the Jetboil pot.

I took both **hand sanitiser** and a mini **soap cake** of the sort you get in motels. I carried both **sports strapping tape** and **duct tape** and would do away with the latter next time, as you can use a good brand of strapping tape for nearly anything. I carried an **emergency beacon** which I borrowed from the NSW National Parks and Wildlife Service after filling in a form and giving them a refundable deposit. I also carried a **pencil** and **tiny note book**. I navigated with a basic **Sunnto compass** and I carried **16 local maps** in total, which were placed, a few at a time as needed, in my food drops. My food drop containers were **25-litre wide-mouth plastic water drums** from Bunnings. I carried both a small **lighter** and **waterproof matches**. **Zip-lock bags** proved invaluable for storing food and collecting water from shallow streams or puddles. I took **headphones** but never used them. My small water bottle was a **Quechua 1.5-litre aluminium bottle with quick-open cap** from Decathlon. I loved it because it was so easy to open and close. My large bottle was a **two-litre plastic mineral water bottle** from the supermarket. Plastic bottles are surprisingly durable and if your hike is less than a few weeks, I wouldn't hesitate to take one.

And of course, I took **trekking poles**, which were actually my carbon fibre ski poles. I can't remember their brand or recommend another brand, but you'd be mad to attempt a long hike without poles. For the record, I still haven't given up on recovering my stick-and-pole combo from Mackeys Hut. One day soon, with luck.

AUTHOR'S NOTE ON SOURCES

High Country huts and apostrophes

Mapping authorities across Australia generally do not use possessive apostrophes in place names. That's why we have Kings Cross, Surfers Paradise and so on. Geographical features also do not take possessive apostrophes, which is why we have places like Johnnies Top, Taylors Crossing and Marums Point, to use just three examples from this book. Buildings in Australia generally *do* take the apostrophe, which is why Sydney has a suburb called St Marys and St Mary's Cathedral in the city.

High Country huts are an exception to this rule. They are buildings clearly marked on maps, yet generally *don't* take the apostrophe. Hence this book has Wallaces Hut, Ropers Hut, Mackeys Hut and many others. Why no apostrophe? I put this question to Klaus Hueneke, author of *Huts of the High Country*. He reckons it's because they are places, not mere buildings. I loved that answer.

* * *

The Robert Macfarlane quote on page 17 is from his book *The Old Ways: A Journey on Foot*, Penguin, 2013. The interview with Cheryl Strayed that I quoted from on page 23 can be found on *Forbes* magazine's website at https://www. forbes.com/sites/alexandratalty/2019/07/31/wild-author-cheryl-strayed-on-her-greatest-legacy/#15d1b3cd5b6e. The quote from Phil Zylstra on page 44 is from the January 2020 issue of *Meanjin* https://meanjin.com.au/blog/the-unlearned-country/. All other Zylstra quotes are from my interview with him. The quote on page 76 regarding blood in urine is from the Mayo Clinic website https://www.mayoclinic. org. The 'Fun Scale' on pages 92–93 was discussed by Kelly Cordes in a 2009 article on his website: https://kellycordes. com/2009/11/02/the-fun-scale/. The quote from Klaus Hueneke on page 137 comes from Hueneke's book *One Step at a Time*, published by Tabletop Press, 1999. The quote on p. 174 is from *The Australian Alps Walking Track* by John Chapman, Monica Chapman and John Siseman, published by John Chapman, 2009. The letter from members of the Australian Academy of Science to John Barilaro quoted on page 180 can be found at https://www.science.org.au/files/userfiles/ support/documents/letter-aas-jb-re-kosciuszko-wild-horse-heritage-bill-2018.pdf. It was sent from the Academy direct to Barilaro on 1 June 2018 ahead of the bill going through state parliament. The letter from Dave Watson mentioned on pp. 180–81 in which he resigned from the Threatened Species Scientific Committee and which he shared on social media can found at https://twitter.com/D0CT0R_Dave/sta tus/1004537089025662976?s=20. The quote on p. 205 from Tony Sponar comes from his book *Snow in Australia? That's*

News To Me published by Tabletop Press, 1995. The quotes on p. 206 come from *World Ski Atlas*, Mark Heller, published by Marshall Cavendish Books, 1978. The quote from Alan EJ Andrews on p. 221 can be found in his book *Kosciuszko: The Mountain in History*, published by Tabletop Press, 1991. Quotes on pp. 228–30 and 245–46 are from Elyne Mitchell's book *Australia's Alps*, Angus & Robertson, 1942. The quote on p. 276 from Klaus Hueneke's poem, 'If I Was a Mountain Hut' is reproduced with his permission. The full poem can be found in Hueneke's book *Charlie Carter: Hermit, Healer and High Country Legend*, Tabletop Press, 2017.

ACKNOWLEDGEMENTS

Thanks firstly to John and Monica Chapman and John Siseman, for your invaluable Australian Alps Walking Track guidebook. I know of nobody who has attempted this track without it, nor anybody who should. Thanks also to the first John for sharing your thoughts on the track and on hiking in general. If Australian bushwalking has a godfather, that title is deservedly yours, John.

Thanks to Jemima Headlam – whose surname is seven-eighths of a crucial piece of hiking equipment – and all the staff of Trek & Travel for your advice, and for never making me feel foolish.

Thanks to Dad for driving me to Walhalla and to Mum for driving me crazy with your worry during the hike.

Thanks to Peter Maffei for your local knowledge and for helping keep Baw Baw beautiful and (mostly!) walkable.

Thanks to left-wing Steve and right-wing Steve for your kind offers of a lift and for your ongoing interest in this project.

Thanks to Phil Zylstra, Tom Fairman, Brodie Verrall and all the scientists interviewed during the writing of this book who took the time to break down their expertise in a way that even I could understand.

Thanks to all the trail angels. To Simone for your phone cord and your ceaseless advice, ideas and encouragement. To Ferg for your beef jerky and beautiful thoughts. To Dave from Tawonga who is not actually from Tawonga but who shall forever be known as such. To the people of the Benambra district for looking after a lonely traveller in a heatwave and a fire emergency. To Kevin McGennan for being every High Country hiker's best mate, not least mine. To the ski.com.au crew for being the most supportive, knowledgeable and entertaining bunch of idiots in the online universe.

Thanks to Klaus Hueneke AM for your open soul and inspirational work.

Thanks to Ian Dicker and Col de Pagter for being tougher than fire and cooler than water.

Thanks to Rob Gibbs for your integrity, for your work administering the AAWT and for permission to reproduce the AAWT website map.

Thanks to Rivermate for the Zooper Doopers and company, wherever you are now.

Thanks to Shaggy at The General at Mt Hotham for storing a food drop, to Caroline at Christiania Lodge in Thredbo for doing the same, and for being the best cook Southern Alps Ski Club has had since Gerhardt.

Thanks to Catriona Carver, Glenn Cullen, Susie Diver, Ben Doherty, Glen Fergus, Jason Harty, Heath Kelly, Roz Kelly, Ann King, Peter Lewis, Kate Pearcy, Bradley Roche, Simon Sharwood, Dave Sisson, Cam Walker and anyone I've forgotten who read bits of the manuscript, or who offered thoughts, encouragement or expertise before or during the writing of this thing.

Thanks to Rockdale Library, Sun's Noodle and Ibrahim Pastry for sheltering, feeding and coffeeing me in the early days of writing this book when the late summer sun was too hot for the shed and COVID-19 hadn't yet confined us to isolation.

A massive thanks to publisher Sophie Hamley at Hachette for believing in this project. Sophie, the end of the hike was the halfway point of this journey, which continued with this book. That makes you a true trail angel, which is the highest praise there is. Thanks also to editors Libby Turner and Karen Ward, who always knew when I'd made one Dad joke too many, and who trusted their gut and mine to shape the manuscript. Thanks to Luke Causby for his beautiful cover art, to Alex Craig for her foolproof proofreading, to Graeme Jones for his Type A typesetting, and to everyone at Hachette Australia. It has always felt like everyone in the company is fully invested in this thing.

And of course, my eternal thanks to Kate, Stella and Leo for being here.